A BALLAD OF LOVE

By the same author

Novels

THE ASIATICS

THE SEVEN WHO FLED

A TALE FOR MIDNIGHT

Poetry

THE ASSASSINS

THE CARNIVAL

DEATH AT SEA

Translations

THE MEDEA OF EURIPIDES

SOME POEMS OF HÖLDERLIN

THE SONNETS OF LOUIZE LABÉ

FREDERIC PROKOSCH

A

BALLAD

OF

LOVE

FARRAR, STRAUS AND CUDAHY

NEW YORK

While the heart weeps at
what it has lost, the spirit
laughs at what it has found.

Arab proverb

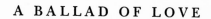

A BALLAD OF LOVE

I

I AM SITTING AT MY DESK in a little room on the Avenue Gabriel which a kindly old lady has lent me for three months. The sun is shining. It is May. The chestnut trees are in flower. The stamp-collectors are browsing among the stalls below my window and a nurse is wheeling a carriage in the shade of the Champs-Elysées. I can see the spray of a fountain in the Place de la Concorde, if I'm not mistaken. There is happiness in the air. Someone above me is playing Mozart.

I open a slender volume and look at a crushed little dandelion. I stare at a thumb-worn snapshot inscribed in a clumsy, childlike hand. I caress an old handkerchief with the letter S embroidered in the corner. These are my talismans. They have brought me luck. I have been carrying them around with me for years. They saved my life once in Tokyo (or so I like to imagine) and one night in Monte Carlo they brought me a shower of gold.

I close my eyes; and suddenly I am swept away on a torrent of images. I see a sail on the brink of the horizon, as white as a sea-gull. I see a lake wrinkled with raindrops, and a veil of doves encircling the basilica. I see the plane-trees along the quay clutching at the fog like great tarantulas; I smell the sweat and the sickly treacle of almonds in the *soukh*.

Is that all? Just a dazzle of half-forgotten patterns, with nothing to weave them together but the dark thread of passion? Well, there it is. Who wants to hear about birth and decay? We want music, we want fire, we want pain and delight! So let me tell you my little tale—or rather, sing my little ballad: for it is a song more than a history, an incantation, not an analysis. The secret is there, the terror is there, and the hydra-headed mystery. But the meaning? The message? That is for you to decide.

2

I was born in the woods of Carinthia one summer morning in 1914—on the very day, as luck would have it, when a shot was fired in Sarajevo. I still remember those woods— towering fir trees, black as night, marching away into the distance in long, silent aisles. I still remember the golden tears which clung to their bark and the great lonely storks that went soaring above their summits. I still remember the velvety moss which caressed my bare feet and the smell of wild strawberries which I tossed in my basket. I still remember the hunter's horn which came echoing through the trees, and now and then the voice of the cuckoo or the low dark warning of the owl.

Now and again I saw a pale, moth-like shape drift through the treetrunks. I caught the murmur of little voices or infinitesimal footsteps. I knew the path that led to the cave where the old witch Hackebacke lived. I peeped into the giant oak-tree where the squirrel Peppi hid his acorns. I knelt by the stagnant pool where the Frog King Waldemar ruled, with a ruby in his brow and a golden crown on top of his head.

One fine day I was sitting on a stone with my basket of strawberries when young Christl, who sold chestnuts down in the town, came wandering by.

"What are you doing there, Henni?"

"Eating strawberries," I said.

"Where's your father?"

"He's down by the stream, chopping birch-logs," I said.

Christl grinned at me slyly. "Well, you'd better go home, Henni. Just look! It's almost dark! The witches are on their way!"

The last threads of sunlight hung from the boughs, like a burning cobweb. So I picked up my basket and strolled down the path. I paused for a moment by the pool, waiting for the Frog King to emerge, and I peeped into the oak for a glimpse of the marvelous silver acorns. I could hear the axe's echo, sharp and clear as a crystal. I tip-toed through the birch-trees and looked down at the waterfall, which was churning bright and coppery in the sunglow. I saw my father raising his head as Christl stepped into the clearing and I watched them wandering into the darkness of the copse, arm in arm.

3

I opened the door and found my mother all alone, playing the piano. The twilight seeped through the curtains, which were embroidered with bees; it fell on her brooding face with its knife-like nose and sunken eyes. I took my box of tin-soldiers and sat down under the piano and watched her white slippers pressing gently on the pedals. It was a fine old piano, built in Vienna in 1884 and bequeathed to my mother by her great-uncle Wenzel. The fluted legs tapered down to enormous claws, like a sphinx's, which rested on sceptres of mirror-bright ebony.

Mother's hands came to rest. She closed the lid of the piano.

"Where's your father?"

"Still in the woods."

"It's almost dark!"

"He's chopping logs . . ."

Mother rose, struck a match and lit the lily-shaped gas lamp.

"Was he alone?"

"Yes," I said.

"You're quite sure?"

"Yes," I whispered.

On the wall hung a row of old Biedermaier silhouettes, some with their pigtails tied in ribbons, some with roses in their hands. Over the piano hung a portrait of my grandfather in a military uniform, with deep liquid eyes, eyes colored like death, where the lustre of blood melted into the glitter of cannonballs.

Mother settled herself on the sofa and started to leaf through an album of photographs. I stood directly behind her and rested my chin on her shoulder.

"This is your old Uncle Franz, dear. He was killed in a duel in Karlsbad. And this is your Uncle Willibald. He died in Prague, of epilepsy."

She turned the page with a sigh and pointed to a thick-set man in an Alpine costume.

"And this is your Uncle Claudius, who studied philosophy. He left Vienna because of a scandal. He lives in Wisconsin."

"Where is Wisconsin?"

"In America, dear."

"What's it like?"

"Rather wild, I imagine."

"Are there tigers there?"

"Quite possibly."

"And elephants?"

"Who knows?"

"What does Uncle Claudius do, mama?"

"He's writing a book, if I'm not mistaken. He's a weird, woolly man. He is married to your Tante Elfrida, who has lived in the Orient and refuses to eat beef, and does queer little exercises."

On the opposite page there was a woman in a hat heaped with hyacinths, with a string of pearls around her neck and a fan of ostrich feathers in her hand.

"And who is that?"

"That, my dear, is your dear old Tante Ursula. She used to sing operettas but she wearied of it all and went to Pennsylvania to live with a lady friend."

"Are there Indians in Pennsylvania?"

"I'm sure there are. Lurking in the woods."

"Won't they kill Tante Ursula?"

"Tante Ursula is a very brave woman. I think the Indians would think twice before attacking your Tante Ursula."

She turned the page and I gazed at a bony, desiccated face. Uncle Adelbert, this was, with a pince-nez fastened to a ribbon and his hair down to his shoulders, in the fashion of Franz Liszt.

"Where does Uncle Adelbert live?"

"In Texas, the poor creature."

"Are there buffaloes in Texas?"

"More than likely," said Mother.

"Won't they kill Uncle Adelbert?"

"I doubt it," said Mother. "Your Uncle Adelbert keeps to his rooms, playing mazurkas on his fiddle."

I pointed to a photograph of a black-haired little girl, four years old or maybe five, with a ribbon tied to the top of her head.

"Is that Stella?"

"Yes, Henni. That's your little cousin Stella."

"Will I marry her some day?"

"Certainly not," said Mother curtly.

"Why not, mama?"

"Little boys aren't allowed to marry their female cousins."

Sorrow gripped at my heart. "Why not?" I said softly.

"It's unnatural, that's why not. It's against the laws of God. It brings sorrow and disaster. Just forget about your cousin Stella . . ."

4

Our house was a silent house. There was the sound of the piano at sunset and at dusk the mewing of the cat, the ticking of the clock, the buzz of the egg-beater. At dinner there was only the sound of knives and forks scraping the plates. My father almost never spoke to my poor, broken mother. They lived in a state of perpetual tension, mute reproaches, noiseless hatred.

After supper I'd sit by the window and watch my father carving at his dolls. The lamplight shone on the chest with the silver coffee pot on top of it, and on the oven in the corner with its blue armorial tiles. My mother would read aloud to me from the fairy tales of Madame d'Aulnoy, nibbling daintily from time to time at a candied prune or a sugared violet.

My father was an itinerant puppet-master. He was a nervous little man with a silky brown mustache and powerful, penetrating eyes. I watched his long nimble fingers as they whittled away at a tiny head, pausing now and again to enfold the stem of his wineglass. He wore a black velvet jacket and puffed at a thick briar pipe. He rarely spoke except with the shrill, bird-like voices of his marionettes.

Year after year he toured the small, provincial towns of Carinthia, performing in cheap little cafés, plebeian wine-houses and crowded market-places. He did "Rapunzel" and "Snow White" as well as "The Boar with the Golden Tusks," "The Chimneysweep and the Empress," and "The Little Blind Princess."

Our house was filled with myriads of strange little fragments: miniature cradles and spinning-wheels, dwarf-like dishes and clocks, stray arms that needed mending or moth-eaten wigs; tiny baskets filled with vegetables, tiny coronets and cutlasses, tiny helmets and wands, tiny thrones and sedan chairs. The dolls themselves hung from the wall, row upon desperate, wild-eyed row of them, carved from birch-wood or hickory wood, with luridly painted faces: beggars and knights, witches and wolves, maharajahs and khans, dressed in shimmering sequins and faded old taffeta. During the dark winter months dust and cobwebs gathered upon them, and when a window swung open the icy draught would set them trembling, giving them a macabre little life of their own. Through the rustle of frozen boughs and the whine of the weather-cock I heard the sighs of tiny princesses or the baleful muttering of a sorcerer.

There were times when my father perched me on his knee, lit his pipe, and proceeded to leaf through a battered copy of *Max und Moritz* or *Struwelpeter*. I stared with fascination at the drawings of little children devoured by flames or baked in an oven. The scent of tobacco mingled with another odor, a twilight musk, like that of a hickory tree. My father would look at me and say: "What will you do when you're grown up, Henni?" And a looming sadness filled my soul, a sneaking dread, a dark resentment. But when he placed his hand on my head and smiled at me teasingly, a terrible longing surged up in me, I wanted to fling my arms around him and bury my face in his hairy neck. But I never dared; I blushed; I stammered; I looked away.

I wore short leather pants and suspenders embroidered with *edelweiss*. Only on Sundays and Name-Days I wore my suit of black worsted, with woollen stockings up to my

knees and black shoes with six buttons. Sometimes my
mother would take me along when she visited the Schloss.
On these occasions she wore gloves and a polka-dotted
veil and over her shoulders a little fox ferociously biting
his own tail. I crouched on the love-seat, munching almonds, while my mother sat at the piano, racing briskly
through a rondo by Schubert or Mendelssohn.

Now and again the Baron turned and rested his llama-
like gaze on me: "He's a thoughtful little boy, isn't he?"

"He is indeed," said Mother.

"Beautiful eyes. Like a water-spaniel's."

"Yes, it's true, isn't it?" said Mother.

And then at dusk we'd wander home again, down the
hill with its shuddering poplars, past the monastery
walls and through the dark little town. It was hardly a
town, really: scarcely more than a village, with a small
cobbled market-place surrounding the church of St. Stanislaus. The gloom of post-war desolation still hung in the
air, like the smell of soot. At the end of the square stood
a tiny black smithy where Christl's husband, the swarthy
Peter, stood sweating beside his anvil. Behind the church
stood a fountain with a naked boy riding a dolphin, and
around the square stood a row of shops—the butcher and
the apothecary, the vintner and the saddler. As I passed I
caught their odors welling forth from their recesses:
sausages, leather, wine, witch-hazel, tinged with the scent
of old masonry.

5

Winter came. Shiny icicles hung from the overhanging roof and the sound of iron hooves echoed along the frozen road. Little globes of fresh horse-dung lay steaming on the ice and the snow was pitted with jets of yellow urine.

Christmas arrived and a heavenly fragrance filled Herr Krahwinkl's pastry shop. At dusk all the townsmen gathered on the shore of the lake. The musicians played a polka and Frau Hegelberger poured the fruit punch while the boys went racing across the ice in their woollen caps. High on the hill stood the castle with its windows all lit, and after a while the Herr Baron came riding along in his sleigh and tossed little marzipan eggs to the children.

As I hurried back home I heard the sleigh-bells tinkling in the distance and the far-off voices singing *Kommet Ihr Hirten*. The door of the living-room swung open. I rushed up to the blazing tree. There was an aroma of rum and cinnamon, dripping wax and fresh evergreen. I prowled on tiptoe around the tree, staring wildly at the glittering ornaments—the gilded walnuts, the silver posthorn, the china mushrooms, the bird-of-paradise.

I ripped open my gifts: a mechanical tiger and a gingerbread soldier, as well as a pair of woollen mittens, poppy red with black dots.

Then my father took me on his lap and opened a book and started reading:

"Once upon a time in the middle of winter, when the flakes of snow were falling like feathers, a Queen sat by the window sewing, and the frame of the window was made of ebony. And while she was sewing and looking through the window, she pricked her finger with the needle and three drops of blood fell down on the snow. And the red looked very lovely upon the pure white snow, and she thought to herself: 'Would that I had a child as white as this snow, and as red as this blood, and as black as the wood of the window-frame . . .' "

And as he read I kept thinking about my tiny cousin Stella, with the snow-white ribbon tied to her ebony-black hair. I thought of her living out in the wilderness, among the buffaloes and vipers; mysterious and inaccessible, shadowed with doom.

6

My father usually returned from his journeys at dusk. I'd be sitting by the window breathing mist upon the pane. And then I'd suddenly hear the sound of the echoing hooves and the sleigh bells, and I'd see my father in his astrakhan cap jump down from the sleigh, cover the mare with a thick red cloth and come striding into the kitchen.

One night, soon after Christmas, he was later than usual. My mother was making pancakes; I listened to the spoon rattling in the bowl. And then I heard the familiar sound of the tinkling little sleigh bells. I saw the mare stop by the door and my father lolling in his seat with the whip on his lap.

I waited; nothing stirred. Not a sound. Nothing at all. It was as though the world had come to a halt, like a clock that needs winding.

I opened the window and called "Papa!"

But my father didn't answer. He sat motionless in his sleigh, staring up at the moon.

I stepped out through the kitchen door and strolled up to the sleigh. I saw the snow shining like gold dust in the light from the kitchen window.

I cried: "Papa!"

But he didn't answer. Not a sound. Not a whisper. And then I saw the dark blood pouring from a gash in his temple, trickling down over his gloves and dappling the hard, rutted snow.

7

For three days my poor mother lay in a kind of garrulous delirium. Frau Hegelbauer, the apothecary's wife, sat beside her during the night, and now and again I heard my mother cry out in the darkness: "There they are again! Look at them! All horrible and hairy! God help me!"

During the day she calmed down a little and clutched me to her breast. She said in a whisper: "You'll never leave your poor little mama, will you, dearest?"

"No, mama."

"You swear it?"

"Yes, mama," I said. "I swear it."

On the day following the New Year the effeminate young Baron came down to visit us. He was accompanied by a thickset woman dressed in black bombazine and an elderly gentleman with a rust-colored goatee. Frau Hegelbauer regarded them solemnly, wiped a tear and shook her head.

"What do you think, Herr Baron?"

"I think it's best. Just as you said."

"But the poor little lad. . . ."

"It can't be helped. We'll take care of him."

The next morning they took my mother to the "sanitarium" in Weinsiedl, and the Herr Baron came down from the Schloss to fetch me in his sleigh.

8

From my window I could see the walls of the monastery, bearded with hoar-frost; and below the monastery rose the onion-shaped spire of St. Stanislaus, with an empty stork's nest on top of the steeple. And around the church huddled the village with its chocolate-brown roofs all cushioned with snow like great slabs of whipped cream.

I went roaming through the castle, stroking the heads of the glass-eyed stags, tapping at the icy coats-of-mail and peeping into the rose-painted cupboards. Sometimes, when no one was looking, I groped furtively among the drawers and found moth-eaten muffs, ancient pistols and tarnished opera-glasses.

The great salon was filled with rosewood side-tables and gilt rococo mirrors. There were toy canaries which twittered merrily under little glass bells, and there was a Directoire clock which played a minuet by Haydn on the hour. In the cabinet there were rows of damascened snuff-boxes and periwigged monkeys playing the flute and the violin.

Sometimes I wandered into the kitchen where old Trudl

was stirring the gravy. I caressed the dead pheasants which lay limp on the enormous table or stole a stray hazelnut from one of the Prinz-Regenten tortes. Or I climbed the back stairs to the deserted children's play-room, where the toys of fifty years ago lay scattered in the dust. There were Chinese dolls made of wood, each one tucked inside of another, and tumbling dolls fastened to poles, kicking their heels when I pulled the string. There were horses on wheels and little blocks painted with the alphabet and a small Noah's ark filled with lacerated beasts. There was also a "polyorama," as the Baron used to call it—a collection of colored cards with pictures of ruins and waterfalls, which could be interchanged at random to form a variety of landscapes.

As I sat in the lonely room, creating vivid new sceneries and zealously populating them with Arabian steeds and Russian witches, something of the mystery and terror of the past few months melted away. I was lost in a world of dreams, gentle, melodious, picturesque. And the world beyond, the world of reality, with all its manias and enigmas, gradually receded into the mists that hung over the twilit monastery.

9

Months passed. The great forest grew fragrant again and the Baron went hunting with his dark young groom, whose name was Sepp. They'd return to the castle with a brace of pheasants or a bleeding chamois, and bowls of hot water were brought upstairs for the Baron's bath. Then we'd gather for dinner: Frau Maritsch and I on the right, and the Baron and his good-looking groom on the left. Periodically the Baron would appear in *décolleté:* in a Spanish mantilla, for instance, with heavily painted eyes; or in a sleek Fortuny gown with a pair of huge rhinestone ear-rings; or in a blue satin turban with a row of ringlets clinging to his brow; or in an elaborate tulle hat laden with lilies-of-the-valley, with a feather boa around his shoulders and a black lace fan in his hand. Sepp, the groom, would sit with a grin on his satyr-like face, twisting his thick black mustachioes and sniffing knowingly at the wine; while Frau Maritsch, the *châtelaine,* an amiable creature with an enormous bosom, would phlegmatically sip at her strawberry mousse.

After dinner we'd go wandering across the smooth green lawn. Sepp, the groom, and Frau Maritsch would sit under the beech-tree for a game of checkers while I accompanied the Baron for a stroll in the park. There were neatly clipped hedges shaped like sphinxes and pyramids and a group of lichenous dwarves surrounded a hexagonal fish pond. Here we paused and dropped wafers into the dark, mossy water.

"Look at that sunset!" said the Baron, pointing his long bejeweled finger. "The sheer elegance of nature takes my breath away, positively. Look at those branches, my dear, silhouetted against the gold like Venetian lace." He sighed and patted my head. "It's moments like this, my precious child, that I feel a Presence, a Mystical Spirit, a Celestial Pattern pervading the universe. . . ."

The Baron was a willowy man with a drooping face like a bloodhound's. His lips were thick, almost negroid, and his eyes were grape-colored, like a baboon's. He was a romantic of the old school—an exalté, with a taste for the decadent. He loved the paintings of Böcklin. He doted on the novels of Huysmans and the music of Scriabin. Once a month he paid a visit to Vienna, half esthetic and half amorous. He attended the opening of some new opera by Richard Strauss and paid his customary visit to the Turkish baths. And he'd return three days later, rather pale and attenuated, with a slender volume of experimental verses or perhaps a Nymphenburg shepherdess.

After these excursions his meditations beside the fish pond grew more melancholy. "Life is a miserable spectacle, my boy. Man is corrupt. The flesh is vile. Remember these words, my little Henni, and you'll be spared many a pang!"

The castle looked down over a mosaic of little meadows, some black with earth, some gold with mustard, some silvery with young barley, which swayed in the wind like ripples in a lake. There was an alley of lime-trees where the lap-dogs played in the shade, and between two black cypresses stood a small rococo pavilion with narrow pink columns and latticework of roses. Here the Baron had his chocolate served each morning on a silver tray.

One evening we both sat there, watching the roe-deer in the distance; their antlers shone in the sunset like bright twigs of coral. Trudl had brought us some tea with sugared pigs' ears and anise-seed wafers, and the Baron lit his pipe and started to play solitaire. They were old-fashioned cards from Switzerland, with the knaves dressed like shepherds and the queens all encircled with garlands of roses.

"Would you like," said the Baron gently, "to visit America, my child?"

"I have a cousin living in America. Her name is Stella," I said.

"Stella? How charming," said the Baron. "Stella means star, my boy, in Latin."

"She is very beautiful," I said, and suddenly I blushed and lowered my eyes.

The Baron picked up the ace of diamonds and regarded it thoughtfully, and then placed it on the table, lifted his eyebrows and smiled. And in his eyes, dilated with mascara and a kind of nineteenth-century soulfulness, I detected a hint of slyness, a Machiavellian appraisal.

I heard a desolate, far-off cry. "What is that, Herr Baron?"

The Baron pointed. "Don't you see them? It's the wild swans flying."

"Where are they going, Herr Baron?"

"God knows, my dear boy. To lonely little lakes hidden among the palms and the tamarisks."

"What will they do there, Herr Baron?"

"Ah," said the Baron, rolling his eyes. "They'll nestle in the rushes at night and make love."

I watched the swans fly overhead on their way down to Africa. They floated effortlessly, like withered leaves, scarcely moving their wings at all, tinged with the blood-colored glow from the sun which had already vanished, so that their feathers looked like ivory encased in strands of gold. Where were they going? To what dark joys? To what strange rendezvous among the cat-tails? I watched till they were lost in the deepening haze beyond the monastery.

And for days I was haunted by the vision of these beautiful wild swans, with their hoarse, horrible voices and far-off destinations.

10

That year was a year of bad omens up at the castle. One of the cows gave birth to a miscarriage; the peas all wilted away in their pods. Sepp the groom broke a tooth on a walnut and Frau Maritsch developed jaundice. So one day old Herr Krusius, the village exorciser, was invited to the Schloss. He stalked asthmatically through the fields and copses, giving his blessings to the cattle, fluttering his wand above the vegetables and warding off the devils with his "emanations."

After he left poor Frau Maritsch raised her head and muttered hoarsely: "I feel better already, dear. There's a certain gleam in his eyes, did you notice? There's no question about it, that man has Powers. . . ."

Occasionally, after our lessons in English were over, I sat by the bed and listened to Frau Maritsch reminiscing about her youth in the Balkans: in places like Bucharest, Sofia and Constantinople.

"I was as slim as a sylph," she said, "back in those days, my lamb. My legs were like a gazelle's. My breasts were like champagne glasses."

I gazed thoughtfully at her rheumy eyes and henna-dyed curls and her sagging old cheeks peppered with caper-like warts.

"What did you do in Bucharest, Frau Maritsch?"

"I used to dance, my little pet. I swirled about in a purple veil, rattling away with my tambourine."

"Did you dance in a theatre, Frau Maritsch?"

"Not as a rule, my chick, unfortunately. I danced for

small private gatherings. Gentlemen, chiefly, as it happened."

"And what did you do in Constantinople?"

"I ran an establishment in Constantinople. A kind of *café chantant*. With silky cushions and soft music."

"Did the sultan come to your café?"

"I don't remember the sultan specifically. But my clientèle was very select. Gentlemen, exclusively," said Frau Maritsch.

Matters improved, after Herr Krusius' visit, out in the stables and in the fields. But in the castle itself things were not what they should have been. One of the big rococo mirrors started to dance about one evening, suddenly leapt from its hook and burst into thousands of fragments. The Directoire clock played its minuet at unpredictable moments. And Trudl the cook declared that one of the old coats of mail in the gallery had raised its hand as she passed and made a pornographic gesture.

So the Baron called the groom. "Get the ghost-chaser, Sepp."

"Where is it, *gnädiger* Herr Baron?"

"In the front hall closet. With the umbrellas."

Sepp returned with a powerful stick which was shaped like a cricket-bat. He strode through the twilit foyer and from chamber to chamber, beating at the air with his stick, chasing the ghosts back to their crannies.

When he had finished I sat down on the stairway beside him.

"Well, my boy, you'll be going to America soon, they're all telling me."

"Will I really? Who told you, Sepp?"

"The Herr Baron. And the Herr Doktor."

"How does one get to America, Sepp?"

"You cross the ocean on a ship."

"What will I do when I get there, Sepp?"

"You'll be staying with your Uncle Adelbert."

"Will I really? Tell me, Sepp. What's it like in America?"

Sepp had never set foot in America; but his mind started roaming and he conjured up miraculous images with names like Wyoming, Nevada and Utah. He told me about Niagara Falls, where the water roared like a million steers and sent up geysers that glittered like an Aurora Borealis. He told me about the Mississippi, which rushed through a wilderness studded with orchids; and about the Grand Canyon, with its opal-colored cliffs; about the Petrified Forest, haunted by bandits and cut-throats, and the great Painted Desert, littered with gold-pieces and skeletons. He told me about Texas, vast and desolate as the Gobi, and about the sunlit Carolinas where the peaches grew as large as watermelons. He told me about St. Louis, where hyenas prowled among the tents, and Philadelphia, where temples of porphyry rose from the prairies, and Chicago, where the millionaires crouched in their fortresses, waiting for the murderous attacks of the Mohawks.

"In America," said Sepp, "they are building a wonderful new world for us. No more poverty and intolerance. Only equality and freedom. Just wait, my boy, and one of these days we'll all be sailing to America—you and me and the Herr Baron, and even poor old Tante Maritsch. . . ."

It was strange how they all kept thinking of America. Even the Herr Baron breathed a lugubrious sigh now and again, and murmured wistfully: "Oh, to live in those infinite forests, like noble Savages! To lie under the moon and sing songs, or recite poetry! To feel the limitless freedom of those sapphire-blue skies! To roam on the shores of Lake Huron with not a care in the world! How lucky you are, my little Henni, with that paradise awaiting you!"

11

Once a fortnight or so I was taken to visit my mother in Weinsiedl. I was led down a long green corridor to her small, stuffy room where starfish and sea-horses danced about on the wallpaper.

She looked desperately frail; her voice was feeble and hesitant.

"Kiss your poor, sad Mama, Henni. Have you been polite to everybody?"

"Yes, mama."

"Have you practiced the violin?"

"Not yet, mama."

Her voice trembled. "Are there still those t-t-terrible creatures lurking in the corners?"

I started to answer but all of a sudden she burst into tears, and I was led from the little room back to the Baron's victoria.

Winter came once again and the Carinthian woods were filled with snow. The little dwarves in the park wore peaks of snow on their caps and the sphinxes in the hedge wore snowy shawls over their shoulders.

One day a strange terror came over me all of a sudden. I ran down the stairs and out through the snow-filled garden. I took the road past the monastery, with St. Stanislaus looming in the distance. The little houses in the town looked deserted and empty. The naked boy in the fountain was coated with ice. I passed by the sweet-shop and pressed my nose against the pane; there were bowls of sugared almonds and jars of mint pastilles, there were chocolates shaped like daisies and tiny bottles wrapped in gold foil.

Suddenly, the tears burst from my eye-balls and I ran down the street. I hurried on through the outskirts; I entered the forest; I followed the path through the birches and past the white waterfall.

Finally I came to our old house. All the shutters were closed. I knocked at the door. No one answered. There was only a faint, lingering echo.

I heard sleigh-bells behind me and a voice called out gruffly:

"Is anything wrong, child?"

It was a bearded man in black fur cap.

"I'm looking for my mother," I said timidly.

"Where does she live?" said the old man gently.

"In Weinsiedl," I said, and collapsed into tears.

The old man stepped from the sleigh, picked me up in his arms, tucked me tenderly under his blanket and drove off toward Weinsiedl.

The sky grew leaden and ominous. The clouds churned like whirlpools. Soon the snow began falling in a thick silent veil. We rode by the edge of the river and finally we crossed a wooden bridge and entered the little village of Weinsiedl.

Sister Perpetua looked at me gravely when she opened the door for me.

"Mercy, child. What brought you here?"

I started to sob. "Where's my mother?"

Sister Perpetua took my hand and led me down the gloomy corridor. "Your poor mother is very ill, my little child," she said quietly.

Mother lay motionless in the twilit room. She turned her head when she saw me. Her lips trembled slightly. Then she sighed and stared at the ceiling.

Suddenly she cried: "There he is! All black and hairy! He's come to get me!"

She sat up in her bed, flailing about with her skeletal arms. Her eyes rolled deliriously under their moist purple lids.

"Help!" she screamed. "Save me! Save me! He's trying to rip me to pieces! . . ."

Her whole body began to shake in an uncontrollable paroxysm. Sister Perpetua flung open the door and called "Quick! Sister Rosa!" Then she lifted me in her arms and carried me down to the kitchen, where I sat close beside her while she kneaded the dough.

I stared silently at the old copper pans above the oven, dented with decades of use, so that they glittered like mosaics. The bulging molds, shaped like roosters or cavalry officers, hung motionless over the flames, as though awaiting some dreadful verdict.

A little later, half an hour perhaps, Sister Rosa strode into the kitchen. She crossed herself and cast a sombre, significant look at Sister Perpetua. Then she took my hand firmly in her cold, calloused hand and said huskily: "Try to be brave, my boy. Come, say good-bye to your poor dead mother."

12

The snow had ceased and the stars were out when we drove into the forest. The hooves sank soundlessly in the darkness as though they were treading clouds. I could see the waterfall gleaming with its long, frozen fangs. The whole world was steeped in a breathless, phantom-like stillness.

Sepp the groom sat beside me, holding the reins in his furry mittens; his breath hung in the air like a long blue feather.

"It's a cruel world," he kept muttering. "It's a miserable world we all live in."

For several days I was treated with a strange and almost menacing solicitude at the Schloss. "It's best that it happened the way it did," said Frau Maritsch, "my poor little duckling." And the Baron murmured: "We all must learn to live in the Shadow of Disaster, child, and the sooner the better."

At first my brain, numb with bewilderment, rejected the idea of my mother's death. It kept insisting, savagely almost, that she was still alive and would return at any moment and sweep me back into her arms. Then, when the truth grew inescapable, I fled into an orgy of lamentation. I reveled in histrionics. I basked in my tragic self-importance.

Then suddenly the real grief took hold of me, in all its secrecy and power. The sense of irreparable loss was mingled with the sense of a strange, hovering nearness. Even while I grasped the sickening fact that I would never see her again I felt that her presence was close beside me, that she was lingering by my bed, and that her desperate, sunken eyes were still watching me constantly.

But after a while even this childish little stratagem began to fail me and I was faced with the full, gigantic reality: the black unbearableness which somehow simply had to be borne, and the wild incomprehensibility which had to be somehow comprehended.

II

O NE FOGGY MORNING in early April I sailed from the city of Hamburg on the *Transylvania*. A friend of the Baron's, Herr Dortmeyer, was discreetly put in charge of me. He was a stout little man with a bulging neck and protuberant eyes, and his clothes filled our cabin with a scent of pipe-smoke and garlic.

During the day I wandered about amongst the intricacies of the deck, fondling the brightly polished brass and the thick, moist cables; sniffing at the tar and the grease, at the fresh white paint and the huge gray sea; listening to the churning of the motor and the clinking of bouillon cups and the tinkling of the ship's musicians as they played their Léhar and Suppé.

At night I leaned over the railing and watched the foam of the Atlantic, white as a ghost under the floating rays of light from the port-holes. I saw the moon perched in the distance like a fat white sorcerer, casting his mercury-cold magic over the boiling wake. Once a ship passed in the dis-

tance, all aglitter like a crown of diamonds, and one of the
ladies said calmly, "It's the *Berengaria,* isn't it, my dear?"
And I was filled with a sense of inexplicable mystery and
splendor. Slowly the ship slid past us and was lost in the
windy infinitude.

2

Herr Dortmeyer said gently, as he placed me on the train
for St. Louis: "Remember, my boy. Go straight to your bed
at nine o'clock sharp. Don't talk to strangers. Drink plenty
of water and don't eat too many caramels!"

"Good-bye, and thank you kindly, Herr Dortmeyer," I
said.

"Good-bye, my little friend. And remember, from now
on your name is Henry!"

I held my atlas in my lap as we raced through the interminable landscapes. I thought each state would be different, according to the colors on the map. Pennsylvania
a sultry blue—a land of torrents and thunderstorms; Ohio
a mossy green—a land of jungles and serpents; Indiana a
flaming red—the terrible domain of the man-hunters; and
Missouri vast and golden, strewn with palms like the
Sahara.

But the land remained flat and monotonous. I saw wheat-
fields that shimmered like quicksand in the blaze of noon.
I saw cornfields that pierced the withering light like a million swords. I saw muddy black streams coiling through
sprays of wild elderberry and muddy red streams where
naked boys splashed in the shallows.

My heart grew expectant as I read the names on the little railroad stations. But, alas, there were no loons to be seen in Loon Lake, there were no temples in Sparta, there were no castles in Heidelberg. Nor did I see a single Indian as we passed Mohawk Junction, or even a trace of a poplar in Poplar Bluff. No mantillas were to be seen as we rattled our way past Cordoba, no trumpets were blowing as we shot through New Jericho. Here and there stood a lonely house with shingles patterned like a moccasin; or a lonely figure stood by the tracks, wrinkled and rigid, like a corpse; while a freight-train ground past, black, endless, sepulchral, and steely poles crossed the horizon like praying mantises, absurd and sinister.

Dusk fell and the little three-pronged candelabras were lit in the coach. I gazed at the mahogany panels and the tulip-shaped lampshades. I ran my finger across the pane and over the rose-patterned plush. The land outside grew ocean-blue; we raced through vast, empty steppes. And as we rumbled into the night toward the lonely shores of the Mississippi, I felt a strange new excitement, half terror, half expectancy.

We changed trains in the middle of the night. A red-haired man in a chequered jacket led me through a black and cavernous concourse to the coaches that were labeled "Missouri-Kansas-Texas."

"Where are you going?" said the red-haired man.

"San Pedro," I said dejectedly.

"That's way past Waco," said the man, with a leer. "They're nothing but bandits down there! You'd better be careful or they'll slice out your belly with a butcher knife!"

3

My uncle's house in San Pedro was set in a thick group of trees: fig and crabapple trees, persimmon trees, mulberry trees. Its white latticed porches, etched with cracks by the grinding sunlight, shone through garlands of foliage like the bones of a skeleton.

"I hope, my child," said Uncle Adelbert, "that you will develop a taste for music."

"My mother," I said virtuously, "played the piano every day."

"What did she play? Do you recall?"

"She played the Moonlight Sonata."

"Did she play Chopin?"

"I think she did."

"Did she play Brahms?"

"I think so, Uncle."

"Well, in any case," said Uncle Adelbert, "I think we'll start you on the violin. An hour a day, that's all I ask. You can practice out in the chicken yard when it's not too hot."

There was something spectral, ectoplasmic about my Uncle Adelbert. His mouse-colored hair hung down to his shoulders. He wore high-buttoned shoes and a black mohair suit, and a silver-rimmed pince-nez was perched on his nose. I still can see him lolling in his chair, thoughtfully peeling a hot tamale: the trembling hands, the bony body, the arid brow and the haggard cheeks, the mournful eyes deep and festering as the bottom of a well and the beautiful thin voice, remote and crepuscular as a nightingale's. I still can see him standing alone in the hot little

parlor amid the maiden's hair ferns and the chirping
canaries; turning the leaves of the album, the electric fan
stirring his hair and rippling the fringe on the lampshade;
and the emaciated face, full of tiny pink wrinkles which
continually rearranged themselves like the shifting flakes
in a kaleidoscope.

Uncle Adelbert was a composer. He gave violin lessons
on Tuesdays, but the rest of the week was given to the
process of creation. He was working at this period on a
great cantata about Semiramis. He had written a Humor-
esque in the style of Schumann and a little wind octet in
the manner of Mendelssohn, as well as a tone-poem called
"Attila" and two or three Slavonic Rhapsodies. None of
them, as far as I know, was ever publicly performed; but
now and again he played brief snatches of them on the fiddle for his wide-eyed pupils. He lived alone with his
dreams, sad and tender and obsolete, still encased in the
cob-webbed echoes of the Prater and Marienbad.

Occasionally he said: "You look sad, child. Are you
lonely, by any chance?"

"Not especially, Uncle Adelbert."

"Why don't you play with the other boys?"

"I'd rather not," I said guiltily.

"Well, then, play with your cousin Stella," he said, with
a weary sigh.

And I wandered into the garden, looking for my little
cousin Stella.

4

The play-house stood in a dark, shaggy corner of the garden, which was littered with rusty hoes, rotting melons and old bicycle wheels. Strips of wall-paper hung from the walls, yellow and torn, like antique banners; and the floor was strewn with corpses—broken dolls and punctured teddy-bears.

I found Stella sitting on the steps with a large white rabbit in her lap.

"Hello, Stella."

"Hello, Henry."

"What are you doing?"

"Just thinking."

She leaned her head back importantly and drew her skirt down over her knees.

"What were you thinking about, Stella?"

Stella glanced around furtively. "I have Indian blood in my veins. Daddy said so. Isn't that interesting?"

"It certainly is," I agreed.

"Daddy says that I ought to be proud of it. That I'm a pure-blooded American." She glared at me fiercely.

I nodded discreetly and sat down on the floor.

"Do you love your father?" said Stella casually.

"My father is dead."

"Oh, I see. Do you love your mother?"

I stared at the ceiling. "She's dead too."

"Oh," said Stella, raising her brows. "You're an orphan, then, aren't you?"

"Yes," I said, trapping a ladybird. "I'm an orphan, I guess."

"What," said Stella, "is your favorite color?"

I paused for a moment. "Royal blue."

She narrowed her eyes. "Do you want to kiss me?"

"I don't know. Not especially."

"I hate boys," said Stella rapidly. "They pick their noses and bite their fingernails. They have holes in their stockings. And nasty things between their legs."

I picked up a pebble and stared at it judiciously.

"Lizards and snails," remarked Stella. "And puppy dogs' tails. That's what they're made of!"

She wore a red-dotted dress and bright red shoes with silver buttons. An ebony braid hung over her shoulder with a large pink ribbon tied at the end. Around her neck hung a string of shells and on her wrist a bracelet of coral.

She wasn't pretty; not in the least. She was too dark-skinned for one thing. Her legs were too bony and her ways were too sudden. Her eyes were abnormally large and strangely luminous, almost feverish. They glistened like bloodstones on her silky brown skin.

She dropped the rabbit in a basket and pressed her fingers into a triangle.

"What is your favorite fruit, Henry?"

"Raspberries," I said. "Or maybe strawberries."

"I like strawberries too," she said. "I like grapes. And I like peaches. I don't care for oranges particularly. Have you ever eaten a pineapple?"

I nodded. "Yes. Twice."

"They're best with sugar and a pinch of cinnamon." She cast a veiled, crafty look at me. "Sugar and spice. That's what I'm made of."

She picked up her jacks and started to play, spreading her legs across the floor. "I loathe lizards," she said confidentially. "And spiders. And snails." She tossed the jacks on the floor and held the ball in the palm of her hand. She said haughtily: "I'll show you my sugar-bowl if you promise not to touch it."

"Yes, I promise," I said.

"And you'll have to show me your puppy dog's tail."

"I don't have a puppy dog's tail."

"Yes, you do. All boys do!"

Suddenly her eyes flashed with rage; her mouth tightened dangerously. She reached out and snatched at my hair and tugged savagely.

Tears sprang to my eyes. My lips started trembling. And for an instant a strange, tender smile shone in her eyes.

"Why don't you cry?" she said softly. "Go ahead and cry, why don't you?"

And she sprang to her feet and went prancing across the garden.

5

When I went to school in the fall I wore a jacket with an embroidered collar. It was a gift from Frau Maritsch; it gave me a feeling of magical security.

But every day, as I hurried home through the eucalyptus trees, Billy Baxter leapt from the shrubs and started to throw little pebbles at me.

"Fraidy cat!" he cried as I ran. "Sissy boy! With your prissy jacket!"

When I finally came home I hid in the play-house and wept silently. And after a while I grew ashamed of my Austrian jacket and my Austrian memories.

One fine day Billy Baxter suddenly sprang out of a berry bush. He threw a handful of gravel at me and cried: "Mama's baby!"

A hysterical hatred took hold of me. I lunged wildly at Billy Baxter. I dug my fingers into his neck and hurled him violently to the ground. My whole organism was electric with the intensity of loneliness and persecution. I pounded his face with my fists. I ripped at his shirt, I tore at his throat.

Finally I loosened my grip and gazed breathlessly at Billy. His freckled face was spattered with mud, his lips were puffy and bleeding. He lay flat on his back and stared up at me blearily.

I stood breathless, expectant. Neither of us spoke; neither of us stirred.

And an exultation swept through me, assuaging as honey. I started laughing. Softly at first; and then fiercely, deliriously.

"That will teach you!" I sang merrily. "That will teach you, Billy Baxter!"

I went racing across the field, ripping the leaves from the sun-flowers. I went leaping over the boulders and swung from the boughs of the dusty cedar trees.

On the following evening I saw Billy squatting at the edge of the creek.

"Come on down," he said softly. "I've caught a turtle. Do you want to see it?"

"Not especially," I said.

"It's only a baby. It won't bite."

"I'm not afraid of it," I said. "And I'm not afraid of you either!" My voice darkened. "Do you want to have another fight, Billy Baxter?"

I crawled down and sat on a smooth purple stone beside Billy. I watched the mud ooze through my toes like a row of black snails. The water crept lazily over the moss-bearded pebbles. A bull snake slid past us and vanished among the yuccas.

Billy jabbed at the turtle with a long yellow stick.

"Don't," I muttered. "Stop teasing it. Or I'll fight you, Billy Baxter!"

He rammed the stick into the ground. "Do you want to know something?" he said.

"What about?"

"About Stella."

I tossed a pebble into the water.

"She's half-nigger," said Billy.

"It's not true," I said. "It's a lie."

"Chester Halliburton told me."

"Chester Halliburton is a liar."

"Look," said Billy, "how dark she is. She's as dark as a Mexican!"

"She has Indian blood in her. I happen to know," I said solemnly.

"Well," said Billy, scratching his elbow, "let's go and catch frogs."

"All right," I said darkly. "But stop telling lies!"

So we waded upstream through the copper-bright reeds, watching the spiders weaving their webs and the water-bugs dancing. It was almost dusk when I wandered home again through the lonely pecan grove. I heard the sound of women laughing down at the edge of the alfalfa field, and the baying of hounds along the banks of the Colorado. Night came crawling like lava down the slopes of Mount Avis; and a train shot through the distance, dazzling and venomous.

6

Winter swept over the plains with its chilly blue northers, and then spring with its clamorous torrents and floods. The thunder came roaring. The rain slashed at the cactus-land and the lightning went rippling across the sky like a white-hot artery.

On the following morning the sun came out again. A reddish ooze filled the garden. The tomatoes were coated with an iridescent slime.

"Come," said Stella. "Let's go wading."

"There'll be lizards," I said. "And snails."

"Don't be a coward," said Stella contemptuously. "Come. Let's climb to the top of the tree."

So we climbed up the fig tree and sat huddled among the foliage.

Stella brushed an ant from her skirt. "I'm going to get married. I've just decided."

"Oh, really? Whom will you marry?"

"I don't know. Someone rich."

"Someone here in San Pedro?"

"Certainly not. A duke. Or a count." She plucked at a silky wisp of hair. "I'll go to Paris, or maybe London. I'll be as famous as Norma Talmadge, or even Pola Negri."

"You'll be an actress?" I said, wide-eyed.

"Or maybe a dancer," said Stella casually. "I'll have diamonds and furs. I'll wear nothing but taffeta."

I grew thoughtful. "I don't suppose . . ."

"Well? What?"

"That I'll ever be rich."

"Certainly not," said Stella scornfully. "You're too shy. And too stupid."

"You'd never marry me, would you?"

"I wouldn't dream of it," said Stella.

"What will he look like? Do you imagine?"

"Who?"

"The man whom you're going to marry?"

"He'll have beautiful white teeth. And curly hair. And masses of money."

"Will you kiss him?" I said miserably.

"Of course I'll kiss him," said Stella.

"Will you let him see you naked?"

"Well, I might," whispered Stella.

One warm evening we were sitting alone in the canna-bed at dusk. The sphinx moths were beginning to gather, swift and vibrant as humming birds.

"I'll buy you a necklace," I said softly, "if you marry me, Stella."

"Don't be ridiculous," said Stella. "You don't have the money. And you never will."

"You'd look like a beautiful Egyptian princess."

"I don't want to look like an Egyptian princess!"

A feeling of desperate and unappeasable longing swept through me. The sky was darkening to a deep sea-blue. The scent of the cannas filled the air. I caught the musk of Stella's body—resinous and tart, like sun-soaked juniper.

I plucked at one of the canna blossoms and held it under my nose: a strange and insinuating, unmistakably female smell.

I said hoarsely: "Do you remember what you told me one day?"

"I have no idea," said Stella coldly.

"That you'd show me your sugar-bowl?"

"Don't be ridiculous," said Stella.

"You said it! I swear!"

"Well," said Stella, "I've changed my mind."

"Please," I begged. "Let me look at it!"

"Don't be ludicrous," said Stella.

"I'll keep it a secret. I swear I will!"

"What will you give me?" said Stella craftily.

"I'll buy you a bag full of jelly beans."

"It's not enough. Not anything like."

"I'll buy you a doll at the five-and-ten."

"I'm weary of dolls. Dolls bore me."

"I'll buy you a bracelet," I whispered.

"What kind of bracelet?" said Stella sulkily.

"With emeralds," I said. "Or even diamonds. . . ."

I still can hear the whispering leaves, conspiratorial, expectant; and the tense, breathless silence as she lifted her skirt. I still can see the curves of her flesh, downy pink like the skin of a peach, and the satin-smooth, amber-hued area of the abdomen; and the coy little crease, shimmering faintly with moisture, suavely curved like the lip of a shell and daintily lined with a silky shadow.

"There," said Stella, straightening her skirt. "You'll have to swear not to tell!"

"I'll never tell as long as I live. I swear I won't, Stella."

"I'll let you touch it," she added primly, "if you bring me a diamond bracelet."

I ripped the petals from the blood-red blossom. "All right. Don't forget!"

7

Billy Baxter and I went down to the creek one windless evening. We were carrying our nets. We were out to catch moths. The creek trickled feebly among the smooth violet boulders, which were crusted with layers of mud, hexagonally veined, like the shell of a tortoise.

The great heat had fallen. The fields all lay blistered. The streets were quaking with heat and the boughs were seething with blood-red caterpillars.

We tossed our pants over a bough and lay down in the shallow water, waiting for the moths to come floating through the gathering twilight. As we lay there Zenobia came wandering through the cedars.

She stood by the shore with her arms akimbo. She was wearing a crimson dress. Her hair was divided into geometrical black tufts.

"Come for a dip," I said, "why don't you?"

She shook her head. "I don't dare, honey."

"It's lovely and warm," said Billy coaxingly.

"I'd never dare! All staring naked!"

The fireflies burned in the dove-grey dusk and a huge white moth sailed through the shrubbery. We jumped ashore and snatched at our nets and went racing through the cedars.

When we came back we found Zenobia lying in the pool, nude and grinning.

"What have you got there?" she gurgled.

"It's a Luna moth," said Billy.

He held the frail, miraculous creature between his fingers for her to see.

"Lordy me! What will you do with it?"

"I'll frame it," said Billy.

"Lordy me!" sang Zenobia. "What a queer thing to do!"

Her skin shone like ebony. The stream passed over her thighs and the drops clung to her furry black hair like drops of blood.

We grew silent as we watched her. Finally she waded ashore. She stood motionless in the gloom, almost invisible, like a part of the night.

Then she sat down beside us, dripping and grinning. Her eyes rolled like marbles and her gold teeth glistened. She leaned back her head and drew her palms over her breasts. The stars peeped through the afterglow and the land sank into secrecy.

Zenobia started to sing: very softly, like the sound of a lullaby. She sang "Look, Jehovah," and "My Lord, What a Morning." Then she started caressing us ever so gently; until she finally whispered, "There. Lie down and I'll teach you, honey . . ."

First it was Billy and then I and then it was Billy and then I again as she guided us deftly through the mysteries of coition. "There," she said. "Take it easy . . . Not so fast, honey boy . . ." She lay heaving on the mud, primordial and sinuous, while her thighs enveloped our hairless little limbs like a great amoeba.

Finally we lay back panting, listening to the crickets in

the meadow and watching the moon rise up from Mount Avis.

Zenobia purred: "Well, I'd better be going."

We lay motionless while she dressed.

Finally we said: "Good night, Zenobia!"

"Good night, honey. And say your prayers. . . ."

We walked home slowly. There was a feverish brightness in the glow of the moon. It seemed to draw a new pungency from the sour-smelling shrubs. The American Beauties drooped from the lattices in fleshy festoons. And the jet-black shadows cast on the asphalt suggested a land of hallucinations, a mesmerized little world without depth, without memory.

8

A fierce, fiery wind started to blow across the land. The cottonfields crackled and hissed in the brassy light. A terrible glare hung like a halo on top of Mount Avis, and the air was filled with grains which tickled the nostrils and burned the retina.

I was obsessed, in San Pedro, with a feeling of impending violence. The very light suggested recklessness, fanaticism, bloodshed. Those coiling creeks, studded with stones which had faces like an embryo's; those carmine slopes where the scorpions lay basking in the blaze, tense, heraldic. Something hideous was going to happen. Fever and vastness shone in the air. At any moment, I thought, some tiny spark might fall from the sky and the world would burst into a great yellow flame.

Sometimes I would sit in the bay-window, fondling the leaves of a rubber-plant while Uncle Adelbert performed some intricate piece by Paganini. A spray of colored glass glittered and tinkled in the breeze. Two beaded cushions from Chihuahua lay on the wicker settee, and on the piano stood a basket made from an armadillo's skin and filled with old postcards from Vienna and Nuremberg.

On the walls hung the following: an autographed portrait of Meyerbeer; a watercolor of Capri; an old engraving of a scene from *Parsifal;* a small Turkish rug; a strange collection of little daggers, boomerangs, assegais, stilettos, and in their midst, like some perilous deity, a sepia photograph of Stella's mother against a background of roses daintily framed in bamboo.

I used to stare at this portrait to the accompanying strains of the violin: Aunt Rosita, still casting her spell over the melancholy household. She wore a white linen blouse with a high lace collar and a heart-shaped locket which hung dangling over her bosom. Her luxuriant black hair looked like the coat of a poodle and on top of it was perched an Uhlan's cap with a feather. There was an enigmatic leer on her thick, sullen lips. She looked like a Papuan belle groomed for a fancy dress ball.

One day, as I sat there listening, my uncle's eyes began to water. He crossed the room and ran his fingers over Aunt Rosita's face. "She had eyes," he said, "like Duse's! She was lovelier than Lola Montez!" Tears went trickling down his cheek and suddenly his Adam's apple began to quiver, his eyes rolled uncannily and his head swayed like a cobra's. His whole body shook spasmodically. "Oh, my child, where have you gone? What have they done to you? What have they done?" And he fell to his knees and tore at his tresses.

I took my violin-case and stepped out into the yard. A lazy breeze was silvering the locusts; the smell of wood-smoke filled the air. I heard the voice of the hot tamale man wailing in the distance and the wheels of the water-melon wagon creaking on the gravel. Lola Belle Haines was out on the sidewalk, playing hop-scotch with Suzy Long, and Stella was squatting under the fig-tree, playing mar-bles with Billy Baxter.

I scraped my bow over the strings, producing horrible little squeaks that made the Rhode Island Reds flutter their wings with hysteria. Even the rabbits flattened their ears and wiggled their nostrils in disgust. Finally I tucked my violin in the shade of a bush, counted the pennies in my pocket, and slipped out through the gate.

I walked down Guadaloupe Street toward the confec-tioner's shop on the corner, where I bought some licorice shoe-laces and a lump of pink rock-candy. Then I strolled through the empty lots on my way to the river. Tiny hum-ming-birds were hovering over the blossoming honey-suckle and sharp tongues of light shone like tinsel on the broken glass. Centipedes crawled over the dust, looking for crannies of moisture. Doodlebugs hid at the base of their conical traps. Pigs lay twitching and groaning in their little black pens and swallowtails danced over the scrawny chrysanthemums. I heard the twanging of a Jew's harp on a shady veranda. And then nothing but stillness: a huge, soaring stillness.

9

The Cochrane Mansion stood in a grove at a curve in the river. All around rose the drowsy moss-bearded trees. The Doric columns reared through the shadows, suffocated with ivy. Thistles and milkweeds filled the paths and the castiron stag was scabby with lichen.

One fine day I found Stella skipping rope in front of our house. Suddenly she tossed her rope on the grass. "Come, let's go to the Cochrane Mansion."

"What will we do when we get there?"

"Look for ghosts," answered Stella.

"Real ghosts?"

"Naturally," said Stella. "Suzy Long told me about them."

"What did she say?"

"There's a man without a head down in the cellar."

"Heavens. What else?"

"Up in the bedroom there's a skeleton on the bed."

"My. Anything else?"

"And there's a treasure up in the attic. A box full of pearls and a chest full of gold pieces."

"I don't believe it," I said.

"That's what Lola Belle told me. We might as well go and make sure, don't you think?"

So we walked to the end of the street and followed the path by the river. Stella's hair blew over her face as the wind rolled over the sand-bars.

"Do you believe in ghosts, Henry?"

"I'm not sure. Do you, Stella?"

"Last night I looked through my window and saw a man down in the bushes."

"Really?" I said. "What kind of man?"

"Big and black. Like a burglar."

"What did he do?"

"He waved a stick at me."

"And what then?"

"He just waited."

"Was it a ghost?"

"It might have been. And then it mightn't, of course," said Stella.

Finally we came to the Cochrane Mansion just as the sun was ready to set. A lazy light tipped the shutters like a puff of golden powder. Nothing stirred except for the grasshoppers that swarmed in the thicket and the hornets that buzzed over the rotten crabapples.

We slid through the gate and stole around to the side of the porch. The steps creaked uneasily. We stopped and peered through a broken windowpane.

The enormous dark room looked like a cave under water. The last rays of daylight pierced the blinds on ladders of dust. The broken chairs, the tattered curtains, the disemboweled sofa—they looked like a tangle down in the bottom of the sea.

Something strange lay by the window. I picked it up gingerly. It was a shriveled little sack filled with a pale, mysterious fluid.

"How peculiar," said Stella. "What's inside it, do you suppose?"

I untied the rubber knot; the evil liquid flowed out.

"How revolting," said Stella. "What do you think it is, Henry?"

I peered at the thumb-shaped tube and slipped it furtively in my pocket.

We found a window half-opened and climbed into an oak-paneled library. The floor was littered with volumes, as though some maniac had flung them about. I glanced at some of the titles: *The Secrets of Tibet; A Wanderer in Abyssinia; The Loves of Napoleon.*

"Come. Let's look for the man down in the cellar," I whispered.

"No," said Stella. "Let's hunt for the treasure up in the attic."

So we tiptoed into the hall and climbed the great stairway which spiraled into a limbo-like gloom. All around us, suspended in the haze like mythological spirits, were dusty little statues of nymphs, fauns and centaurs.

Finally we stepped into the attic. It was like the air in a jungle. The glow from the sunset seeped through the misty panes. It lit on a quagmire of tattered dresses, dank portfolios and rusty birdcages. We plucked uneasily at rotting petticoats, we stared in horror at peeling mirrors.

"Stella! Look!" I said suddenly.

It was a tarnished silver bracelet, chastely decorated with little blue beads, like forget-me-nots.

Stella slipped it over her wrist. "Isn't it gorgeous?" she murmured.

"Do you remember what you promised? If I gave you a bracelet?"

"No," said Stella. "What did I promise?"

"Don't you remember? Out in the canna-bed?"

"Oh," said Stella. Her eyes grew hazy. She pursed her lips cunningly.

"Nobody will see us," I whispered.

"Well," said Stella, "I'll think it over."

I snatched the bracelet from her wrist. "A promise," I snapped, "is a promise!"

A little smile crept over her face: sly, cruel, mongolian.

"All right. But you'll have to swear to be my slave. For ever and ever!"

The last shred of light fell on her skin like a golden feather as she lifted her dress and stood naked by the window.

It was a strange little moment. Savage and sad and yet exquisite. Even in my ignorance and folly I was subtly aware of the flavor: of the mingled pathos and enchantment, of the splendor and squalor.

"Get down on your knees," she said.

I sank to my knees in front of her.

"You can touch me now," she whispered.

I passed my finger over her flesh, which seemed to enclose, like the skin of a plum, some dusky and mysterious sweetness.

"And now kiss me," she said.

I pressed my lips to her olive skin. It felt sleek and curiously frail, like a butterfly's wing. And again I caught that fragrance: tart and tantalizing, like sun-soaked evergreen.

"There," she said, dropping her skirt. "Give me the bracelet now, please."

"Wait a minute," I pleaded. "Don't you want . . . wouldn't you like. . . ."

Her eyes gleamed like a snake's. "Give me the bracelet. Or I'll go and tell on you."

The light suddenly died. A cavelike gloom gripped the place. The stuffed owl and the wooden rocking-horse were changed into monsters.

Stella whispered: "Did you hear something?"

"It sounded like footsteps!"

"It's the man without a head!"

"Or the skeleton in the bedreom!"

We rushed down the stairs and groped our way through the littered library. The broken chairs and the velvet sofa crouched in the dark like beasts of prey.

A batlike shadow stirred in the curtains; a tiny voice cried out from the woodwork.

"Quick!" said Stella. "I see him!"

"Who? Where?"

"There! In the doorway!"

We went scrambling hysterically through the half-open window; we raced wildly across the porch and through the dusk-hooded garden.

Finally we reached the path by the river.

"Lord," gasped Stella. "He almost got us!"

"Who was it?" I panted.

"Didn't you see him?" said Stella.

"Was it a ghost?" I said softly.

"Don't be stupid," said Stella. "It was a horrible black burglar! With a stick in his hand!"

"What did he want?"

"You fool!" cried Stella. "He wanted to kill us!"

The arc-lights blazed on the lonely road. Everything turned to an icy white: blank, inhuman, inexorable, like the end of the world.

III

It was a blistering day in August when my uncle suddenly went mad. I was sitting under the fig-tree, whittling away at a hickory stick, when the door was flung open and Uncle Adelbert rushed out, stark naked except for a pair of high-buttoned shoes.

"What have they done to her?" he shouted, brandishing a Florentine stiletto. And he ran into the street, screaming, "I'll get them! I'll get them!"

That evening two men in black suits arrived at the house and took Uncle Adelbert away in a limousine. He was weeping resignedly. It was the last that I ever saw of him. I sat by the window and watched the car head for the road to San Marcos.

After a while the sky turned green. Puffy clouds squirmed over the cotton-fields. A sickening wind, hoarse and stifling, crawled down from Mount Avis. The yucca plants shook spasmodically, shedding their stiff parchment petals. Suddenly the rain started falling—large, widely spaced drops that rattled like bullets on the corrugated roof of the play-house.

The storm raged for ten minutes. Then it stopped abruptly. The sky cleared with an eerie swiftness and the blaze of the sun shot down the street, where a few tiny drops still puckered the flame-tinted roofs.

An elderly lady, a Mrs. Sammons, had come to take care of us. She was sitting in the parlor fanning herself with a raffia fan. I walked stealthily down the hall and stepped out on the veranda. Then I walked across the garden and entered the dank little playhouse.

Stella was sitting in the corner, clutching her rabbit in her arms. She stared at me wildly with her huge frightened eyes.

"Go away," she said softly. "Leave me alone. I hate you!" And as I stood there idiotically, longing to comfort and appease her, she suddenly screamed, "Go away! Leave me alone! Or I'll kill you. . . !"

2

Three days later Mrs. Sammons drove me down to the railway station and I climbed on a train bound for the dark, enormous north.

I went rumbling through Arkansas, past thorny blue swamps where the wild fowl went soaring into the sullen air. And then up through Missouri, past great stony pastures where the cattle stood motionless in the dusk, as though petrified. And on through Illinois with its black, haggard towns which lay spellbound under the horrifying glare of the arc-lights. And over the hills of Wisconsin, still pearly with dawn, shedding their wrinkles of mist like a snake shedding its skin.

Finally I entered the cool, wooded heart of Prairie du Loup. The sun was just setting as I stepped off the train.

An enormous man with a shaven skull and a blue glass eye strode down the platform. He seized my hand and crushed it violently, so that I whimpered with pain.

He leered at me playfully. "So you're Henni," he growled.

"I've changed it to Henry," I stammered.

"Bravo!" he roared. "That's the spirit! We'll make a man out of you even if it kills you!" He lowered his head in a formidable way. "What's the capital of America?"

"Is it Washington, Uncle Claudius?"

"And what's the biggest state in the Union?"

"Is it Texas?" I said.

"Right!" he bellowed. "And what's the smallest, while we're on the subject?"

"I've forgotten, Uncle Claudius."

"Well," he said, "never mind. We'll talk it over in the morning. Come along, now. Don't dawdle."

Prairie du Loup was a salubrious hamlet poised on the banks of the Wisconsin River. A little church of red brick rose at the far end of Water Street and a gilded eagle shone over the porch of the Eagle Hotel. We passed Muhleisen's Pharmacy, with a big red jar in its window, which shone with a secret luminescence, like an enormous egg-shaped ruby. And then we passed Heckmeyer's Ice Cream Parlor with its frilled lace curtains, its braided wire chairs and its brightly colored calendars. We passed Schmaltz's Smart Fashions and McGillicuddy's General

Store, Van Druten's Garage and Fratellini's Fresh Fruits, and finally we came to the embankment and I stepped in the little rowboat which was fastened to the edge of the moss-lacquered wharf. Uncle Claudius tugged at the prow, threw the oars into the locks, planted his thighs on the creaking seat and started to row toward the opposite shore.

A wooded island loomed to the west of us. Slowly the boat moved upstream toward the dark, tangled gully that lay a mile above the bridge. I dipped my finger in the current; the water was muddy, olive-colored. We passed some hills shaped like thimbles and covered with millions of blue-bells, and then a broad, fan-shaped estuary paved with little white pebbles. The boat touched the shore. The reeds slapped at the oars. We slid into an inlet and tossed the boat-chain over the edge of the pier.

"Well, my boy," said my uncle, pointing to a big brown house on a knoll, "there's your home. You'll be washing the dishes and fetching the water, so you'd better get used to it!"

We passed the pump, where Uncle Claudius filled a wooden bucket for me to carry; we climbed the path past the flowering iris, cautiously straddling the discs of cow-dung; we paused by a raspberry bush to pick a handful of berries; and finally, just as the sun was setting, we stood by the door of the house.

The door swung open and a weather-beaten woman rushed out on the veranda.

"Dearest boy!" cried Aunt Elfrida, enfolding me in her arms. "What a sorrow we have had! He was a saint, in his little way . . ."

She was quite different from what I had imagined: broad

and dark as an Apache. She wore red-beaded moccasins and a rough brownish smock patterned with zig-zags and triangles, like an Indian rug. Her head was too large for her squat shapeless body. She had a philosopher's brow and an immense, beak-like nose, bloodshot eyes and a loose, rather gluttonous mouth, like a carp's.

She looked like a demented squaw, with a touch of the teutonic—an air of hectic expectancy, of lonely fanaticism. She was a fierce vegetarian as well as a dedicated sun-worshiper. I caught a glimpse of her in the woods on several occasions, lying nude on a khaki blanket with a battered copy of the *Bhagavad-Ghita.* Or out on the veranda a pass-ing breeze would tug at her robe and expose her sagging breasts, brown and burnished, like a leather purse. And once or twice I saw her poised on the edge of the pier like a loney Buddha, arms folded symmetrically, perform-ing her Yogi exercises.

She would go for long walks, picking berries as she went and kneeling to drink from the cool mossy streams; or pausing thoughtfully in a thicket to identify some tiny toadstool; or cutting the bark from a birch-tree as she muttered a phrase from Lao-Tze.

"Well, now tell me," she said, as we entered the living room, "what has happened to your poor little cousin?"

"You mean Stella?"

"Quite. Stella."

"She's gone off to Amarillo."

"Mercy me. Where is that?"

"It's up in the Panhandle."

"And what will she do in the Panhandle?"

"Go to school. With some nuns."

"Nuns," said my aunt, growling slightly. "How extremely old-fashioned. I wonder what struck poor old Adelbert. Is she a pretty little girl?"

"Well," I said, "not exactly."

"Is she intelligent, by any chance?"

"She's very bright," I said, "at arithmetic."

My aunt stared at me indulgently. "What beautiful eyes you have, child. Soft and brown, like a doe's. Well, I'll do all I can for you . . ."

I glanced about rather uneasily. An oil-lamp stood on the huge black table, which was littered with curious roots, bits of crystal, lumps of resin, fossilized twigs, giant beetles, rattlesnake rattles and broken arrowheads. Towering bookshelves were heaped with rows of dusty old manuscripts, disintegrating catalogues, and unsavory-looking bottles. On the wall hung some lithographs left behind by an earlier tenant—"A Rescue in the Alps," "The Fisherman's Pride," "The Wreck of the Hesperus."

After a casual little supper of cabbage and rhubarb we sat reading for a while by the thin yellow light: Aunt Elfrida with her *Dialectics,* Uncle Claudius with his Schopenhauer and I with *The Mystery of Edwin Drood.* Finally I crept into my bed and lay in the naphtha-scented gloom, listening to the rats that went scurrying across the rafters; falling to the floor now and again in a paroxysm of lust and squealing with their horrible little voices.

3

Autumn drew her stupendous golden net over the hills. The leaves yellowed and fell. The pears reddened and rotted. During the day I roamed through the woods, trapping beetles and arachnids. After dusk I stayed at home under the eyes of Aunt Elfrida and studied my French and Latin and Geography. The glow of the kerosene lamp lay trembling on the rivers of Uganda, on the invectives against Catiline and the fables of La Fontaine.

The cold weather came. The woods darkened swiftly from a spectacular crimson gold to a drab, drizzling violet. And then one morning I awoke and the thimble-shaped hillocks were cloaked in a billowing, blazing white.

For a week we were snowbound. There was nothing but snow. Snow lay heaped on the sills and the porch was knee-deep in snow. The gooseberry bushes were little waves in a great white ocean. We dug a path past the woodshed to the small shingled outhouse. We opened jars of pickled crabapples and sat huddled in the kitchen, listening to the wind rattling the panes and the water boiling in the kettle.

The sun came out; the drooping boughs shone like bundles of diamonds. I put on my boots and went prowling in the woods. All that whiteness around me! So marvelously pure, so utterly still! I plucked at the snow, sniffed at it curiously and licked it with the tip of my tongue. It tasted thin and a little salty, like sweat from the clouds. A sunny breeze dove past me. I scooped the snow from a twig and tossed it into the river, where it floated like foam. A passionate joy took hold of me. I rolled over in the snow. I felt the softness surge around me like a giant caress. And overhead hung the sky, bluer and lovelier than I had ever seen it—so radiant, so intensely real that I lifted my hand and tried to touch it.

One day a postcard arrived for me. It was from Amarillo, Texas, and was written in a juicy, circular handwriting with little circles like moons floating over the i's. It was a photograph of the Amarillo County Court House, a mournful edifice surrounded by scrawny red pillars, and it read:

"Dear Henry: How are you? It is perfectly ghastly in Amarillo. I have taken up archery and I'm writing a play with a friend of mine, Cecilia Boggs, who is terribly talented. As always, your cousin Stella."

I gazed thoughtfully at each word, hoping to detect some hidden message. I stared at the luridly colored Court House, probing for some secret association. I even sniffed at the little card, trying to detect some tenuous aroma. Finally I tucked it in my copy of *Dracula* and proceeded to other matters.

My Aunt Elfrida continued patiently to supervise my studies, and periodically my Uncle Claudius indulged in an oral examination. There were fleeting sorties into geometry and physics. There were spelling sessions, with equivocal words like "diarrhoea" and "sassafras," or the names of strange cities such as "Tallahassee" and "Ocon-omowoc." But most of the time was spent on matters such as the decay of Rome under Caligula, the corrup-tion of Florence under the Medici, and the degeneracy of France under the Bourbons.

I passed from Cicero to Virgil; from Lepanto to Aus-

terlitz; from the sorrows of Werther to the peccadilloes
of d'Artagnan.

"You might as well," said my Aunt Elfrida, "steep your
mind in the grandeurs of Europe. When you go to Cliffdale next fall and come under the influence of your old
Aunt Ursula it will be nothing but cabbage and Cheddar,
and Thackeray and Trollope, and similar nonsense."

But my greatest interest lay in geography. I stared at
my maps by the hour. I fell in love with the multitudinous
little corners of the world. As I drew my finger along the
wrinkled black line of a coast or a river, tempestuous landscapes rose before me—the reedy stretches of Patagonia,
the crystal domes of the Aleutians, the poisonous thickets
of Sarawak.

"Where would you go, Aunt Elfrida, if you could ride
on a magic carpet?"

"Mercy, child. I'd stay where I am. In the bosom of
Nature."

"How about the Galapagos Islands? Or the Great Wall
of China?"

"You're too restless, my boy. There's nothing in the world
that's any better than what you can find right here in
the woods. The Egyptian sphinx is no grander than an oak
tree in autumn! The Taj Mahal is no lovelier than a forest
by moonlight!"

One day I showed her a little poem I had written: "To
a Snowflake." Aunt Elfrida read it thoughtfully, drew her
fingers through her hair and lifted the kettle from the
oven with a sigh.

"Well," she said, "I wouldn't be surprised if there's a
spark of the poet in you. Don't squander it, child. Keep in
touch with the world of Nature. Avoid postures and affec-

tations. Avoid decadence and artifice. Avoid slogans. Avoid hypocrisy. Study the birds and the insects. . . ."

And she stared into the night, her golden tooth ablaze in the lamplight and her desperate little eyes peering through the gloom like a marmoset's.

4

Finally spring began to crawl over that great lonely territory. Fragrant streams came trickling from the hills and foaming waterfalls poured into the gullies. The deep of the forest was filled with infinitesimal bubbling noises. Under the fresh new sunlight the pebbles in the river shone like topaz. Puffy clouds moved luxuriantly over the empty black fields and the cows wandered forth through their soggy pastures.

And soon the woods by Prairie du Loup were drenched in a buzzing sensuality. The cowslips came out and the berry-bushes blossomed. I was enchanted with all that loneliness, that calm, that animal secrecy. I watched the grasshoppers with their hard, thorny legs and horse-like faces, and the small Lycaenid butterflies rubbing their iridescent wings. I lurked in the woods and watched the wood-peckers and the baby squirrels. I studied the scaly pattern on the skin of a dead rattlesnake and I pored over the glassy wings and steel-blue bodies of the dragon flies.

I gathered wild flowers—violets, cat-grass, valerian. I peeled the bark from the birches, tense and velvety, like snowy leather. I stepped on the syrupy cow-dung and felt the warmth ooze through my toes, and I reached into the water to trap little black tadpoles.

Sometimes my uncle took me by the hand for a lesson in natural history. "This is *Datura stramonium,*" he said, pointing to a fiery trumpet flower. "Don't eat the fruits. They'll make you sick. They're good for asthma and sunburn."

Once he pointed to a tall pale mushroom. "*Amanita philloides!* You'll die in terrible agony if you eat it, my boy." And now and again he'd point to a butterfly and mutter: "*Argynnis idalia!* Do you see those silver spots?" Or: "*Grapta interrogationis!* Do you see that little question-mark?"

I invented names for various landmarks as I strolled through the wilderness: The Sorcerer's Den, the Sultan's Throne, the Pond of the Wicked Troll. But these names, after a month or two, seemed strangely incongruous; they seemed to evaporate in the atmosphere of sumach and wild crabapples, and I changed them to the Gray Wolf's Cavern, the Moose's Lair, Powhatan's Pool.

And when I finally came home again I found my uncle dozing in his rocking chair, with a daddy-long-legs prowling across his hairy abdomen. He'd open his eyes and flutter his nostrils, as though scenting some dangerous adversary, and embark on a long digression on the Council of Trent or the Punic Wars. He kept watching me with a brutal, suspicious love in his blurry eyeball, heaving uneasily now and again like some restive old pachyderm.

"Do you believe in God, my boy?"

"I'm not sure, Uncle Claudius."

"You're not sure!"

"Well, maybe I do."

"Make up your mind! You do or you don't!"

"I suppose I do," I murmured, blushing. "Is there a God, Uncle Claudius?"

"Jesus and Mary," bellowed my uncle. "Of course there's no God! He's a relic of the jungle! A mirage! A *fata morgana!* An anachronism!"

After supper he lay down on his cot on the porch and I watched the moonlight seep through the screen, silvering the rose-patterned sugar-bowl. And as I stared at the wild old man lying on his back, monstrous and comatose, a desolation crept over my soul, a wild, aching loneliness.

5

One day I went strolling down the path toward the shore. The air smelled like honey and the grasshoppers were swarming. The woods were thick with briars, which scratched at my arms like little witches.

The path turned. I saw a lean, sun-tanned boy on the edge of the pier. His feet were dangling in the water; he was whittling at a long black twig.

He turned casually when he saw me.

"Hello there."

"Oh, hello."

"You live in that big old house, don't you?"

"Yes, I do. With my Uncle Claudius."

"I live at the crossroads. With my Uncle Pino."

"Oh. I see," I said affably.

"Are you an orphan?" said the boy.

"Yes," I murmured, with dignity.

"Funny, isn't it?"

"What's funny?"

"Being an orphan!"

I scowled thoughtfully.

"I hate my uncle," said the sun-tanned boy.

"That's too bad," I said tactfully.

"My name's Tony. What's yours?"

"Henry," I said, lowering my eyes.

"Look," he said, flourishing his knife. "I'm making a bow and a couple of arrows."

I sat down on the pier and dipped my finger in the current.

"I'm going bird-hunting," said the boy.

"Are you really? Which birds?"

"Quails. Pheasants. Bob o'links."

"Oh," I said. "That sounds interesting."

Tony grinned at me slyly. "Come along. If you feel like it."

I blushed with delight. "I'd love to," I said.

I looked at him cautiously. He was older than I by a year or two. He had curly black hair which clung to the nape of his neck and mocking green eyes shaded by long, heavy lashes. There was something about his lips which was cunning and cruel. There was a cleft in his chin and a little scar on his cheek. His voice was furry and hoarse; his movements were supple and feline.

"Come," he said. "Let's go for a swim."

He stripped off his jeans, tossed them lightly over a bough and stood for a moment on the edge of the pier. Then he rose on his toes and dove into the water.

I watched his lithe, tawny body glide easily through the

depth. Then he shot toward the surface. His head bobbed
up like a cocoanut.

"Come on in! It's wonderful!" he shouted, kicking
vigorously with his legs.

"Is it cold?" I said wanly.

Tony laughed. "Are you scared?"

"No," I said. "I'm not scared." I started unbuttoning
my trousers. Then I turned my back shyly and jumped
clumsily into the water.

A crazy delight gripped me suddenly. I struck out for the
middle of the river. The touch of the prickly-cool water
made my flesh feel electric. Bubbles of foam shot through
the air like iridescent balloons and the dome of the sky
looked dazzling, stupendous.

I rolled over on my back and paddled along gently. I
saw nothing but the clouds, great motionless coils of snow-
white marble. I was filled with a passionate longing to soar
through the air and land on those bright, paradisical
cascades.

The chill of the water seeped through me. A steely blade
slid down my legs. And all of a sudden a claw of ice ripped
viciously at my belly.

I gasped for air. I doubled up. I flailed at the water with
my arms. A sinister weight, like a chain of lead, started to
tug at my abdomen. I lunged desperately toward the shore
but my legs dangled helplessly, numb and inert with the
violence of the cramp.

I howled "Help!" A torrent of water went rushing down
my windpipe. The sky capsized suddenly; splinters of
flame shot through the air. I tried to scream but there
was nothing but a thin little gurgle. I went spiraling down
toward the pit of the river.

Great weeds swarmed around me, dark and vicious like eels. Something slimy clutched at my thighs. I kicked wildly and shot up again.

I caught sight for a moment of the dazzle of sunlight. But this time it was shrill and unearthly, apocalyptic. The clouds looked like smoke from some huge conflagration. I closed my eyes, overwhelmed with a hideous indifference.

And then I felt something tugging at me, like a great tawny octopus. I twisted frantically. Then I collapsed. I felt the tentacles around my neck, drawing me gently and relentlessly through the needle-cold water.

The light exploded all of a sudden, like a Roman candle. I opened my eyes and saw Tony sitting astride me, like a rider. I felt my arms raised and lowered, I felt his knees pumping my chest. I felt the slime ooze out of my nostrils and ears, even my eyeballs.

Gradually the pain started to leave me. I breathed in gingerly little spasms. Tony lifted me cautiously and laid my head in his lap. I could feel the throbbing in his chest and the silky warmth of his flat hard belly. A strange and luminous joy, heady as wine, trickled through me.

"God," I said. "I'm an idiot."

"You certainly are," whispered Tony.

"You saved my life, didn't you, Tony?"

"Hush," said Tony. "Don't talk."

6

Spring deepened into summer. The billowing hills grew
bright with sumach. The air grew caressive, so that I
spent my days on the sandbanks, gathering mussels and
building castles and watching the catfish bask in the shallows. Now and then in the early morning a pearly fog hung
over the banks: I'd hear the cow-bell tinkling in the distance and see the cows move through the reeds, only their
black sickled horns just barely visible above the mist. And
then the mist gradually dissolved, the leaves grew bright
in the sunlight, the slimy banks grew iridescent and the
stench of rot oozed from the water. The morning dew still
shone on the cobwebs like tiny glass beads and the smell of
fresh coffee went drifting over the cat-tails.

My Uncle Claudius spent most of the day in a pair of
pink-striped pyjamas, powerfully stained with streaks of
syrup, perspiration and olive oil. He'd sit in his rocking-
chair in the shade of a maple tree, scribbling away with a
colored crayon—blue one day, red the next—on an "En-
cyclopedia of the Human Spirit": a general compendium,
as he called it, of all the dogmas and doctrines, supersti-
tions and taboos, panaceas and utopias that have plagued
this planet. He wore an old cowboy hat and had a bottle
of ginger ale beside him. Sometimes toward dusk he fell
asleep and the chair would rock with his snores.

When he awoke again he fixed me with his ambiguous
glassy eye. His voice slowly emerged, not from his vocal
chords, it seemed, but like some powerful vibration issuing
from his drum-shaped torso.

"Have you done your lessons, Henry?"

"Yes, I have, Uncle Claudius."

"What have you learned? Anything useful?"

"I'm not sure, Uncle Claudius."

"What's eleven plus four?"

"Is it fifteen?" I pleaded.

"What's twelve minus seven?"

"Is it five?" I said meekly.

"Where is Timbuktoo, my boy?"

"Is it somewhere in Africa?"

"Who was Hamlet?" roared Uncle Claudius.

"He was a sad young man in a play, with long black stockings," I said joyfully, "and a skull in his hand."

"Olé!" roared Uncle Claudius. "That's the attitude I approve of! Just keep broadening yourself, my boy, and you'll be a millionaire some day!"

And he'd sip at his lukewarm bottle, pick up his crimson crayon and dash off a fresh paragraph about hypnotism in Hungary, or levitation in Borneo.

Soon after daybreak every morning I followed the cowpath over the hill to fetch the milk and the eggs from the Svensen farm a mile away. When I returned through the bushes I caught the scent of hot bacon and saw my uncle laying the toast out on the table under the trees. After breakfast Uncle Claudius worked for an hour in his kitchen garden. Then we rowed across the river and I waited in the boat, studying my lessons, while Uncle Claudius gave his lecture on Ancient History at the local summer school. Then we picked up the ice at the icehouse and the morning mail at the post-office, and Uncle Claudius had a glass of root beer at the drugstore. Then we slowly rowed home again and I wandered amongst the hills while my aunt stood in the kitchen, stirring a broth of red beets, and my uncle sat in his rocking-chair with his rainbow-colored manuscript.

There was a curious relationship between my uncle and aunt. After thirty years of love, of mushroom gathering and Spinoza and Grillparzer, they seemed curiously remote from each other, much as a Peruvian llama might seem remote from the Tibetan yak in the adjoining cage in a zoo. They gazed gently at one another with a kind of mute, puzzled tenderness, but nothing happened which seemed to diminish the peculiar loneliness of their exile.

Toward sunset we went strolling down to the sand-bar for our swim. Uncle Claudius tucked his pyjamas on the end of a birch twig and waddled majestically into the water. I caught the scent of his body, rich, formidable, alien; I peered at the hairs on his dangling breasts and the thin blue veins on his genitals. He lay on his back in the water, floating blissfully with the current, only his toes and belly and nostrils protruding. Finally he waddled ashore again and made his way through the weeping willows, dripping and snorting and expectorating like some old pagan river-god; with a ribbon of eel-grass dangling from his elephantine buttocks or maybe a little red water-spider clinging to his scrotum.

In the evening he read aloud to me by the flickering kerosene lamp; a scene from *Goetz von Berlichingen,* possibly, or a soliloquy from *Timon of Athens.* Or he'd ramble on about the finer subtleties in Kant or Hegel. The mosquitoes clung to the screens and the smell of the night seeped into the room, fresh and sweet and suggestive as jasmine tea. The boughs of the maples were delicately outlined against the moonlit clouds and the slow-moving river shone like a glacier through the tree-trunks. Sometimes a joss-stick was lit and the smoke went coiling across the table and my uncle's sagging face resembled a Chinese idol's.

Suddenly he'd toss his book aside, stare me in the eye, and mutter fiercely:

"What's three times eleven?"

"Thirty-three?"

"And the capital of Portugal?"

"Is it Lisbon?"

"Who conquered Mexico?"

"Was it Cortez?"

"Bravo, Henry! You're learning! Mark my words, you'll be sitting in the White House some day!"

And I stared into the night, listening to the chirping of the crickets and watching the fireflies dance their minuets down by the estuary.

7

August came and the goldenrod flowed through the valley like a torrent. The Black-Eyed Susans speckled the fields and the Monarch butterflies soared over the cow-paths.

I waltzed through the days like a fritillary; hiding in the shadows when it rained, basking in the sunlight when it shone, lolling drowsily in the haze of the dusk and savoring the mysteriousness of night.

Wherever I looked there were bees, ants, spiders and grasshoppers. The place was seething with a passionate woodland vitality. A hidden music filled the air: rustling and buzzing and chirping, the playful laughter of the brook and the furtive whispering of the leaves, even the infinitesimal sound of the cracking bark and the drinking roots, and the lapping of the wavelets down by the cat-tails.

I'd lie on the pier with my new friend Tony, fishing for minnows with my little red fish-net. Or we'd stroll about with our bows and arrows, waiting for a jay to dip through the leaves. Or we'd climb into the rowboat and row down the shore toward the small sandy inlet where the bull-rushes grow.

We'd lie naked in the reed-scented sun and tell stories.

I glanced at him furtively from time to time with a puerile adoration. I was almost as tall as he but he was much more mature. His voice was hoarse and low, silky hairs surrounded his nipples, and even the smell of his flesh had a certain ripeness about it. His face was as smooth and ruthless and beautiful as a girl's, with only a shadow above the lips and a cleft in the chin to give it masculinity. But in the way he picked up a pebble and hurled it at a Coca Cola bottle, or the way he spread his legs and tugged at the oars in the rowboat—in these casual, contemptuous gestures I detected a virile splendor.

Once I said: "Tony, what will you do when you're a man? Do you suppose?"

He drew an elaborate T in the sand with his finger.

"I'll get away from Wisconsin. As fast as I can."

"Yes? And then?"

"I'll look for a rich old widow and marry her."

"And after that?"

"I'll put poison in her coffee."

"Oh? Why?"

"I'll inherit her money."

"What will you do with all that money?"

"I'll go sailing around the world," said Tony. "I'll shoot tigers. And sharks. And boa constrictors."

"Yes? And then?"

"I'll retire. I'll buy a palace and marry a princess."

He wrinkled his brow and started to draw an enormous landscape in the sand. A bulging mosque at one end with a little minaret beside it; a row of palm-trees; a bridge; a great palace covered with turrets. And in the corner he drew his own inscrutable symbol, like Whistler's butterfly: a sword with a two-headed serpent coiled around it.

"It's very unusual," I said eagerly. "Is there a place like that anywhere?"

"Certainly," said Tony. "Somewhere or other. I'm not sure. Africa, maybe. . . ."

8

I woke up every morning while the dew still lay on the grass. I sipped at my coffee and studied my Latin with a hovering expectancy, waiting for the moment when I'd race down the path to the pier and find Tony lying on his belly, fishing for carp or reading the comic strip. We clung together through the long, sweet, spicy afternoon, wandering deeper and deeper into the dangerous woodlands; Tony in his jeans and threadbare T-shirt, which hung loose from his snake-like hips, and I in my khaki trousers and faded blue pullover. We discovered a tiny lake, a hidden swamp and empty quarry. Once we followed a stream and came to a ruined old mill, all festooned with wild grapes and overflowing with nettles. Once we caught a wild pheasant and roasted it over a fire, but the flesh was so stringy that we tossed it into the underbrush. And once we found a dead bullock trapped in a tangle of barbed wire: a vast, swollen horror, green with flies and seething with maggots. I was sick with disgust, but also a deeper disquietude; I had never imagined that death could be so hideous, so prolific.

The moon was rising when we finally returned to the river. The hazy green afterglow still clung to the ripples and all around us the sounds of the wilderness still lingered —the distant call of the quail and the fevered hammering of the woodpecker, the creak of the heavy boughs, the dry falsetto of the cricket.

My heart surged with longing. I sat silently beside Tony, dangling my toes in the water and brushing the gnats from my face. I told Tony about Texas, about the scorpions and the Luna moths, about Zenobia and Billy Baxter, and then finally about Stella. I told him about that evening in the canna bed, and about our little excursion to the Cochrane Mansion.

Night fell as we sat there and looked at the moon.

"If you could fly to the moon," I said, "would you do it, Tony?"

"There'd be nothing but craters, and deserts, and dust."

"Maybe the ground would be covered with diamonds," I hinted.

"Maybe it would," muttered Tony. "But what good would they do you?"

I cried: "Look, Tony! A shooting star!"

"Make a wish," whispered Tony.

So I did. We sat quietly, feeling night creeping over us.

"Tell me, Tony. What will happen when we die, do you think?"

"We'll just die. We'll be buried. And we'll turn into skeletons."

"It's so terrible," I moaned. "I just can't believe it."

"I'd rather be dead," grunted Tony, "than turn into a ghost. Or even an angel."

A sense of the unutterable crept over my soul. I had fallen in love with Tony: with his reckless and roving ways, with his dark, supple grace and his golden-green eyes.

But under it all I caught a lingering whiff of criminality. I sensed the tension, the bravado, the feverish drive, the bluff, the vainglory.

Now and again I thought of the ruined old mill beside the stream. I thought of building it anew and living there forever, in peace and gentleness.

But then I heard in the gathering twilight, ever so faintly but irresistibly, the roar of the mighty seas and the catlike scream of far-off cities.

9

One night I was wandering home through the dusk. A fiery horizon still shone through the network of willows. A loon started to cry from the opposite shore of the river: a wild and unearthly sound, like a cry from prehistory.

The river! That slime-embroidered, snake-haunted river! Swollen at dawn, sleek and idle, tinged with an emerald-tinted foam; radiant at noon, with its millions of water-bugs skimming across the shadows; shrunken at dusk, when the fireflies wove their glitter over the paths; and ominous at night, when the squeal of the distant freight-train mingled with the whine of the mosquitoes and the rustling of half-seen shapes among the overlapping sumach.

The night was suddenly filled with an inexplicable terror. I raced back through the willows and across the white-pebbled estuary. The lamp was shining in the kitchen, flickering on the kettles and salt-cellars.

Uncle Claudius stared at me blearily.

"Well," he said, "what's wrong, Henry?"

"Nothing special," I said guiltily.

"You look scared. Have you seen a ghost?"

"I saw an Indian prowling in the bushes."

"Nonsense," growled Uncle Claudius. "You're letting your fancy get the best of you. You need discipline, that's what you need. What's eleven from twenty-seven?"

I hesitated a moment. "Twenty-one?"

"Certainly not!" snapped my uncle. "You're not concentrating, you rascal! What's the capital of Denmark?"

I whispered: "Is it Amsterdam?"

"Wrong again! You're an idiot!" He pounded the table with his ginger ale bottle. Then he leaned toward me menacingly, narrowed his one blue eye and muttered: "Who wrote *Faust?* Do you remember?"

I lowered my eyes. I was close to tears. I murmured pleadingly: "Was it Shakespeare?"

Uncle Claudius rose from the table. There was a hideous little silence. He was panting like a walrus. Tears of sweat poured down his cheeks.

He seized the bottle and hurled it violently against the opposite wall, where it burst like a firecracker.

"Get out of my house!" he screamed hoarsely. "You're just like your father! A fake and a liar! Get out and stay out, you miserable little bastard!"

He started slowly in my direction, like a beast about to charge. I ran through the door into the gloom of the ravine.

10

I found Tony down on the moonlit shore, smoking a cigarette.

"Come," he said, "Let's get in the boat and row over to the village."

"What will we do when we get there?"

"Go to the movies," said Tony.

"Have you got any money?"

"Not a penny," said Tony.

We slid into the boat and started rowing across the moon-bubbled current. My terror had evaporated. The zest of adventure filled my soul. The creak of the oar-locks pierced the silent immensity of the night. I trailed my fingers in the swift warm water.

Finally we fastened the boat to the moss-bearded wharf, climbed up the embankment and went strolling down Water Street.

The town seemed curiously empty. The stores were all closed. Two men were sitting on a bench in front of Van Druten's garage, smoking their pipes, and two old ladies were chatting in their rocking-chairs on the porch of the Eagle Hotel. We crept past Muhleisen's Pharmacy with its ruby-red jar and past Heckmeyer's Ice Cream Parlor with its fancy lace curtains. The fruits at Fratellini's gleamed in the dark like colored glass, and the plaster ladies at Schmaltz's peered through the gloom like grinning vampires. We came to a halt in front of McGillicuddy's General Store and gazed at the baskets, the fishnets, the rolling-pins.

"Come," said Tony. "I have an idea." He glanced up and down the street, then beckoned and slipped into the alley behind the store. All was still. Not a trace of life. The only light we could see was the moonlight shining faintly on the tapering windows of the Lutheran Church. Tony fondled the window in the back of the store, then tugged at it gently. "It's bolted," he said. So he took out his pen-knife and ran it neatly around the pane, chipping away the old putty until the glass fell loose in his hands. A spray of dust drifted down on us as we peered through the empty casement.

"I'll go first," whispered Tony. "Take it easy. Don't stumble."

I could see the sarsaparilla bottles gleaming darkly on the shelves. The odor of burlap and nutmeg, of tobacco and mothballs mingled with the smell of the dew-drenched asphalt that welled through the open window. We groped our way past the counter; we caressed the great shelves; we lifted the lids of the cigar boxes and fumbled lightly among the sweets.

"A carton of Camels," said Tony.

"And a fountain pen," I said.

"And a pair of tennis shoes," said Tony.

"And a box of chocolate-covered almonds. . . ."

We slid back into the night and followed the deserted little alley, which ran through the edge of the village toward Lover's Lane. The fireflies were out, weaving their golden parabolas, and down in the swamp the bull-frogs were bellowing.

We crossed a stream, which shone in the starlight like India ink, and crossed the tracks, which exuded a faint stench of creosote. A feeling of triumph, of complicity surged in my heart; but it was tinged with an aroma of treachery and obsession.

Finally we reached the main highway which went winding into the hills. The scattered lights of Prairie du Loup hung reflected in the squirming river.

"Easy, wasn't it?" said Tony.

"Easy as pie," I agreed. I ripped open the candy box and pulled out an almond.

Tony lit a cigarette and puffed at it thoughtfully. "It just shows," he said softly. "A bit of nerve. That's all that it takes."

The road dipped into the woods again. The smell of mushrooms coiled about us. A faint glow swam in the foliage; a car was parked under the evergreens.

"Hush," said Tony.

We crept closer, threading our way through the tree-trunks. Something stirred among the ferns—two ambiguous tangled shadows. There was a low, pleading murmur; a stealthy rustle; a long-drawn sigh.

Tony tiptoed to the side of the car and reached in toward the dashboard. He flicked deftly at the door-handle; we slipped in and he stepped on the starter.

It was a two-seated Essex. We went screeching up the

hillside, sending sprays of white gravel as we whirled around the bends. The woods fell behind us as we kept on climbing. The road twisted sharply. The engine began to splutter.

"A Packard," said Tony. "That's what I'll have one of these days."

"Or a Cadillac," I said. "Or what about a Pierce Arrow?"

"Or a Mercedes," said Tony. "Have you ever heard of a Mercedes?"

"Bright red. With wire wheels. And silver pipes coming out of the hood."

"I might even consider a. . . ."

"Look!" I shrieked. "Quick! Oh God. . . ."

The blaze of the headlights shot down at us. Tony tugged at the wheel. The car struck a rock, shuddered and moaned and turned over.

11

Six days later, on the fifth of September, I departed for Pennsylvania.

"Don't harbor any illusions," said Uncle Claudius, "about poor old Ursula. She's a snob and a martinet. Her heart is kind but her brain's like a linnet's."

And Aunt Elfrida declared, as she kissed me on both cheeks: "We've explained to her about that nasty little accident. It's pure luck that you're still alive. It wasn't your fault, I quite realize. It was that nasty Cavallero boy's. Serves him right, breaking his arm. He'll end up in the penitentiary one of these days."

My uncle rowed me across the river and accompanied me to the railway station. There he patted me on the head and gently inquired:

"What's five times seven, my boy?"

"Thirty-five?" I said sadly.

"And where's the Ganges?"

"In India?"

"Who wrote *Cinderella?*"

"The Brothers Grimm?"

"Absolutely perfect!" roared Uncle Claudius. "You'll be president of Harvard, if you put your mind to it!"

A little later, as we waited for the train, I caught him peering at me with an air of melancholy. There was a tear in his little eye; of self-pity perhaps.

"My child, just forget what I told you about God. I've been hard on you, I'm afraid. Maybe there's a God—who can tell? If it gives you comfort to think there's a God up in the clouds, gazing down on you, well, keep on thinking it. We'll never know the truth of the matter!"

A butterfly came dancing over the platform. The train was whistling in the distance. The dry, yellowish air hung trembling over the tracks, which glittered like needles as they pierced the heart of the wilderness.

IV

My aunt ursula lived in Cliffdale, a spruce little sub-
urb near Philadelphia. The streets were shadowy and
prim. The lawns were velvety, luxuriant. The houses were
chaste and substantial, Colonial or Georgian for the most
part, with an occasional touch of the Palladian or even
the Rococo.

There were ivy-covered stables enclosed by neatly
clipped hedges. There were squash-courts edged with holly-
hocks and swimming pools surrounded by fuchsia. There
were ladies' colleges with grassy lawns well suited to Eurip-
idean tragedies and Tudor folk-dances; there were antique
shops filled with china poodles, pewter beer-mugs and
castiron weather-vanes.

Aunt Ursula's house stood at the end of a winding lane
called Dogwood Drive. It was a neat half-timber cottage
surrounded by a bristling hedge of privet. Aunt Ursula
was an Anglophile: she lived with a spinster named Phyllis
Abercrombie, who had endowed their little dwelling

with a stern, Edwardian atmosphere. The paneled hall was cluttered with golf bags, badminton racquets and croquet mallets. The living room was done in chintz, with a warming-pan beside the fireplace, rows of Spode upon the shelves and the *Cries of London* dappling the walls. The library was filled with sets of Trollope, Disraeli and Meredith, with an occasional volume on the excavations in Thessaly or the initiation rites in the Solomons. On the table lay copies of the *Tatler*, the *Connoisseur*, and the *Country Gentleman*.

Tea was served in the afternoon, with buttered scones and gooseberry jam, and for dinner we had a curry of lamb or roast beef with Yorkshire pudding, with a trifle for dessert or perhaps a semolina pudding. Miss Abercrombie owned a Sealyham named Dogberry and an irascible parrot named Yorick; Aunt Ursula had a Siamese cat whom she chose to call Mata Hari.

"You must have an ambition in life, Henry," said my aunt, stirring her tea. "Otherwise you will go to seed. Do you have an ambition, my boy?"

"Not particularly, Aunt Ursula."

"Wouldn't you like to be famous?"

"I suppose I would," I said. "In a way."

"Have you ever thought of archaeology?"

"What is archaeology, Aunt Ursula?"

"Digging for pottery. Like Phyllis."

"Did Miss Abercrombie dig for pottery?"

"Yes, dear. In Thebes and Gnossos."

"Did she find anything, Aunt Ursula?"

"Some broken funeral urns, I believe. She gave them to Bryn Mawr, along with some old Etruscan cutlery. . . ."

Occasionally after dinner, while the light of dusk still

played on the lawn, the two old ladies stepped outside for a little game of croquet. I would sit in the library with my *Three Musketeers,* peering through the window now and again when I heard a brisk, contralto cry: "Bravo, Phyllis!" or "Jolly good shot, my dear Ursula!"

They looked, as they prowled through the twilight with their sagging tweeds and floppy hats, like ancient priestesses or sybils engrossed in some crepuscular ritual. An air of the impenetrable hung over the cottage on Dogwood Drive: a blending of stoicism and nostalgia, of erudition and witchery.

2

Little by little my Aunt Ursula developed a dry, disparaging affection for me. She'd sit on the terrace after dinner with a cup of coffee and reminisce. She had sung in Innsbruck and Graz in the days of the Emperor Franz Josef, and she showed me yellowing photographs of herself in *Casanova* and *Die Perle von Iberien.*

In those days she had been a voluminous blonde, sheathed in sequins and ostrich feathers. But now her hair was iron-gray, clipped short like a man's, and her face was a mosaic of infinitesimal pink veins, as though it had been exposed to generations of fog and cabbage. She had taken on Miss Abercrombie's texture, both physical and cerebral, by a kind of osmosis. Like Miss Abercrombie, she wore rusty suits, starched blouses, and sensible shoes.

"Those were gay, busy days," she said, tapping her bosom somewhat wistfully. "I was very beautiful, I might add. My stage name was Fifi de Medici and I was the toast of the Tyrol. I still remember the ovations, the marriage proposals, the champagne! People came all the way from Bad Ischl and Zell-am-See. . . ."

On the sixth of September I started my course at the Rosedale High School. I studied English under Miss Halleck and mathematics under Mr. Silliman. For Mr. Gooch I parsed the orations of Cicero, for Miss Mulholland I read *Colomba,* and for Miss Kalbfleisch I did watercolors of pears, plums and pomegranates.

But aside from these momentary pleasures the atmosphere of the High School filled me with melancholy. I hated the smell of chalky blackboards. I recoiled from the fervor of the weekly football games. I was shocked by the tittering that went on in the cafeteria, and by the lewd repartees which I overheard in the lavatories.

My real moments of happiness were passed in the jungle-like gloom of Miss Abercrombie's library, where the sombre green bindings gleamed like a latticework of ivy, dappled with stray oblong touches of nasturtium or cineraria. Here I roamed through *The Cloister and the Hearth, Henry Esmond* and *Rob Roy.* And little by little I recreated a vision of Europe: a continent of ruined castles, of kegs of wine and roasted chestnuts, of periwigs and crinolines, of marble nymphs and golden cherubs, of markets bulging with umbrellas and the sound of bells in a far-off monastery.

One day, as I was reading *The Moonstone,* Aunt Ursula entered the library. She gazed at me ominously. "You read too much, Henry. You're turning into an absolute little book-worm. It was the same with your Uncle Amadeus, who lived down in Klagenfurt. He drowned himself in the Wörthersee one dark winter night. And all because he'd been reading *The Critique of Pure Reason.*"

"I'm sorry to hear it, Aunt Ursula."

"There was always something rather odd in your family, I'm afraid. My own family, the Freilassings, were cheerful, wholesome folk. But your father's line ran to anxiety. Your Aunt Rosa, for example. She played the harp like an angel but she died of a heart-attack in Portofino."

"What a pity," I said.

"It was more than a pity. It was a tragedy. That is the penalty that people pay for an over-heated imagination. Try to control your fancy, Henry. Don't read these wild romances. Read *Framley Parsonage,* my boy, or *Daniel Deronda.* They'll calm your nerves."

But Trollope and George Eliot were too prosaic for my lurid appetite. As I browsed among the shelves I came across some rather unusual items. One day I found an old Bavarian treatise on sexual abnormalities. I leafed through the chapters avidly, absorbing such spicy bits of information as:

"Excessive masturbation produces impotence, paralysis and madness." "Masochism flourishes in England, where it is accompanied by a preference for boots and birch-rods." "Among the Bontoc Igorot the cult of the dead is conducive to necrophilia." "Transvestitism is generally frowned upon, except in China, where it is linked with ancestor-worship."

Sometimes I read until midnight. The two old ladies were sleeping soundly, Dogberry and Yorick were snoring in the kitchen and Mata Hari lay coiled on her cushion. And imperceptibly the little library would begin to expand, the dimly illuminated shelves would slowly recede. Dark presences stirred in the hidden corners. The air took on a mysterious density, a mushroom-like fragrance. Time and place crumbled away. I sat alone in a starlit vastness. I listened tensely; and I grew aware of a strange procession passing in the distance—hooded nuns and bearded abbots, armored warriors and ermined emperors. And then the night suddenly deepened, the world of books crumbled apart and the passing shapes took on the feverish precision of reality. They were people whose existence I would never have suspected: old men clutching at staves, monstrously fat, hairless as porcelain; old women shaggy and foul as the roots of an oak-tree; naked beggars, hideously misshapen, with flesh striated like the skin of a melon; and behind them the uncontrollable idiots, the fools and hunchbacks and epileptics; and finally the beautiful ones, the lucky and seductive ones, with eyes like lapis lazuli and bodies exquisite as ferns. More and more floated past, unimaginable millions of them; until finally the air grew hazy and the last of the caravan faded away. All were gone, nothing was left, nothing but the aridity of a dream.

3

And little by little I grew aware of myself as a human being: a separate and unmistakable identity, with thoughts and feelings of my own. And the more I thought, the more insistently remained the mystery at the core: why was I born to be myself? How did it happen, this little miracle?

Why wasn't I a small greenish bird in Indonesia, or maybe a blade of grass in the plains of the Pampas? Why was I suddenly thrust into the world, at a particular moment in a particular place, with chestnut hair and a mole on my cheek and a hundred odd little instincts?

Outwardly, as my Aunt Ursula used to tell me, I was a gentle, "sensible" boy, with "wholesome" impulses and "respectful" manners and a strong healthy body. I liked to walk through the woods, to climb trees, to trap beetles. I liked the wind and the sun, the breath of the sea and the smell of pines.

But beneath this innocuous surface lay a second, more secluded self: sly, patient and calculating, anxious to please but thoroughly unscrupulous, inquisitive and touchy, tenacious and vain. Under the skin of a dog lurked the spirit of a cat. I played a deft, cajoling role, tortuous almost to the point of criminality; with no opinions or convictions, without faith, without dogma, guided by the instincts of the jungle and an irrepressible lust for freedom; forever poised on the edge of a bough, ready to jump into safety; sensual, sceptical, nimble, luxuriant and moody.

And somewhere in the depths, beneath this feline second self, lay coiled a dark and passionate and unpredictable third identity, waiting for its moment to leap forth and commit some wild, irrevocable folly. This was the self that lay hidden, that spoke in a whisper. This was the self that was capable of obsession: that baffled and tormented me. This was the self that under it all gave its mystery to existence; its savagery, its sadness, its touch of the miraculous.

4

There was a copse of red bushes just below our little cottage, and a slate-colored stream edged with lilies-of-the-valley. Here Aunt Ursula, in an alpaca jacket, would set up her easel and paint little water-colors of birds, flowers and butterflies. Miss Abercrombie joined her occasionally with a basket of needlework or a copy of *Emma*, wearing a green-checkered cap and a black and cream waistcoat. Dogberry lay in the shade, snapping at gnats and mosquitoes, while Mata Hari prowled through the grasses, stalking small green-eyed grasshoppers.

When dusk descended Aunt Ursula placed her brushes in their grooves, gazed at the sky through her lorgnon and lit a cigarette.

"You look pale, my good Henry. Are you feeling unwell?"

"Look at those rings around his eyes. It might be his liver," said Miss Abercrombie.

"The boy looks worried, to be quite honest. He needs friends," said Aunt Ursula.

"And exercise," hinted Miss Abercrombie. "I wish he'd learn to play badminton."

"I feel guilty about the lad. I never take him to church. Did poor Elfrida ever take you to church, my little pet?"

"Tante Elfrida didn't believe in God," I said gloomily.

"She was an atheist, was she?"

"She was a Buddhist," I said.

"Oh, well," said Miss Abercrombie, "she believed in God, if she was a Buddhist. A very different sort of God, but a genuine God all the same."

"She never killed a chicken, or even a fly," I said cautiously.

"She was always a bit of a crackpot," muttered Aunt Ursula.

"Well, I happen to be an Anglican myself," said Miss Abercrombie, "and your dear Aunt Ursula is ostensibly a Catholic, if I'm not mistaken. But follow your instincts, child. Don't you feel the need of God?"

"I'm not quite sure that I do, Miss Abercrombie."

"Well, in that case, you obviously don't. All that we have a right to ask of you is that you do your lessons and watch your table manners."

"And discipline your bowels," said my aunt.

"Needless to say," said Miss Abercrombie.

"And be practical," said Aunt Ursula. "Keep your head out of the clouds. Forget these silly fads that Elfrida goes in for. Remember one thing, my dear. Money is everything in life. It gives you freedom to live as you wish, and love as you wish, and die as you wish. With money in the bank you're an emperor. With nothing but debts, you're a slave. Art, romance, spirituality—they're all luxuries. You have to pay for them."

I wandered wearily back to my room, lay down on my feather mattress, opened a box of peanut brittle and embarked on a crossword puzzle.

Oh, the boredom and misery, the utter squalor of adolescence! The bloom had faded from the world, the pristine freshness had evaporated, and what was left was lust and laziness, a brooding gloom, a sickly self-regard. The world of nature had slipped away like some half-remembered paradise and I was trapped in my little prison of suspicions and innuendoes.

5

One day Aunt Ursula announced, as she poured the milk into her teacup:

"Your cousin Stella is coming to pay us a little call, incidentally."

"Is she really, Aunt Ursula?"

"Next Tuesday. On her way to Connecticut."

"What will she do in Connecticut?"

"Go to school, I presume."

"She hated her school down in Texas."

"I am sorry to hear it," said Aunt Ursula. She cast a cool, sloping look at me. "Is she pretty? Your cousin Stella?"

I grew thoughtful. "Not especially."

"Her mother, I hear, was quite a beauty. How very odd of dear old Adelbert. He was such a prim little creature. To go running off with a voluptuous Mexican half-breed. . . ."

Three days later Stella arrived. I scarcely recognized her when she stepped from the cab. She had grown surprisingly tall and awkward and skinny. Her luminous black hair was wound in a braid around her head and her great shining eyes looked shy and uneasy. She wore an asylum-like dress of glossy blue serge, and black buttoned shoes with black cotton stockings.

She looked at me with indifference.

"Well, how are you?" I stammered.

"Perfectly well. Thank you kindly."

"How was Amarillo?"

"Hot and horrid."

"And how was school?"

"Utterly hideous."

"That's too bad," I said with sympathy. "What will you do up in Connecticut?"

"I have no idea," said Stella icily.

"Will you study acting, by any chance?"

"What a ridiculous notion."

"You use to dream of being an actress, didn't you?"

"Did I really? Perhaps I did."

"Have you given it up?"

"Of course I have. I've become a realist," said Stella.

She peered at me from the corners of her eyes. Her expression grew gentler. The ghost of a smile hovered on the edge of her mouth.

"Come into the garden," I said. "I'll show you the hydrangeas, if you'd like."

"You haven't changed one tiny bit," she said as we strolled across the lawn.

"Haven't I really?"

Her voice grew teasing. "Except for your pimples, of course. And something queer about your voice. And those little hairs on your upper lip."

I blushed fiercely. I was going through a phase of physical self-detestation.

My Aunt Ursula and Miss Abercrombie stepped on the terrace for their tea. I saw them sitting side by side, smearing jam on their biscuits and watching us through their dark-colored glasses. I felt troubled; chilled, mystified. And Stella herself seemed suddenly alien, as though caught in some cryptic, unmentionable spell.

"Are you still ambitious?" I said.

"Heavens. Not in the least," said Stella.

"You always wanted to be rich and famous."

"I was an idiot," said Stella.

"And wear diamonds and furs, and so on."

"Well, I'm through with all that nonsense." She tilted her head defiantly. "I've grown up. The Lord be praised."

"You wanted to travel to Paris and marry a count, or even a prince."

"I'll never marry," said Stella. "I loathe men. I can't abide them."

"What will you do, then?" I said, kicking a ball through the wicket.

Stella's lips curled up haughtily. "There's plenty to do now-a-days. Women are free. Women are liberated. They don't need men any longer."

I looked at her thoughtfully. "No, I don't suppose they do."

"I'm going to take up a career. Medicine, perhaps. Or maybe Law."

"You'll have an office, I suppose?"

"In New York," said Stella sternly.

I felt curiously sad: as though some exquisite memory had been blighted and some beckoning, far-off hope had been crushed forever.

"I'm sure that you'll be a success in New York," I said politely.

Stella glanced at me with a quick, furtive look of alarm.

"And I'm sure you'll be rich and beautiful," I said in a moment of cruelty.

Stella blushed and lowered her eyes. "I don't want to be beautiful," she whispered.

We both stood motionless, just the two of us, touched by the shadow of something menacing. And for a strange, fleeting moment I felt close to her again. She pressed her fingers together tensely; her lips moved; her eyelids trembled. I wanted desperately to lean over and kiss her wild little face.

We crossed the lawn silently. Finally we stood on the edge of the terrace.

"Well, anyway," I said, "it was nice to see you again."

"Thanks," she said in a brittle tone. "I enjoyed our little talk."

"Maybe we'll meet again some day. In Paris or Monte Carlo."

She pursed her lips, shrugged her shoulders and stepped on the terrace.

6

The same evening after dinner my aunt sat down with me for a game of dominoes. The parchment light fell obliquely across her splendid old face, which has a damascened sheen to it, like rose-tinted moiré. Her wrinkled mauve eyes looked inhumanly wise, like a mandrill's.

"Your cousin Stella," she said, "is a rather unusual girl, isn't she, dear?"

"She's changed quite a bit. She's grown bitter and cynical."

"She is passing through a phase, I presume," said Aunt Ursula.

"She used to be much more vivacious. And pretty."

Aunt Ursula glanced at me sharply. "You are blushing, my boy. I hope you don't cherish any illusions about your cousin. She is not the type for you—that I can tell you with some certainty. I suspect that her tastes lie in another direction." She picked up a domino and placed it firmly on the baize. "You must grasp the fact, my good Henry, that the role of women has been changing. You mustn't expect them to be pretty or amusing necessarily. Women are exploring a new and highly significant role in our society."

"Stella is planning to be a doctor. Or even a lawyer," I said mournfully.

"You must realize, my boy, that women are superior to men, *au fond.* Their instincts are finer. They are more sensitive. And more fastidious."

I nodded submissively. "I suppose they are, Aunt Ursula."

"Men are vain and licentious. There are moments, my dear Henry, when I almost wish you were a niece instead of a nephew."

I blushed and stared at my row of dominoes, which stared back at me equivocally.

7

Miss Abercrombie gave me a small mahogany phonograph for my birthday, which came in April; and on Sunday afternoons I crept up to my little room, lit a pyramid of incense, and put on the *Liebestod* from "Tristan." I would lie on my bed and look out at the sunlit clouds: they changed from horses to swans and from swans into odalisques. And occasionally I stole a glance at Miss Dalrymple's School, just down the street, where girls in green bloomers went racing across the hockey field.

My flesh started to tingle. I stood at the gates of my secret paradise. My breath came faster. My mind was roaming. I remembered the shadows of the canna bed, and the spectral gloom of the Cochrane house, and the whispering waters of Prairie du Loup. The familiar visions swept over me. The music soared to a climax. And once again I was plunged in a chasm of guilt and remorse.

One afternoon, as I glanced through the window, Dusty Peabody rode by on his bicycle. He waved his racquet at me merrily. "Come along, why don't you, Henry?"

"My tennis is ghastly," I said.

"Well, come anyway," said Dusty. And he swatted at a bumble-bee with his pea-green racquet.

So I picked up my racquet, which was slack and slightly warped, and rolled my rusty old bicycle out of the toolshed. We rode past ivied walls and rose-festooned fences and finally we slid through the wrought-iron gates of the Cliffdale Cricket Club.

I followed Dusty into the locker-room, where we slipped into our ducks. He bought three brand new tennis balls; we stepped out on the smooth green lawn. I had scarcely ever played, but a strange new zest shot through me suddenly. The delicious smell of new-mown grass, the snow-white ball darting toward me, the joy of watching it leap from my racquet and sail triumphantly over the net: it was like discovering an ecstatic new universe. I gamboled wildly after Dusty's volleys, I swung exuberantly at his backhand drives; I patted foxily at his spinning services and leapt ferociously for his floating lobs.

"Well," said Dusty, when the game was over, "you aren't bad, you know, Henry."

"I've never played on grass before. I'll have to get used to it, I'm afraid."

"You made some beautiful stop-volleys. But your drives," said Dusty, "are a bit erratic."

"My racquet," I said apologetically, "needs re-stringing, I've noticed."

We strolled up to the veranda and ordered some lemonade. Leathery women with beady eyes and raucous voices sat under the awnings. Some of them were playing bridge, others were sipping at their highballs. Three old gentlemen in checkered sport-jackets and plus fours were puffing at their pipes. Now and then a Pierce Arrow or a LaSalle roadster drove up under the *porte-cochère* and a pampered young athlete in a blue-striped blazer would step out. In the distance some elderly cricketers were practicing their bowling, and four dark ladies in bandanas were playing doubles on the center court.

"In a couple of years," said Dusty gravely, "I'll be playing at Forest Hills."

"You'll be a champion," I said, "if you just keep practicing, Dusty."

"I'll play at Wimbledon," said Dusty happily. "I'll play with Perry and Vines."

"It sounds marvelous," I murmured enviously. "Maybe the Queen will come and watch you."

We strolled back to the locker-room, slipped off our jock-straps and stepped in the showers.

"Can you play tomorrow?" said Dusty.

"I'd love to," I said.

"We'll practice our back-hands."

"An excellent idea," I said breezily.

Dusty started shampooing his rebellious mop of red

hair. Bubbles of iridescent lather rolled down his freckled chest. Then he lobbed the cake of soap at me and turned the spiggot briskly. He squealed with excitement as the ice-cold water shot down at him.

"Isn't it wonderful?" he said, rubbing his buttocks with the towel.

I nodded, somewhat wistfully. "It's terrific," I said.

8

After this I developed a fanatical craze about tennis. I practiced my shots against the wall of the tool-shed, where I drew a line at the height of the net. I borrowed books from the village library—treatises by Tilden and Lacoste —and immersed myself in the legends and lore of the game. I dreamed of Lenglen and Larned, of the great Gobert and the sly little Shimizu, and at the club I studied the silver trophies, the painted shields, the ancient photographs. I was thrilled by those majestical figures with straw hats and walrus mustaches, those shapely ladies with waving coiffures and underhand services. I studied the newspapers for the summaries of obscure tournaments on the Riviera and the latest exploits of Didi Vlasto or the Baron de Morpurgo.

Ah, the green of those velvety courts! the glittering pattern of whitewashed lines! the tarry web of the long black net and the snowy ball stained with sap! the ping of the racquet, the crash of a smash, the delicate click of a half-volley! Love-thirty, love-forty, game, set, match, tournament! My heart still beats in the obsession of a perpetually recurring dream, at the sight of those new-mown courts, with the thrill of those rhythmic drives, and with my magical liberation from the world of secrecy and solitude.

9

In the middle of June I went and stayed with Dusty's family in Sycamore Point, which was a rocky little fishing village on the coast north of Boston.

We played tennis every day. We went sailing around the cape. We ate lobsters and clams. We lay basking on the sand.

"I'd like to do something really wonderful in the world," murmured Dusty.

"What kind of wonderful?" I said judiciously.

"Oh, to eliminate suffering, for instance," said Dusty.

"What kind of suffering?"

"So many people are lonely and sad, I've decided. They need a philosophy or something. I'd like to become a great philosopher."

"Would you really? You'd have to read a lot of books, I imagine."

"I wouldn't mind. I'm going to major in philosophy in college."

"Where will you go?" I said softly.

"Harvard," said Dusty. "And you?"

"Oh, Llewellyn, I suppose."

"Llewellyn? Really? How dreary."

Tiny wavelets were lapping away at the sand like glassy

tongues. A flurry of gulls was pirouetting along the edge of the promontory. And on the brink of the horizon, like triangular chips of ivory, hung three little sail-boats with billowing white sails.

We were lying on large yellow towels embroidered with starfish. I was lying on my back, looking out toward the sea; Dusty was lying on his belly and building a pyramid of sand.

"You know," said Dusty, "I can't help thinking that the world is fundamentally wrong, Henry. The poor workers living in slums. And the idle rich riding in Cadillacs."

"You're turning into quite a philosopher already, aren't you, Dusty?"

"I wish I were," said Dusty modestly. "I'm just trying to face reality."

"There will always be unhappiness in the world, don't you think so, Dusty?"

"Not if you stamp out injustice. And banish poverty," said Dusty.

"There will still be sickness," I said. "And death. And loneliness. And sorrow."

"Not necessarily," said Dusty. "There'd be wonderful new medicines, to cure the sicknesses. And clubs and societies, to cure the loneliness."

I glanced across the beach. The sand lay furrowed under the sun, patterned with finely sculptured waves, like a miniature Sahara. Here and there lay a fan-shaped shell or a small sun-baked skeleton. Two tiny sandpipers were scampering by, daintily eluding the glossy ripples.

"And what about death?" I said thoughtfully, sifting the sand through my fingers.

"Oh, death," replied Dusty. "We'd stop worrying about

death. We'd have places for old people, full of flowers and birds. And when they'd die they'd disappear. Nobody would know anything about it."

"It sounds cruel," I said.

"It's perfectly sensible," said Dusty touchily. "You're old-fashioned, that's all. You aren't interested in progress."

He tossed a fistful of sand at me and went racing across the beach. Then he climbed to the top of a rock and dove into the agate water. When he stepped on the shore again his body was puckered with goose-flesh and his hair clung to his forehead in blood-red bangs.

We picked up our towels and strolled lazily up to the house, which was a gray shingled structure surrounded by larkspur and petunias. There was a loggia sprinkled with little glass tables and bamboo couches, and a rose-garden with a castiron bench, a striped umbrella and a stucco cupid. At the end of the driveway stood a painted sign: "Wistaria Cottage."

Lunch was served in the loggia: cold shrimps and to-mato salad. Mrs. Peabody and her daughter Evelyn were dressed in eggshell-colored muslin. Evelyn was a bony girl, red-headed like her brother, with a square bulldog jaw and suspicious gray eyes. Mrs. Peabody was a hand-some woman with a low, rasping voice, Diana-like gestures and a bloodthirsty glance.

"Well," she said, "how was the beach?"

"Terrific," said Dusty.

"Were any of those Portuguese boys there?"

"I didn't see any," said Dusty.

"It's such a pity," said Mrs. Peabody, "about Sycamore Point, you know. Ten years ago it was perfectly lovely, with nothing but nice old families. But little by little some rather unfortunate elements have drifted in."

"I saw Jane Wilcox talking to that Pereira boy," said Evelyn darkly.

Mrs. Peabody glanced at me affably as she speared a shrimp with her fork.

"Is your family from Poland, Henry?"

"From Austria," I said discreetly.

"And what was your father's profession, dear?"

"He directed a well-known theatre."

"Henry and I," said Dusty placidly, "are playing in the tournament next week."

"How very pleasant," said Mrs. Peabody. "I hope you've been practicing your strokes."

"Henry's game is rather weird. I was watching him yesterday," said Evelyn.

"Weird?" said Mrs. Peabody, raising her brows.

"Lots of slices and lobs, and so on."

"Don't be intolerant," said Mrs. Peabody. "As long as he wins. That's what matters."

"Henry is weird in other ways, too."

"You don't say," said Mrs. Peabody.

"I caught him reading a French novel."

"For school," said Mrs. Peabody, "presumably."

"And he needs a haircut," said Evelyn viciously.

"Come, come, dear," said Mrs. Peabody.

She folded her napkin and cast a white, steely smile at me.

10

Life at Sycamore Point had its own hidden frenzies. From the windows of Wistaria Cottage one could look across the golf-course, which was washed by the silvery light of the Atlantic. I'll never forget Evelyn Peabody in her terra-cotta tweeds, swinging her club like a venging fury on the seventeenth tee. Or Harry Blakeslee in his little garden, clipping the hedge with his big black scissors. Or Agatha Potter crouching on the edge of a lichenous cliff, daubing paints on her canvas while the fishermen set their lobster-pots. Or Sammy Tiffany emerging from the showers in the Country Club locker-room, fat and paunchy as Bacchus, coquettish as Ganymede.

Now and again Dusty and I went for a drive in his little roadster. We drove through the glades of Massachusetts, sunlit pastures, drowsy hamlets. Drooping elms cast their shadows on clapboard walls and vined verandas; and the smell of sour crabapples came oozing from old graveyards. Occasionally we paused at some nautical museum or dowdy little antique shop, or had tea at a rustic inn called the Copper Kettle or the Old Red Barn. And from the sea in the distance drifted the odor of shell-fish, of decomposing weeds and of barnacled driftwood.

And as the afternoon deepened a strange glow slid over the landscape, a violet-gold sheen almost supernatural in its clarity: things looked trapped and arcane—a cat, a bicycle, a sail-boat on the horizon, all took on an oracular and faintly malignant lustre.

And by seven o'clock in the evening we'd be back in

Wistaria Cottage, with its cocktails and canapés, its cross-word puzzles and Sunday bridge games, its hooked rugs and copper warming-pans, its etchings of poodles.

"They're having a tournament next week," announced Dusty one day.

"Oh really? How exciting. Maybe you'll win it," I said.

"They've seeded Mike Pereira and Tommy Van Alstyne," said Dusty. "But I think I can beat them. Tommy's much too erratic. And Evelyn would be horrified if I lost to that Pereira boy."

"Well, I'm sure you won't, Dusty. Just keep concentrating, that's all. And one of these days you'll be playing in the Davis Cup matches . . ."

11

The finals of the Sycamore Point Championship fell on a Sunday. I had squeezed past Tommy Van Alstyne in the semifinals by the skin of my teeth, and Dusty had triumphantly swept aside Mike Pereira.

It was a hot, gusty day. The ladies sat on the shaded porch, sipping thirstily at their gin fizzes and applauding drowsily as we stepped on the court. I started badly. I was sickeningly nervous: I had never taken a set from Dusty. He slammed his services into the corner and passed me at the net with his looping drives. He won the first set, 6-0, in less than ten minutes.

Then I gradually steadied down. The wind began to favor me. My slow, coiling slices seemed to wilt on Dusty's racquet. His game grew uncertain; he started to double fault. I chopped assiduously at the ball, sending drop-shots that grazed the net and angling my volleys into un-expected corners. Finally, after a feverish rally, I won the second set, 7-5.

In the third set Dusty crumbled. His backhand drives went out of control, soaring high into the backstop or dribbling abjectly into the bottom of the net. I won easily, 6-0. We shook hands across the net and Mr. Bainbridge, the tournament chairman, presented me with a silver platter.

That night we had a clambake down on the beach at Dooley's Neck.

"I don't see how you did it, Henry," said Mrs. Peabody. "You were inspired, my dear."

"It was those sickening slices and lobs," said Evelyn contemptuously.

"And the wind, of course," said Dusty. "It was awful. I played like a fish."

"Dusty is infinitely better than I. I was horribly lucky," I said smugly.

Agatha Potter was pouring the martinis while Ethel Bates mixed the salads. Sammy Tiffany and Harry Blakeslee were hovering tipsily over the clams. Aside from the clams there were broiled lobsters, fried chickens, and deviled eggs. For dessert we had blueberry pie and one of Mrs. Etting's custards.

A strange depression crept over me as the evening wore on. I sensed an ominous condescension, a prowling sus-piciousness in the air. Gin bottles and whisky bottles were rolling haphazardly across the sand. Fatty Dexter was playing "Honeysuckle Rose" on his portable gramophone.

I wandered down past the point. A full moon was shining. The ocean looked smooth and serene, faintly treacherous. It kept nibbling at the beach with its steel-blue ripples. They looked fragile as cobwebs and sharp as a razor blade.

I leaned thoughtfully against a boulder and looked out over the sea. The warmth of the August sun still clung to the furry stone, which lay warm under my palms, like the hide of a beast. There was no one in sight. I felt suddenly at ease again. I slipped off my clothes and crept cautiously into the moonlit water.

It was surprisingly warm. I lay down in the balmy shallows and felt the ripples swirl gently across my belly. It was a marvelous sensation—the feathery caress of that mighty ocean, so vast and so murderous, so forgiving, so calm. I swam out into the blackness. The moon looked eerily close—it hung from the sky like a great pomegranate, spraying its seeds into the ocean. Where would I land, I wondered vaguely, if I just kept swimming, on and on? Lisbon, possibly? Or maybe down by the beaches of Morocco?

I swam back and stepped on the sand and went racing across the beach. I had never before felt so miraculously at peace with the world. It was as though I had changed into an animal—a dolphin, perhaps, or an otter—with the pulse of the night throbbing away in my blood.

Suddenly I saw a dark figure standing in the shelter of the rocks. I paused for a moment. Then I ran toward my bundle of clothes.

A woman's voice called out casually: "Is that you, Henry, dear?"

I snatched at my shirt. "Yes, it is, Mrs. Peabody."

"You've been for a dip in the ocean?"

"Yes, I have, Mrs. Peabody."

"How very odd. Come and talk to me. There is something I want to say to you."

"Just a moment, Mrs. Peabody. . . ."

"Oh, don't bother to dress, dear. You don't need to feel embarrassed. I have a son of my own, you know. . . ."

I slipped nimbly into my slacks and strolled sheepishly toward Mrs. Peabody. She stood motionless, with folded arms, puffing away at a cigarette. She looked rather flushed. Her graying hair was fluttering in the wind.

"I don't blame you for wandering off. Fatty Dexter was making a spectacle of himself. And I've never seen Agatha like that. She must have thought she was Theda Bara."

"I suppose it was rude of me."

"Not in the least. It was perfectly natural. Sit down, dear. Here, where it's dry. I want to have a little chat with you."

I sat down beside Mrs. Peabody on the soft, balmy sand. I could smell her L'Heure Bleue, faintly tinged with the scent of gin. Her eyes shone like a cockatoo's, glazed and dilated. Her voice was peculiarly hoarse and spasmodic.

"I'm so happy that my little Dusty has made friends with you," she said. "You're so different from the rest of the boys. More artistic. More sensitive."

"Thank you," I murmured, "Mrs. Peabody."

"Well, I'm glad that you're taking it as a compliment, dear. I know several young men who would loathe being called artistic."

"Oh, I'm sure that you didn't mean . . ."

"Of course I didn't," said Mrs. Peabody. "I meant it in a perfectly nice, wholesome way. You read books and like music. There is nothing fundamentally wrong with books or music."

I gazed at the moon noncommittally. I was beginning to feel chilly.

Mrs. Peabody's voice grew pensive. "There's so much in the world that one misses, you know, when you stop to think of it."

"How right you are, Mrs. Peabody."

"My little Dusty, for instance. I'd love to see him spend more of his time with books, to be quite frank about it. Good ones, I mean, like *The Fountain*. As long as he doesn't turn queer."

"I don't think that there's any danger of that, Mrs. Peabody."

"Well, you never can tell. Take Sammy Tiffany, for instance. He was married for twenty years to Lola Weatheridge, poor dear. And then suddenly, one fine day. . . ."

"Yes? What happened, Mrs. Peabody?"

"Lola died of a stroke. And five days later he sailed on the *Europa*. He stayed in France two whole years. When he came back he was a different person."

"Really. How?"

"He wore spats. He grew a mustache and carried a cane. He smoked Turkish cigarettes and kept talking about Picasso. It made me blush, positively. I have always been suspicious of men who are elegant."

"Well, I don't think that you need to worry about Dusty, Mrs. Peabody."

Mrs. Peabody narrowed her eyes. "Dusty tells me you've written some poetry."

"Just a sonnet or two," I said hastily. "Nothing special."

She drew closer. "I can't quite figure you out, you know,

Henry. You puzzle me, dear. You're, well, somehow a bit unusual."

I recoiled imperceptibly. "I'm perfectly ordinary, I'm afraid."

"Oh, no, you aren't. There's something definitely *outré* about you, Henry. Going off like that for a swim. Not that there's anything wrong with it."

"Perhaps," I hinted, "I had just a drop too much to drink, Mrs. Peabody."

"Not at all," said Mrs. Peabody. "I was watching you like a hawk." Her gray eyes glittered and her jaw was set like a boxer's. She tossed her cigarette into the night and her voice grew tense and arrowy. "Tell me, Henry. You think of me as an old, old woman, don't you, dear?"

"Goodness, no, Mrs. Peabody."

"How old do you think I am?"

"Thirty-one. Thirty-two."

"Well, it's sweet of you to say so. I was only a girl when I married Mortimer. I shouldn't have done it, to be quite honest. I was much too naive. Much too easily shocked, if you know what I mean. . . ."

I nodded sympathetically.

"It was all most unfortunate. Mortimer was twenty years older than I. He had been a football hero at Yale, as well as a member of Wolf's Head and Psi Upsilon. He loved his business. He did brilliantly. He was on the Board of Directors. He belonged to all the best clubs. But something went wrong. He lost some money on the stock market. And then he started to drink rather heavily, poor darling."

"What a shame," I said gently.

"Am I boring you?" said Mrs. Peabody.

"Not a bit. It is fascinating. What finally happened to Mr. Peabody?"

Mrs. Peabody lowered her voice. "He was found in his garage one night, as dead as a doornail."

"How terribly sad."

"Poor old Mortimer. I was never sure that it was an accident." Her voice was trembling; she stared at me wildly. "I don't know why I'm telling you this."

"You've had a difficult life," I said, "Mrs. Peabody."

She took my hand and held it for a moment. "You are wonderfully kind, my dear. I do appreciate it."

The sound of laughter rose suddenly from the darkness behind the dunes. Three goat-like silhouettes came lurching in our direction. It was Sammy Tiffany and Fatty Dexter, with Agatha Potter between them.

"Heavens above, Helen," cried Agatha. "We thought you were drowned, my poor angel."

"I merely went for a walk," said Mrs. Peabody wanly.

"So it seems," roared Sammy Tiffany. "You wanted a whiff of the ocean, didn't you?"

"Come and join us," said Fatty Dexter. "We're going to drive to Magnolia. Leslie Pattison is having a party. With Japanese lanterns and guitars."

Mrs. Peabody rose wearily. "Well, all right, if you insist. Though I've grown rather bored with Leslie's parties, to be quite frank with you. . . ."

12

I wandered back along the beach. The picnic party had broken up. The broken whisky bottles shimmered in the glow of the dying embers. In the distance I saw the headlights racing feverishly toward Magnolia.

Finally I reached Wistaria Cottage. The moon had disappeared. Puffs of mist came drifting up over the lawn like apparitions. There was something intensely bleak, almost corpse-like about the house, with its rhinoceros-colored shingles and its odor of rotting clams.

The front door was open. I crossed the hall and stepped into the living room. There was a stench of damp wicker, mouldy cushions and stale tobacco. I turned on the lights: a greenish glow fell on the cretonne curtains, the candy-striped davenport, the Audubon prints.

A voice whispered: "Is that you, Henry?"

I swung around nervously. Dusty was lying on the couch, tousle-haired, bleary-eyed.

He groaned. "I feel ghastly."

"You had six martinis, didn't you?"

"I know I did; I felt awful. I felt that the world was going to pieces."

"Poor old Dusty," I said.

"That horrible tennis-match," said Dusty.

I sat down on the couch and patted his poppy-colored head. "Cheer up. You'll win at Wimbledon one of these days. In front of the Queen."

I lifted him up by his arms and led him out into the garden. The roses shone in the foggy glow from the loggia windows. I felt a pang of compassion for poor little Dusty, with his turned-up nose and his brick-red freckles, his sweetness, his stupidity.

He stared at me desolately. "I feel frightened to death, sometimes."

"What of?"

"Of something happening to me."

"Such as what?"

"Insanity, for instance."

"You'll never go mad. Don't you worry."

"Or syphilis. I might catch syphilis."

"They have medicines," I said, "for syphilis."

"Or I might be a failure in business."

"You'll never be a failure, I'm sure of it, Dusty."

His voice darkened. "Or I might be a pansy."

"What on earth makes you think so?"

"Dad kept warning me against it. He said he'd cut me off in his will if I ever turned into a pansy."

Great violet-black clouds were churning ominously overhead. A streak of lightning shot down at us, turning the roses to platinum. A gust of wind scurried past, rippling the petals from their stems. And then stealthily, conspiratorially the drops began to fall.

V

LLEWELLYN COLLEGE is a group of disconsolate little buildings set in a park full of poplars, Japanese cherries and gingko trees. The dormitories are Georgian; the library is Gothic; the chemistry building is a wistful Tudor and the gymnasium is furtively Moorish. There is a pond surrounded by willows and inhabited by swans. Beyond the pond lie three tennis courts, a football field and a cricket pavilion.

My room-mate during my first year at Llewellyn was Latimer Peck. I found him crouching over his bags in our little study in Warburton Hall. He was a scrawny young man with shaggy hair like a Scotch terrier's, a large Adam's apple, thick glasses, and a high-pitched voice. He lurched forward, gave me a limp wet hand and said desperately:

"My name is Peck. My home is in Pittsburgh. Where is yours, may I inquire?"

"Mine?" I said, disconcerted. "I don't have one, I'm afraid."

"What? You don't have a home?"

"Not really."

"How refreshing . . ."

He put a record on the gramophone: a sonata by Scarlatti. Then he placed his hands on his hips and glared at me challengingly. "Do you really think it's worth our while? Going to college, I mean?"

"I'm not sure," I said blandly. "It might be, in a way."

"We'll soon find out. I'm prepared for the worst, quite frankly," said Latimer.

I peered through the window. "Look, Latimer. Do you see the swans?"

"I certainly do. They're rather ridiculous, don't you think?" snapped Latimer.

I glanced at a book on the table. *Antic Hay,* by Aldous Huxley.

"Are you reading this, Latimer?"

"I just finished it. It's rather devastating."

"Do you like Galsworthy?" I murmured wistfully.

Latimer froze. "He writes for chambermaids."

I looked at my watch. "It's almost six. I'd better take a bath before dinner."

Latimer stared at me vacantly. The record ground to a halt. He sighed, shrugged his shoulders, and sank back in his Morris chair.

I opened my bags and gazed dejectedly at my humble belongings—a tennis racquet, *The Forsyte Saga,* a lithograph of the Piazza San Marco. Then I slipped off my clothes, threw a towel around my waist and went tiptoeing down the gloomy, freshly varnished corridor.

I was soaping my body when Latimer joined me in the shower-room.

He tossed his towel over a hook. "You probably think that I'm terribly cynical."

"Just a little," I said, "perhaps."

"I'm not actually," said Latimer. "I'm an aristocrat, that's the point. I hate things that are vulgar."

I washed the soap out of my eyes and glanced through the window. Dusk was settling on the campus; a violet sheen tinged the ivy. A few straggling silhouettes were wandering aimlessly toward Goodspeed Hall. The great bell began to toll. The lights went on in the quadrangle.

And quite suddenly, for no reason at all, a wave of horror passed over me: a sourceless and uncontrollable feeling of menace, as though a serpent-like shadow were threading its way through the gingko trees, casting its spell over the lawns, dropping its poison in the swan-pond.

2

I pored dutifully over the *Georgics* and *La Princesse de Clèves*. I memorized *Ozymandias* and the dates of the Kings of England. I drew sketches of isosceles triangles and dismembered lobsters. I practiced my trudgen crawl and my overhead smash.

And at night I lay in my bed-room, chewing butter-crunch candies and reading one of Latimer's books—*Dorian Gray*, or *The Aspern Papers*. I'd glance at my little etchings of Florence and Salamanca; I'd catch a phrase from a record—a bit of Handel or Prokofieff; I'd watch the glow of the lightbulb reflected in the mirror and I'd wonder about Existence—the insoluble enigma of human identity, the possibilities of an after-life.

Sometimes Latimer opened the door and sat down at the foot of my bed.

"Well," he said, "what did you think of old Bramble-bottom's lecture?"

"About Wordsworth, you mean?"

"About that ode on immortality. He talked as though he were addressing a group of cretins, I must say."

"I wasn't listening very carefully."

"Of course you weren't. Neither was I. He talked about Heaven as though it were a field full of buttercups."

"What do you think Heaven is like?"

"I don't believe in Heaven," purred Latimer.

"Do you believe in Hell?" I said.

Latimer's eyes grew darkly luminous. "It depends on what you mean, dear. If you mean a Hell after we're dead, full of cauldrons and prancing devils, I must say that I'm not convinced."

"What kind of Hell do you think exists, then?"

"The Hell," said Latimer, "of being alive. Haven't you ever felt it, Henry? Lying alone in your bed and wondering what you're born for? Feeling dreary and pointless, day after day and night after night? Seeing nothing ahead but just boredom and decay? Hating yourself? Hating everybody? Picking up a bottle of iodine. . . ."

"Good God, Latimer," I said. "You've never seriously thought of suicide?"

"I certainly have. Many a time. When life seemed sickeningly futile." His voice grew tenuous and brittle; his Adam's apple began to quiver. He looked down at me accusingly. "Nobody would care if I suddenly died."

"Oh, I'm sure they would, Latimer."

"Who, for example?" bleated Latimer.

"Your father," I said. "And your mother."

"They both loathe me," said Latimer.

"You're wrong," I pleaded. "I'm sure of it, Latimer. They really love you. They just don't show it."

"And anyway," said Latimer, "why go on living? You just grow older and older. You grow bald and repulsive. And nobody would dream of falling in love with you."

"You're a pessimist," I said.

"I look facts in the face," said Latimer.

"But you're young still," I ventured. "You won't grow bald for a while yet, Latimer."

"Yes? And then?"

"You'll be married, won't you, and have plenty of children, and all the rest of it?"

"Fiddlesticks, dear. I'll never marry."

"Oh? Why not?"

"I loathe women."

"Do you really?"

"They revolt me."

"Come, come, Latimer," I said.

"Those spreading hips. Those droopy breasts. Those puffy buttocks," said Latimer, wrinkling his nose.

"There are plenty of women," I said sternly, "who don't fit that description."

"Women," said Latimer, "are made for childbirth. They should stick to it, in my opinion."

"Aren't you being just a wee bit old-fashioned, perhaps?"

"When have women," snapped Latimer, "ever achieved true greatness?"

"What about Catharine of Russia? And Queen Elizabeth? And Madame Curie?"

"In the world of art, I mean," said Latimer. "That's the only world that counts."

"Well, there's Rosa Bonheur. . . ."

"Try to be serious, please, Henry."

"And there's Sappho," I muttered.

"Sappho. Precisely," said Latimer. He leered at me triumphantly. "Sappho was a Lesbian, my dear Henry."

"I beg your pardon? A what?"

Latimer bared his teeth in a smile. "Poor little Henry," he murmured. "You're still a babe in the woods, I see."

He fondled a pimple on his cheek, then picked up a pencil and jabbed his chin with it.

"Is there anyone in the world that you really love, Henry?"

I pondered a moment. "I am very fond of my old Aunt Ursula."

"I mean *love*. Not just dreary old fondness," said Latimer snappishly.

"Love? . . . Love?" I repeated the word. It sounded incongruous, bizarre. It rhymed with glove, dove, above, and should have been the word for a kind of garment, or perhaps a green vegetable, or a kitchen utensil.

That night I dreamed of Stella. We were walking beside a lake. Dark clouds hung bubbling in the distance like billows of lava. A wind came roaring out of the south, a hot, gelatinous wind that plucked Stella like an orange-blossom and deposited her in the lake. I plunged in to rescue her; we sank slowly into the depths, and as I clung to

her she turned into an old, wrinkled harridan. Her flesh
grew black, her eyes grew yellow, barnacles covered her
thighs and the worms began to gnaw at her shriveled
breasts.

3

Snow clung like a rash to the Ionic columns of Quigley
Hall and matted the Chinese gables of the cricket pavilion;
it lit on the grinning gargoyles above the library door and
dappled the Sevillian traceries of the Whipple Memorial
Gymnasium. Snow covered the tennis courts, it dappled
the swan-pond, it shone like a skeleton on the emaciated
poplars.

During these crisp winter evenings, when the stars began to glitter, I'd go wandering through the college library toward one of those little alcoves that smelled of
crumbling calf-skin and mildewy paper. On my way I
passed the desk where Miss Eschleman sat like an ogress,
surrounded by crenelations of black buckram volumes.
I passed the green ramparts of the card catalogue and the
spattered portcullis of the magazine rack. I paused to
glance at the forbidden joys of the "Locked Case," where
behind the luxury of glass and bronze lurked Martial and
Rabelais, *Justine* and *Fanny Hill.* I'd leaf through
ancient treatises on Mandarin costumes or Tuscan villas;
I'd browse through old engravings of Brazilian waterfalls
or Hessian stage-coaches; and for a while I'd find a refuge
from the Quakerish aridity of Llewellyn.

Sometimes I strolled into the gymnasium, whose grilled
Moorish windows dropped luminous curlicues on the

snow-sheeted quadrangle. I used to squat by the swimming pool and watch Phil Bainbridge doing his back-dive,
or I wrestled in the shower-room with Steve O'Malley, who
played on the soccer team. I found a certain relief in this
spry pagan nudity after the bleakness of Solid Geometry
or the Laws of Probability.

I grew aware, during these wintry months, that I was
gradually maturing. I started to shave more regularly. My
complexion began to coarsen. Fine dark hairs were sprouting from my chest and the muscles on my calves began to
bulge. I grew expert at swinging from the rings, climbing
the rope and twirling the dumbbells. I discarded my herring-bone suit and wore gray flannels and a thick white
pullover. I bought a pair of saddled sport shoes and
ordered a crew cut at the barber-shop.

I noticed that Latimer was glancing at me with gathering chagrin.

"You're going in," he said acidly, "for protective mimi-
cry, I see."

"What do you mean?" I said innocently.

"All this crude collegiate nonsense. It's so frightfully
immature. You're not like the rest of these idiots, Henry,
so why go and imitate them?"

"I didn't realize that I was imitating them."

"That preposterous haircut, for instance. And why do
you go around with that moron Tim Boomer?"

"I play tennis," I said, "with Tim."

"Do you find him culturally stimulating?"

"He doesn't read Firbank, I'll admit. But he's easy to
get along with."

"Well," said Latimer, "mark my words. You'll end by
turning into a Rotarian."

I bought some records at Ye Musick Shoppe down in the village to placate Latimer: *La Cathédrale Engloutie* and the *Rhapsody on a Theme of Paganini.* But he laid them aside contemptuously and put on a bit of Vivaldi. One evening I brought back *The Tattooed Countess* for him from the library. He tossed it aside with a moan and returned to *Mrs. Dalloway.*

I began to feel, in Latimer's presence, a mingling of guilt and alarm. I felt that my mind was decaying. I felt torpid and mediocre. And so it happened that when Tim Boomer asked me to room with him the following year, I hesitated for a moment and then gratefully accepted.

4

My French instructor, Monsieur La Motte, was beginning to take a personal interest in me. Every Monday he asked me to his chambers for a glass of vermouth. Occasionally he played some choice little tidbit on the piano—Satie's *Gymnopédies,* perhaps, or Rameau's *Fanfarinette*—and then he would light a cigarette and gaze thoughtfully down on the tennis courts.

"I have a feeling about you, Henry. There is something unusual in your make-up."

I lowered my eyes demurely and sipped quietly at my Noilly Prat.

"You'll go far in the world, I think. If you only make the effort. If you find some sort of goal. And if you learn some self-appraisal."

I rather enjoyed the cloistered atmosphere in Monsieur

La Motte's little study. It smelled of stale tobacco and powerful black coffee. Some old photographs hung over his desk—a girl in bloomers standing beside a bicycle, and an elderly lady with her hair done in the manner of Queen Alexandra, flanked by two little boys in straw hats with long ribbons. On his desk stood a paper-weight which, when I shook it, showed Mont Saint-Michel in a flurry of snowflakes.

Monsieur La Motte himself was a caustic, disheveled man in his middle thirties. He wore his reddish hair *en brosse:* he looked like a dissolute parrot. He fixed his huge beady eyes on me and sat in silence for a minute or two. Then he said, baring his gums:

"You must find the right terrain, of course."

"What do you think would be the right terrain for me, Monsieur La Motte?"

"Oh," he said, "goodness knows. Have you ever thought of entering the theatre?"

"It did occur to me once or twice."

"You seemed to enjoy *Les Femmes Savantes.* And even *Hernani,* I gather. And then poetry. You took a fancy to Lamartine, didn't you?"

"Well, yes," I said. "Rather."

"You look guilty," said Monsieur La Motte. "Well, you needn't, *mon cher.* There is nothing discreditable in an appreciation of literature."

He took off his glasses and wiped them carefully with a dark blue handkerchief. Then he turned with a sigh and gazed at me myopically.

"I suggest that you go abroad. You have a streak of romanticism in you. Don't let it wither away on the vine. Youth is brief. Gather ye rosebuds."

"You really think that. . . ."

"I certainly do. You have talents. Take advantage of them. You're lively and shrewd. You're good-looking. Don't bother with Economics or Sociology. Believe me, dear Henry, there is more to life than just being respectable."

Some days later Monsieur La Motte called me into his office.

"Your paper on *Le Rouge et le Noir* was unusually good, I thought, Henry. You seemed to grasp intuitively what went on in Julien's soul. And you have a real feeling for the French milieu, I've observed. Here," he said, pushing a paper-bound volume across the desk: "try this for a change. You might find it amusing."

I glanced at the title: *Du côté de chez Swann.* "Thank you," I said. "Is it a novel?"

"It is everything," said Monsieur La Motte, dropping his ash in the crystal bowl. "It is a novel. It is a confession. It is a scientific treatise. It is a philosophical masterpiece. It is history. It is music. It is painting. It is poetry."

I nodded. "I see."

"You'll find it rather unusual for the first few pages. But keep on with it, my boy. You'll find it worth your while, I assure you."

5

Tim Boomer was precisely the opposite of Latimer Peck: blond and stocky, with a powerful neck and an air of animal luxuriance, as though he were basking in the noonday sunlight. He looked peaceful and pastoral, almost at times a little bovine; but now and then a glint of rapacity, even of violence, shone in his eyes.

We played doubles together on the Llewellyn tennis team that spring. His position was up at the net, where he darted about stylishly, stabbing the ball into the corners with a flick of the wrist: while I lingered near the base-line, busily recovering the angled drives and lobbing them back with a kind of agonized persistence.

Sometimes, when the game was over, we strolled into the Baxter Memorial Garden and lay down under the boughs of a black arbor vitae, on which a small plaque announced that it had been planted there in memory of a certain Gertrude J. Aspinwall.

"Do you ever wonder," said Tim, unbuttoning his shirt, "what you're going to do with your life?"

"Oh, now and then. Vaguely." I nibbled lazily at a clover leaf.

"Have you picked a career, for instance?"

"Not exactly. Just yet."

"You're not serious about being a poet, are you?"

"Oh, not really. It's just a hobby."

"I've thought of chemistry," said Tim complacently. "I like to play with all those test-tubes."

"I've thought of botany. Or maybe zoology. I like animals," I said. "And plants."

"I'd like to make money too, of course. I'd like to make a fortune, wouldn't you? Frankly?"

"I suppose I would," I confessed. "As long as it didn't involve office hours."

"Oh," said Tim, yawning slightly, "I don't think I'd

mind an office specially. Not if I were the boss, at any rate. And I'd be the boss. Don't you worry."

"You'll marry," I said, "I suppose?"

"Of course I'll marry," said Tim.

"Latimer Peck," I remarked, "has no intention of getting married."

"I'm not surprised. Latimer Peck is a pretentious old sissy."

"He is highly intelligent," I said.

"He's a scarecrow," said Tim.

"He's terribly unhappy. He's thought of suicide. Many a time. He told me so."

"Well," said Tim, "I don't blame him. I'd cut my jugular if I were Latimer."

The sun shone on our faces and the scent of hawthorn hung over us: it seemed like an embodiment, a distillation of all the aromas of youth: the nameless yearnings, the dark cunning, the haunted pride, the hovering expectancy, with just a hint of something predatory and homicidal.

Suddenly Tim leaned over and whispered: "Tell me the truth, will you, Henry?"

"What about?"

"About sex."

"Well," I said, "what about it?"

"Are you a virgin, Henry? Frankly?"

I paused for a moment. "Not exactly."

Tim looked puzzled. "What do you mean by not exactly, please, Henry?"

"Well, I had a stray little episode or two in Texas, I seem to remember."

"Oh, really?"

"I was only twelve."

"And you lost your virginity?"

"I suppose I must have."

"Don't you remember?"

"I remember perfectly," I said. "But at twelve, you know, it's hard to draw the line."

Tim flicked a small bug from the edge of his wrist. "Tell me, Henry," he whispered: "have you ever seen a girl all naked?"

I grew thoughtful. "Yes. Twice."

"Oh really? Who were they?"

"A girl named Zenobia down in Texas."

Tim's eyes bulged with lust and his husky voice began to throb. "Was she pretty? Did she have big bubbies? Tell me about her bubbies, please, Henry."

But I was thinking of something else. I stared up at the clouds, which shone in that sea of azure like wind-billowed sails. I caught the scent of the wistaria hanging over the garden wall, and through the panes of the adjoining library I caught sight of Miss Eschleman prowling among the shelves devoted to anatomy.

"It's a bit of a bore, being a virgin," Tim was saying. "Don't you think?"

I nodded absently. I closed my eyes. A bee was buzzing over my head.

"It keeps weighing on my mind," said Tim. "I'd like to get over it. As soon as possible."

I glanced up and saw Tim staring disconsolately into space: his cheeks flushed with the sunlight, his pupils narrowed to a point, beads of sweat clinging to the silky blond hairs of his upper lip.

"Well," I said. "I'll ask Bill Mallory. He'll give us some addresses."

"Addresses? What kind of addresses?"

"Never you mind," I said craftily.

6

One afternoon late in April there was a knock on my bedroom door. I slung a towel around my waist and opened the door briskly.

A handsome fellow in a yellow pullover and corduroy trousers stood in front of me. He flashed a dazzling white smile at me. Then he reached out his hand.

"Well, my friend, don't you recognize me?"

"Goodness, Tony. What on earth. . . ."

"I had your address from your Aunt Elfrida. And since I was passing through Llewellyn. . . ."

"What a surprise," I said brightly.

"I thought that it might be," said Tony.

"How is Prairie du Loup?"

"Just the same. A little drearier, maybe."

He sat down on the windowsill and placed his hands on his outspread knees. The light from the setting sun fell on his curly black hair. I noticed a sickle-shaped scar on his cheek—a memento of the automobile accident, no doubt. He hadn't changed: there was still the same Italianate elegance about him. But here in the chaste, aseptic atmosphere of Merriweather Hall his brilliant plumage seemed rather incongruous: he looked like a gypsy.

"Well," he said, glancing me up and down adroitly, "you've put on some muscles, haven't you?"

"Maybe I have. Just a bit."

"You've turned into a regular athlete."

I blushed. "Have I really?"

His voice darkened mysteriously. "I'm taking a trip around the world, you know."

"Oh, Tony. That's splendid."

"France. Italy. And then Turkey."

"God. I certainly do envy you."

"And then Egypt and India."

"And what will you do when you get there, Tony?"

"I've taken up painting. Seriously, I mean."

"I'm delighted, Tony. I really am."

"I'm going to visit the South Sea Islands."

"It sounds marvelous," I said.

"And then the Congo," said Tony.

"You're terribly lucky, I must say."

"Do you really think so?" said Tony. His eyes narrowed slightly. "I'll have to earn a bit of cash before I go, I'm afraid."

"I wouldn't worry about a dreary thing like cash, if I were you."

"I don't especially. I'll manage somehow. Just wait and see, Henry. I'll be a world-famous artist. You'll be proud that you knew me."

His voice grew sly and caressing. His small white teeth shone like a cat's. A thread of fire from the dying sun lit on his velvety olive cheek. And in his eyes I detected a hint of violet in the green—the hidden animal tumult, the old feline restlessness.

And suddenly it all came back to me: the scent of the

woods in the early autumn and the rustling of birch-leaves as the rain started falling; the ominous drumming of the bull-frogs and the marshy smell of the lily-pads and the desolate twilight music of the whip-poor-will calling.

The room darkened abruptly. Dusk was falling across the campus. I could see the cricket players in their long white flannels crossing the lawn.

Tony rose and shook my hand.

"Well, I'd better be going, I guess."

"Thanks for coming to see me, Tony."

"I was curious, you know, a little. I kept wondering what had happened to you. I used to think of all those times we went fishing together, just the two of us."

"I was curious about you too."

"Have I changed?"

"Well . . . not really."

"Nor have you. Not much, anyway." He paused in the doorway. "By the way."

"Yes?"

"Do you think you could lend me some money?"

"Heavens, Tony. I wish I could."

"Just twenty dollars?" he said cajolingly.

I glanced toward the window. "I wish I had it."

His eyes grew fawning, like an Irish setter's. He placed his hand on the nape of my neck. "For old time's sake?" He smiled wistfully. "In memory of the days we went fishing?"

"Well, I really. . . ."

"Just enough to get to New York? Ten dollars, maybe?"

I opened the door of my closet and reached into my herring-bone suit.

"Here," I said. "It's all I've got. Maybe it will help you get to Bali."

Tony took the rumpled bank-note and patted my cheek affectionately.

"You won't regret it, I promise you. I'll give you my first full-fledged masterpiece!"

"Well, good luck to you," I said.

"And the same to you, Henry."

"Good-bye. . . ."

"And God bless you. . . ."

He closed the door with a little wink.

7

One Sunday afternoon I borrowed Bill Mallory's apricot roadster and Tim and I started off down the highway toward Nineveh.

It was a sultry, oppressive day: dead gnats clung to the windshield and the stale smell of tar hung over the turnpike.

"Are you sure," said Tim hoarsely, "that the addresses are genuine?"

"Well, Bill Mallory seemed quite pleased to cooperate," I said.

"What will happen when we get there? Have you any idea?"

"Your guess is as good as mine," I replied, non-committally.

"Will the girls be pretty, do you think?"

"They might be a shade on the sluttish side."

"They'll be clean at any rate, won't they?"

"Well, let's hope so," I said.

"I feel rather nervous, you know."

"That's natural enough," I said judiciously.

Tim whispered: "Wouldn't it be terrible if. . . ."

I tilted the mirror. "Yes? If what?"

"Well, you know. If I made an ass of myself."

I paused discreetly. "How, for instance?"

"Oh, if I couldn't get into the spirit, if you know what I mean."

"Well, they're probably used to that little problem," I said knowingly.

A great cloud of geranium-hued smoke hung over Nineveh. Night was falling. The glow of the foundries simmered dangerously in the distance. The smell of coke filled the streets and the walls were mossy with soot. The very air lay crushed under the pyramids of dirt and desolation.

Finally we found the right address: 712 Cranberry Street. It was a narrow wooden house embedded in a jungle of black tenements. We parked the car two blocks away and sauntered back, whistling casually.

A skeletal woman in a bright red wig opened the door. She regarded us stoically and sent a spray of tobacco juice across the sidewalk.

"Where are you from?" she asked hoarsely.

"From Llewellyn," I said.

"Mm. Who sent you?"

"Bill Mallory."

"Never heard of Bill Mallory."

"He gave us the address. He knows Dolly. And Janice. And Mable."

"Oh, he does? Well, come in. And I'll see what I can do for you."

We entered the parlor, which was draped with persimmon-hued plush and papered with aisles of symmetrical tiger lilies.

"Just make yourselves at home," grunted the red-headed woman. Then she called across the hallway: "Come, girls. Finish your custard. There's a couple of nice, clean boys from Llewellyn."

Tim kept staring at the wall-paper while I fondled the threadbare curtains. The door opened and four rosy-cheeked girls stepped into the room. They wore high-heeled slippers with shell-shaped buckles and tight little smocks of tomato sateen.

"Hello, boys. My name's Mable," cried a large, mellifluous blonde. "And this is Janice. And Edna. And that's Dolly, with the diamond necklace."

"Sit down, boys," said Dolly briskly. She draped herself on the arm of my chair. "Go on Mable, put on *You're the Cream in my Coffee,* won't you, honey?"

8

I followed Dolly up the steep yellow stairs to her room. There was a bed with a pleated coverlet and a tiny lamp with a scalloped lamp-shade. I caught the smell of cheap perfume, damp upholstery, and stale secretions. On the wall hung a faded oleograph: "The Soldier's Dream of Home."

Dolly bolted the door and glanced casually into the blistered mirror.

"Just relax," she said drowsily. "Don't be afraid of me, baby."

I stood awkwardly by the window, running my thumb down the pane.

"There," said Dolly. "Don't look so worried. There ain't nothing to be scared of."

She unbuttoned me deftly and dipped a sponge in a bowl of witch-hazel. "You ain't never been with a girl before, I'll bet, have you, honey?"

"Once," I said. "Maybe twice."

"Well," she said, "I know how it is. If the first time don't go right it takes a while to get over it."

I folded my trousers over the bedstead and lay down on the scented coverlet. Dolly squatted beside me on the edge of the bed. Her damp, rustic face shone in the beaded light like *blanc de Chine:* she looked like a benevolent household deity, eyes lowered, lips parted, engrossed in some elaborate culinary ritual.

Finally she said: "There you are. That wasn't so bad, now, was it dear?"

"Thank you, Dolly," I murmured.

She kissed me affectionately. "You're welcome, darling."

9

An hour later we were heading through the moonlit night toward Llewellyn. The land had mysteriously altered: it looked vast and impenetrable. The green rolling pastures looked like the ruins of the Gobi. The Appalachian slopes stirred with blue, bat-like shadows.

"Well," I said. "How was Janice?"

"Fine," said Tim. "How was Dolly?"

"Very gentle. Very patient. Very motherly," I said.

"So was Janice," said Tim. "Very sweet and understanding."

"Did you get into the proper spirit?"

"More or less," said Tim laconically.

"You lost your virginity, at any rate?"

"I'm not sure," said Tim sadly.

"Why? Did something go wrong?"

"Well," said Tim, "not exactly." He gazed up at the stars. "It was all so sudden. If you know what I mean."

We rumbled across the shallow gray waters of the Susquehanna, which squirmed in the moonlight like a ribbon of lava.

"Isn't it strange?" murmured Tim.

"What, Tim?" I said gently.

"About sex. Just think, Henry. If it weren't for sex we wouldn't be here. If it weren't for sex there wouldn't be anything. Sex is the reason for living, isn't it?"

"I suppose it is. In a way."

"It's the reason for being born, and for growing up, and for falling in love. It's what everyone keeps waiting and hoping for, isn't it, Henry?"

"You're perfectly right, Tim," I said.

"Well, then, answer me this, please. If sex is the reason for being alive, and for love and all the rest of it, then why does it seem so silly and disgusting?"

"I wish I knew. I really do."

"It should be beautiful, don't you think?"

I nodded wistfully. "It should."

"But just look at it," said Tim.

We entered a land of desolation: deserted factories and empty warehouses; great black fields studded with the carcasses of disemboweled cars and stagnant swamps littered with broken bottles, rusty tins and rotting rubber. The light of the moon shone on the chips of glass and coils of metal. And in the distance loomed the aluminum oil tanks, like a horde of giant turtles.

10

In the middle of May an insidious kind of restlessness seized me. I'd lie in the grass by the swan-pond with my *Principles of Trigonometry* and watch the enormous pink clouds sailing over me. They seemed to be wandering toward some fabulous wilderness—the shores of the Caspian or the swamps of the Oxus.

And there were times when I sat in my swivel-chair, usually in the evening toward sunset, and I stared at my compass, my ink-pot, my tennis shoes: which gradually changed, in the gilded light, into something quite different—a paint-brush, a liqueur glass or a pair of ballet slippers. And a sudden panic shot through me—a whiff of far-off excitements, of time slipping away, of something precious eluding me.

I finished my brisk little thesis on "The Seventeen Causes of the French Revolution." I completed my biology notebook, with its loving portraits of fleas and annelids. For Monsieur La Motte I wrote a paper on the plays of

Corneille, and for old Bramblebottom's Creative Writing
I submitted my annual poem:

> *"I would not alter thy cold eyes*
> *Nor trouble the calm fount of speech*
> *With aught of passion or surprise.*
> *The heart of thee I cannot reach:*
> *I would not alter thy cold eyes. . . ."*

I had discovered these dusty verses while leafing through
some old anthology. I changed the title, *Flos Lunae,* to
Lover's Lament. Professor Bramblebottom marked it with
a voluminous cherry-red B, with the annotation: "Deft but
stilted. Words like *aught, fount* and *thy* do not ring with
the unmistakable timbre of true passion."

When the final examinations came I prepared miscro-
scopical lists of the Roman Emperors, of the comedies of
Molière, and of the Linnaean orders of the animal king-
dom, and tucked them astutely under the edge of my
coat-sleeve.

"What did you get in Biology 2?" asked Latimer Peck
as we met in the Library.

"A," I said, with an off-hand air.

"And in French 3?"

"A—, unfortunately."

"And in History 4?"

"A+, as it happens."

"I don't see how you do it," said Latimer acidly. "I've
been slaving for old Hinchcliffe. And all I got was a dis-
mal B."

"Pure luck," I said lightly.

"It smacks of favoritism," said Latimer.

"Well, I did my best. As a kind of swan song."

"What do you mean," said Latimer: "swan song?"

"I've made up my mind. I'm leaving Llewellyn."

Latimer gaped at me. "You're mad."

"I suppose I am," I said meekly.

"And what," said Latimer, "do you plan to do?"

"A bit of traveling. Hither and yon."

"And you're going to abandon Llewellyn?"

"I'm afraid that I am."

"You're an idiot. After all those beautiful A's," said Latimer mournfully.

That night I woke up in the trance-like stillness of early morning. I slipped out of my bed and glanced through the door. Tim was lying on his side, pink and coiled, like a foetus. A silvery sheen fell on his face: it looked ruthless, inscrutable.

I looked out through the open window. The moon was peeping through the clouds. The Gothic portals of the college library shone in the gloom like a spray of ice, and the little dome of the Coxe Observatory was glittering like an igloo. And suddenly the sound of far-off bells pierced that lunar sterility: it was like the sound of humanity itself, wild and intricate and terrible.

VI

A LONELY CROQUET MALLET lay in the shade of a forsythia bush and a spider hung dangling from one of the wickets. The hydrangeas had withered; the bird-bath was dry; a smell of corruption hung over the terrace.

I found my Aunt Ursula sitting in the musty green library. I was shocked by her appearance. She had shriveled uncannily. Her skin had turned into a dusty terra-cotta.

"Dear boy. How well you look. You're as dark as an Indian." She kept stroking Mata Hari, who lay coiled in her lap. "It's a pity about your leaving Llewellyn, of course. A Bachelor of Arts is so useful in getting ahead nowadays. Still, you must have had your reasons. Maybe you were bored just a bit. There was always a restless streak in your family."

The evening light, filtering through the chintz, seemed to wilt on her face. The past few months had created a mysterious reversion in her aspect. The Scottish tweeds were cast aside and she wore a thick écru shawl, a black velvet choker and a heart-shaped garnet brooch. Behind her I still discerned the faded prints of the Epworth Hunt, the set of Disraeli and the Uncle Toby jug: dusty relics of another era, a buried love. But grief had finally drained her of all powers of camouflage and she had turned into a weather-beaten old Tyrolean peasant woman.

"I have arrived at a decision, Henry."

My heart tightened. "What about?"

"About your future."

"I see."

"Do you wish to become a poet?"

"Well, it sounds rather odd, but. . . ."

"It is not a lucrative profession."

"I'm afraid it isn't, Aunt Ursula."

"Wouldn't you like to travel a bit?"

"I certainly would, Aunt Ursula."

"Where, for example?"

"Oh, anywhere. New York for a while. And then Paris. Or maybe Mallorca."

Aunt Ursula sat and looked at me with her sly simian eyes. They grew suave, almost tender. A playful smile slid over her lips.

"You don't seem to be a very practical young man," she murmured.

I glanced guiltily at the bust of Byron which stood on the mantelpiece. He too seemed to leer at me with an acid amusement.

"I suppose," I said glumly, "that I ought to look for a job."

"Indeed you ought," said Aunt Ursula, staring at the dogwood below the window. Her mouth tightened, as though in pain; her eyelids twitched oddly. For a moment

I thought she was going to burst into tears. Then she pressed her hands together and said in a matter-of-fact tone:

"Well, my dear, I suppose you'll do as you wish in the end, so there's really no point in my giving you advice. I've tried to drill the importance of money into your naughty head, but I can see that you didn't listen, and I don't suppose you ever will. I shall give you a thousand dollars a year for the next three years. It isn't much, but it will keep you from starving. Do exactly as you wish. Roam about. Write poems. And try to be happy."

She rose and dropped a dry, leaden kiss on my forehead.

"God bless you," she said. "Go, take a bath and get ready for tea. Felicia has baked some Petticoat Tails."

"I was terribly sorry," I said, "to hear about Miss Abercrombie, Aunt Ursula."

Aunt Ursula gazed at me placidly. "There was nothing to be done," she said softly.

I felt a rush of strange tenderness for the lonely old woman. So much had been left unsaid, so much had been suffered in secrecy. I flung my arms around her neck but she stiffened in horror and recoiled in a brittle, puppet-like movement.

And she waddled off toward the museum-like gloom of the parlor, where some old Etruscan fragments still lay scattered on the table. They shone faintly in the dying light, corroded and yellowish. They looked like the bones of some antique monster.

2

The dark days arrived. The windows glittered; the air grew steely. Ribbons of mist, foul and purple, coiled in from the sea.

Day after day I wandered about in that huge seething labyrinth, peering through half-shuttered panes which seemed to hide mysterious orgies; staring into softly lit shops where jewels lay scattered as in a bandit's cave; sipping coffee under fluorescent lights in dingy cafeterias; sinking into the popcorn-scented darkness of cheap, dirty cinemas; thumbing old Parisian magazines in small dusty bookshops and staring at night from the cidery fragrance of Central Park at those incandescent spires which rose implausibly in the distance. They lay reflected in the inky pond, scaly and serpentine; until I tossed a small pebble and they burst like a Catherine wheel.

For three weeks I lived in a cheap little hotel west of Broadway. Finally one day I rang the bell of an old brownstone house on which a sign hung suspended: *Rooms for Rent. Gentlemen Only.*

The door opened. A squat little woman with a gypsy face glared from the darkness.

"I'm sorry to trouble you, madam. Do you have a room, by any chance?"

She narrowed her eyes, then nodded slyly. "Fourth floor. Cozy. With a view."

I peered into the shadows. "How much is it?"

"A dollar a day," she growled hoarsely. "Come in. Don't be afraid. I am not a cobra, young man."

I stepped into the hall, which was dark and stuffy. A smell of asparagus oozed from the walls. Two Persian cats slid out of the shadows and rubbed seductively against my legs.

"I am Madame Slama," said the woman furrily. "You're fresh from the country, I imagine? Just relax with me, dear. Come, I'll show you the room."

I followed her up three gloomy flights of steps. Her quivering hips rolled laboriously while the cats rippled past us, elegant and weightless as ostrich feathers.

"Here it is," she said finally, opening a narrow green door. "Small but comfy. Nice big mirror. Navajo bedspread. Cheery wallpaper. I'll let you have it for five dollars a week. No women allowed. Do you drink?"

"Very little," I said softly.

"What's your religion?"

"Oh, none especially."

"A heathen, eh? Well, never mind. There are worse things in this world. Here's the key. Don't lose it. Feel this bed! Goose-feathers from Hungary. . . ."

She folded her arms, which were moist and swollen, like giant leeches, and stood motionless by the bed with a sphinx-like expression. She was wearing a dress of greenish crêpe, suggestively stained and frayed at the hems, and over her shoulders she wore a tattered Indian sari. Two drops of mother-of-pearl hung suspended from her ears. On her wrist she wore a bracelet studded with miniature charms—twigs of coral, skulls, elephants, buffalo horns and four-leaf clovers. A tangle of oily, Medusa-like curls hung down to her shoulders. The face itself was puckered and purplish, with two beady little eyes lurking nervously under the wrinkled lids, like an iguana's.

"You can pay a call on me tonight, if you're in the mood," she said impassively. "Nine o'clock sharp. And dress properly. Jacket and neck-tie. And no smoking. There's a full moon tonight. So maybe we'll have some interesting visitors. . . ."

3

Little by little my life took on a vaguely esthetic pattern. I wore corduroy pants and a turtle-neck sweater. I'd sit in the Automat with a liverwurst sandwich and *Trivial Breath*, or in the restaurant by the zoo with *Huntsman, What Quarry?*

Weeks passed. I progressed. My tastes grew more subtle. I grew jaded with Vachel Lindsay and James Elroy Flecker. I wrote odes, triolets, villanelles, ballades and dithyrambics. I lay in my bed, munching nougats as I throbbed to the magic of *Byzantium,* or sipped at my coffee at Nedick's over a copy of *Hugh Selwyn Mauberly.*

To relieve the squalor of my room I set a fern on the windowsill and hung a Gauguin reproduction on the poppy-patterned wall-paper. I placed a row of crystal elephants on the shelf over the sink and by my bed-lamp lay a copy of *The Flowers of Evil.*

And once in a while, out of sheer loneliness, I went and called on Madame Slama. She would sit in her twilit parlor among the potted begonias. On the wall hung an Inca mask, a Tibetan prayer-mill, and two Javanese cymbals. The smell of sandalwood permeated the air, tinged with a whiff of salami and my landlady's own personal aroma, like a pumpkin's.

"Did you ever visit the Orient, Madame Slama?" I said one evening, as we waited for the guests to arrive for the séance.

"Not in body, dear boy. But in spirit, most definitely. I remember it all just as clearly as though it were yesterday. I have hovered in the alleys of Bangkok, I have crouched on the stairways of Lhasa, I have floated like a butterfly through the markets of Samarkand."

"How do you explain this, Madame Slama?"

"There is nothing to explain, my dear friend. It is all perfectly natural. We all have a part in the great All-Consciousness in us. The All-Consciousness floats in the air like an invisible radio. Everything that happens is registered in the great All-Consciousness. The Age of Ice, the Trojan War, the voyages of Christopher Columbus, they're all registered in the great All-Consciousness, in full regalia, you might say. They still keep sending out delicate little rays occasionally, like the music from a far-off broadcasting station. And if we're sensitive, as I personally happen to be, these little rays enter our brains and send forth echoes. We call them ghosts. But they are only echoes from the great All-Consciousness."

"I see."

"One day I might echo to Cleopatra, lolling on her barge on the Nile. Another day I might echo to poor little Marie-Antoinette, lying on the guillotine."

"How very thrilling."

"It is indeed," said Madame Slama, stroking her abdomen.

"Have you seen many ghosts?"

"Well," said Madame Slama, "I don't actually *see* them. I feel their presence. I sense them. Two in particular. They come when I need them."

I nodded tactfully. One of the cats sprang into my lap and started to purr. Madame Slama ran her handkerchief under her nose and continued festively:

"The first ghost is Lady Adlington. Lady Adlington is my Mentor. She is an English lady of considerable distinction. When I start to merge into the All-Consciousness she comes and lurks on my left, just by my chair. All I am aware of is a pale blue haze and a delicate scent, like verbena. She wears a large, flowery hat with a veil, I should imagine. And long white gloves. She had suffered. She has a feeling for love affairs."

"And who," I said, "is the second ghost?"

"That," said my landlady, "is Green Fish. Dear Little Green Fish is an Indian maiden. A Seminole, I suspect. She is my Guide. She never fails me. When I lose my way in the tangles of Space, Green Fish comes to my rescue. I hear the sound of her moccasins swishing through the grasses. She is very loyal. And very brave. But a wee bit meddlesome now and then. . . ."

4

One night the snow fell. The sky turned into a mighty sieve from which a delicate white dust, like powdered sugar, kept falling. It sparkled under the street-lamps and dissolved under my footsteps. I stuck out my tongue; it was crisp and tart, like the blade of a knife.

I wandered aimlessly down Fifty-Seventh Street. A feeling of elation took hold of me. I peered through the windows at the Lowestoft bowls, the Wedgwood platters and Hepplewhite chairs.

Gradually the snowflakes grew larger. They fell more slowly. They seemed to pause in mid-air, trapped in the light like a flock of moths. A little whirlwind swept past and the flakes started dancing, around and around, as though they were chasing each other. They changed from blue into gold as they eddied across the light. The wind died down and they sank into the wet black asphalt.

I paused for a moment, caught up in the magical atmosphere. I found myself staring into an illuminated cavern: gilded chairs and acajou consoles were reflected in Chippendale mirrors.

Suddenly I noticed a dark, slender figure beside me, gazing intently into the breath-misted shop window. She was much slighter than I remembered. And more fragile somehow. She wore a dark blue béret and a greenish coat with silver buttons.

I said: "Stella!"

She turned sharply, with a look of alarm.

"Goodness, Henry! It's you."

"Yes, it is. Don't be frightened."

"How very odd." Her voice wavered. "What in the world are you doing here?"

"I was looking at those cherubs. There in the corner, above the writing desk."

"I mean here in New York, dear. Mercy me. What a surprise." She started to brighten; she smiled. Her huge eyes grew alive. "Of all places to find you. Staring at those fat, silly babies. Come, dear, let's have a nice friendly chat over a cup of coffee. . . ."

We stepped into a cheap little tea-shop on Lexington Avenue. There was an artificial grate in the fireplace, pewter plates hung on the wall, and a squat red candle was burning on each table.

Stella flung her coat over a chair, placed a cigarette in a holder, leaned back and peered at me through her long black lashes.

"Well, Henry. You certainly have changed. What on earth has come over you?"

"What do you mean?"

"Those corduroy pants, dear. And that incredible sweater."

"What," I muttered, "is so incredible about it?"

"You look like an artist, you really do!" She laughed gaily. "Provided one doesn't look too carefully!"

I sipped at my coffee and glanced at her furtively. "And what about you? You look rather arty yourself, you know."

She was wearing a tight black dress with a gilt flamingo pinned to her breast. Her shiny hair was tucked in a bun on the back of her head. The yellow light from the candle clung to the tip of her nose and hung reflected in her enormous blue eyes. She was definitely homely, I decided. She looked greedy and famished. Her mouth was too big and her neck was much too long. The whole effect was rather pathetic, with that black cigarette-holder.

"Arty? Really?" she said. She flicked the ash from her cigarette. "Well, it can't be helped. I'm utterly broke. I'm on the brink of suicide."

"Oh Stella, I'm terribly. . . .'

"Well, not really," she said, with a simper. "It's just that

I feel a shade weary. I've been taking ballet lessons, you know. It's terribly fatiguing. And rather pointless, I've finally decided."

"Pointless? Why?"

"Oh, darling, let's face it, I'll never be a dancer. An actress, maybe. Or even a singer. But not a dancer. I'm too *gauche*."

"Well, take acting lessons, then."

"Precisely. I'm starting on Monday."

I leaned back in my chair. "So you've dropped Law and Medicine?"

"Rubbish, dear. I was just being pompous when I talked about Medicine."

"You were rather sulky that day at Aunt Ursula's, weren't you?"

"I was revolting, I'm sure. I hated myself. I hated the world."

"Really? Why?"

"I wanted to be a man instead of a woman," she purred.

"Oh. And now?"

She laughed gaily. "Oh, don't worry. I'm not like *that*, dear. I'm going to concentrate on being mysterious and frightfully feminine."

"Who knows, maybe you'll turn into another Duse," I hinted.

"Or another Bernhardt," said Stella. "I'm sultry and bony, like Bernhardt."

She glanced at her cup and raised her brows. The same old Stella: defiant and moody. But different too: tense, crafty, remote, somewhat agitated.

She said softly, "And what about you?"

"I'm writing poetry," I growled, with a blush.

"How utterly thrilling," said Stella.

"I wish it were," I said wistfully.

"New York," said Stella, "is dreadfully cruel."

I nodded. "Yes. It certainly is."

"But it's fearfully exciting. Don't you agree?"

"I guess I do. All in all."

"One feels so desperately eager to be glamorous, and rich, and beautiful, and wildly successful." Her eyes glittered; her voice grew tremulous. "One feels that life is terribly short. . . ."

"I suppose one does," I said thoughtfully.

"Oh, Henry, darling, you're still the same. You haven't changed one single whit. Wouldn't it be marvelous if you suddenly grew famous, like Longfellow or somebody? And wouldn't it be marvelous if I turned into a famous singer *and* a famous actress *and* a famous dancer?"

"It certainly would."

"I'd live in Paris."

"A marvelous idea," I agreed.

"Or on the Riviera. In Monte Carlo." She spread her fingers and gazed at her palm. "I'm so weary of being poor, Henry. It's rather frightening to be poor."

I nodded mournfully. "It is. Especially for girls, I should imagine."

She smiled wickedly. "We'll both be fabulously rich some day, won't we?"

"Absolutely," I said. "With a sumptuous villa on the Riviera."

5

After this I began to see my cousin Stella quite frequently. We went to harpsichord recitals and listened to Wanda Landowska. We went to the Dali exhibition at the Museum of Modern Art. We looked at films with Emil Jannings and Ala Nazimova and watched recitals of modern dancing by Mary Wigman or Harald Kreutzberg.

And then we strolled through the icy streets to some small Italian restaurant, the Zia Giulia or the Grotta Azzura, and ate green noodles and Gorgonzola. Or we tried some new bistro, L'Omelette or Chez Mathilde, and dined on onion soup, fried mackerel and spumoni. Or we visited the Frick and then strolled through the park and ate scrambled eggs in the cafeteria by the seal-pool.

"Do you remember San Pedro?" she said one day, licking her fork.

"Yes, I do. Rather vividly."

"I was a disgusting child, wasn't I?"

"Well," I said, "you were a tom-boy. You climbed trees. You threw stones. You caught beetles and frogs."

"How repulsive. I suppose I did."

"And you used to slap my face."

"Oh, Henry, my lamb, did I really?" Her eyes softened; she smiled. She rarely smiled but when she did it was a haunting little smile: shy and reluctant, with a speculative glow in those sapphire eyes.

"You used to tell me about your dreams."

"Mercy. I did? How idiotic." She ran her thumb over

the saucer. "I still have rather amazing dreams. One especially."

"What about?"

"I see a horrible bird swooping down at me," said Stella.

"Yes? And then?"

"It keeps swirling about. As though it were trying to bite me."

"It might be a swan. A wild swan."

"Oh, mercy no, it isn't a swan, dear. Not in the least. It's an ugly, greedy, bloodthirsty bird. . . ."

She looked through the window down at the seal-pool. A lion was roaring in one of the cages. Her eyes darkened for an instant. She thrust a cigarette in her holder.

"You're rather different," she said, "from what I expected, you know."

"Am I really?"

"Much more sturdy. And much more good-looking."

"Oh? Thanks."

"But less interesting. You were such a quaint little boy in Texas. And so sad, with those big brown eyes. Now you're normal and cheerful."

Once she said: "My dear Henry, the weirdest things do keep happening to me. It must be something in my metabolism. I seem to act as a kind of magnet."

"Yes? What happened today?"

"Well, I was sitting under that fountain by the Plaza— that naked lady, you know, with the dripping bowl. Suddenly a man sat down next to me, two feet away. He kept staring and finally he said, 'Would you mind if I say something?' So I said, 'Not especially.' And what do you think he said? He said, 'You're the loveliest girl I've ever seen.' Isn't it amazing?"

"It certainly is."

"He was quite respectable. A Princeton type, I imagine."

"And that's the end of the story?"

"Well, approximately," said Stella. "He gave me his card before he left. His name is Willoughby Cholmondely Pratt. Rather elegant, don't you think?"

"Do you expect to see him again?"

"Well, I might. He was terribly sweet."

I looked at her more carefully. Had someone really thought her beautiful? With her ravenous little face and her sad, searching eyes, and that scrawny little body, like an overgrown schoolgirl's? And yet, as she stared through the window at the seals in the seal-pool, I did notice all of a sudden something striking in her face—just a flicker of something barbaric and passionate.

Some weeks later, in the beginning of March, we were dining at the Automat.

"I feel restless," said Stella. "As though something exciting were going to happen to me."

"It's in the air," I suggested. "Spring fever and what not."

"I'm weary of New York. I really am. I'm weary of eating in cafeterias. I'm weary of all these cheap, drab, boring old clothes."

"Well," I said, "just be patient. You'll soon be another Duse."

"Oh, Henry, don't be ridiculous. I'm not joking. I need a new atmosphere."

I smiled at her playfully. She blushed and lowered her eyes.

Then she whispered: "Tell me, Henry. Should I marry Willoughby Pratt?"

"Good God. Has he asked you to marry him?"

"He is madly in love with me," said Stella curtly.

"You've been going around with him, have you?"

"He took me to lunch today. At the Colony."

"Well," I said, "how very pleasant."

"His intentions," said Stella, "are strictly honorable."

"He sounds," I said, "like a bit of an idiot."

"He is a Yale man," said Stella thoughtfully.

"He has plenty of cash, I presume?"

"He is a capitalist. He works in Wall Street."

"Is he handsome as well?"

"Not bad," replied Stella. "He wears glasses, unfortunately. And his hair is thinning a little."

"Is he charming? Is he witty?"

"Well, now, darling, I must be frank. He's as dull as a dromedary," said Stella, lowering her eyes.

I nodded triumphantly. "Well, there you are. You can't have everything."

"You'll see, dear," said Stella. She stared intently at her long pink fingernails. "I'll be in Paris before long. With or without Willoughby Pratt."

6

Stiff little petals, like bits of vellum, appeared on the dogwood. The jonquils and daffodils were beginning to flower. A strange aroma flowed through the park—a dank, reptilian fragrance, like a lingering whiff from some prehistorical quagmire.

And a new uneasiness crept over me. It filled my room like the smell of pine. It hovered in the dusk like a cloud of fireflies; it pierced the dawn like the cry of a gull.

As April began to ripen, this strange malaise grew more pronounced. There were moments when it almost bordered on panic. I grew obsessed with the idea that my life was a shadow-life; that another, truer life was awaiting me somewhere or other. An amorous, iridescent sort of existence in which I would discover a richer nature, a stronger talent, a deeper happiness.

And I found my mind instinctively gravitating, during these moments of *Weltschmertz,* toward the plain, dark, angular little image of Stella. I kept wondering where she was. What she was doing. Whom she was with. Should I phone her? Or invite her to lunch? Or take her to the Cameo Art Cinema? And, bizarrely enough, I found my flesh beginning to bud with excitement. Something delicate and sinuous was seeping into my nervous system.

One day as we sat by a pond, tossing pebbles into the water, Stella said to me softly: "Tell me, Henry. I've been wondering."

"Yes? What?"

"Don't you ever have sex?"

"Oh, now and then. In a sort of way."

"Sort of way?" said Stella suspiciously.

"Nothing thrilling, I mean."

"You look sexy enough," said Stella. "I should think you'd have an affair." She smiled craftily. "Don't you know any pretty young poetesses?"

"I'm afraid I don't. The only poetess that I've met is tweedy and ferocious."

"I bet," said Stella, "you have Adventures."

I blushed. "Now and then."

"Oh, darling. Tell me about them!"

"Some other time," I said nervously. Then I said: "I know what. Let's call on Madame Slama tonight."

"Good heavens. But why?"

"Maybe she'll tell us our fortunes."

"Well," said Stella, "I've always suspected it. You're superstitious, just like me."

At nine o'clock sharp we knocked at my landlady's door.

"Enter, my child," said Madame Slama in a rich, throaty tone. She patted her bosom suspiciously. "Who is this lady, may I ask?"

"She's my cousin," I said. "She is studying to be an actress."

"Well, sit down, my dears, both of you. Here on the divan, if you don't mind. There'll be some more guests in a moment. I like my people to be punctual."

She drew the Burgundy curtain across the entrance to the dining room and placed a record on the dusty old gramophone. Strange sounds crept through the air as though from an enormous distance—abysmal wheezings and chatterings, with an occasional bark, like a coyote's.

"It's music from the Australian bush," said Madame Slama, belching faintly.

Three visitors arrived at this point: an elderly Italian widow, a pregnant Irish housewife, and a blond young man in suede shoes.

Madame Slama lit a candle and sat down by the table, which was covered with a threadbare Egyptian prayer-mat.

Then she turned to the blond young man. "Would you mind, please, my dear—I don't happen to know your name but I'll call you Percifal, if I may. I shall give my own names to each one of you tonight. Brunhilde. Jennifer. Esmeralda. And Adrian . . . Would you mind, Percifal, my dear, reading a little poem for us?"

She picked up a pamphlet and passed it majestically to Percifal, who opened it at a page marked with an ebony paper-knife. He proceeded to read in his frail, high-pitched voice:

The Slums of Sorrow

"We live in piteous tenements
On sordid avenues
And never dream what mysteries
Lie hidden from our views.

"We drink and smoke and chatter
And sometimes even worse,
Forgetting that we all some day
Must travel in a hearse.

"So let us in humility
Await that shining hour
When all our agonies will burst
Into one gorgeous flower!"

"Thank you, Percifal," said Madame Slama, closing her eyes with a sigh. "And now we can begin. We are in the proper mood, I trust. Empty your minds, please, of all prejudice. Be passive. Relax. Let your spirits respond to the undulations from Outer Space."

There was a creaking and shifting as we settled back in our chairs. The record stopped playing. The flame of the candle swayed nervously, and Madame Slama drew her fingers across her forehead. She slumped back in her chair. Her breath came more heavily. Her jaw sagged, her nostrils twitched; yellowish bubbles shone on her lips.

Presently she said in a thin, dry voice:

"Are you there, Green Fish, dearest? Please come closer. Give me your hand. Thanks. That's better. It's terribly warm here. Is something burning? What's that stairway? And that strange, slimy water? What? The Ganges? What a horrible odor! Where is Lady Adlington, do you imagine? Just a moment. I can't see a thing. It's all blurred. I feel faint. What are those bundles? Corpses, you say? They're burning them up? How perfectly ghastly. Green Fish, please call Lady Adlington. There. At last. I think I see her. She's sitting on top of an elephant. Gwendolyn, darling, do you hear me? Yes, it's me, dear. Dolores. What do they call those things? Howdahs? I see a monkey up in a tree. Green Fish, please run along now. Do you have a message for me, Gwen? What was that? Say it again, please. . . ."

An air of suspense filled the parlor. The candle ceased fluttering. I glanced covertly at Stella: her eyes were glistening with excitement.

Madame Slama lay slumped in her chair. She was heaving spasmodically. Her face had grown pendulous, oily with sweat.

"Yes, Gwen." She moaned slightly. "I understand. You're perfectly right, dear. I feel it now. In the pit of my abdomen. It keeps stabbing. Like an iron claw. Is it . . . well, what I think it is? Really, dear? The Lord be praised. Is it Brunhilde's? It's going to be a boy? When? In June? How perfectly thrilling. What's this now? Come closer, Gwendolyn. Someone is trying to come between us. Is it Green Fish again? Do stop meddling in this, Green Fish. Now. That's better. Do you hear me, Gwen? What's this? News for Jennifer? Wait a moment. Not so fast. I see a ballroom all in crimson. Champagne glasses. Diamond necklaces. Goodness me, it's this terrible heat again. I see a dark-complexioned gentleman. And a mosque. And some palm trees. Swarms of flies. Hills in the distance. I feel ghastly all of a sudden. Something's clutching at my throat. Help me, Gwen! Help! I'm terrified! There. Thank Heavens. That's better. What a sickening experience. What? You're leaving? Thank you, Gwendolyn. You've been perfectly marvelous. . . ."

Madame Slama relapsed with a sigh. Sweat was trickling from her chin. Finally she opened her eyes, which were pink with exhaustion.

"Bless my soul." She surveyed us drowsily. "That was a most unusual journey. A bit exotic for Lady Adlington. But rather fascinating, all in all. . . ."

7

Now it was May. The bees were buzzing and a flood of plumage filled the park. Stella and I used to go for a little stroll after lunch: past the ponds, through the tunnels, over the fields and the flowering hillocks. One day we walked toward the Mall, picking dandelions as we went. Then we hired a row-boat and went rowing on the lake.

In the middle of the lake she opened her bag and took out a tiny book, one of those cheap little bibelots bound in imitation leather.

"A present for you, dear. I know you're mad about

poetry." She plucked a dandelion from the back of her ear and tucked it firmly between the pages.

I opened the book and started reading:

> *"White in the moon the long road lies,*
> *The moon stands blank above;*
> *White in the moon the long road lies*
> *That leads me to my love."*

"Lovely, isn't it?" said Stella. "Terribly lonely and sad, of course."

"A bit old-fashioned," I said, with a touch of condescension.

"How are your own poems coming along, dear?" said Stella absent-mindedly.

"Quite nicely," I said. "I'm developing a new, clinical manner."

"Have you sold any of them yet?"

"Oh," I said, "two or three. I sold my *Ode to an Odalisque* to 'Lyric Moods' for five dollars, and 'The Prairie Pegasus' is going to publish *O, in this trembling hour.*"

"Well," said Stella, frowning slightly as she flicked her ash into the water, "I've been talking to Miss Weinberger. She feels I need some European background."

"Really? Why?"

"Paris, for example. I ought to learn French, Miss Weinberger tells me."

"Is French essential to good acting?"

"Definitely. It gives poise, according to Miss Weinberger."

The little boat drifted lazily under a weeping willow.

The leaves trailed gently over Stella's ebony head, like tassels. She leaned forward and glanced at her reflection. A small blue butterfly lit on her neck. And I noticed the downy shimmer on the curve of her shoulder, and a hint of moisture in the little crease under her chin.

"I can't wait to get to Paris. Everything will be different in Paris."

"You'll be living at the Ritz, no doubt. And wearing dresses by Chanel."

"Don't be a beast," said Stella sulkily. "I'm not interested in luxury. I want to be free. I want to be myself. I'm weary of all this hurly-burly."

"I thought you were rather intrigued by New York."

"I despise New York. With a passion," said Stella.

I grew thoughtful. "How about money?"

"Oh," said Stella in a quick light tone, "I'll manage, dear. Just wait and see. I'll live in a nice, colorful garret. I'll eat in cheap little bistros, with the rest of the artists."

"Even so," I said mournfully, "you can't do it on nothing. The boat trip, and so on. You can't be penniless in Paris."

Stella gazed at the sunlit foliage and placed her finger in the pit of her neck. The filtered light fell on her flesh like incandescent dust. I felt a quick little twinge: a tiny pang of recollection.

I raised the oars and said carefully: "Well, do as you wish. I shan't stop you."

Stella lifted her brows. "Thank you, dear. That's frightfully generous of you."

"The whole idea is perfectly lunatic, of course," I said grimly.

She shrugged her shoulders. "Very well. Then it is. I can't help it."

I watched the drops fall from the oar-blade, scattering slow, silky rings. Suddenly I said: "Have you been seeing that Willoughby creature, by the way?"

She turned her head; her eyes grew distant and icy, impenetrable.

"Willoughby Pratt, do you mean?"

"Yes. Exactly. Willoughby Pratt."

"And, pray, why shouldn't I see him?"

"No reason at all, my dove."

"Are you hinting at something?"

"Mercy, no. I wouldn't dream of it."

"Listen, Henry. I know what you're thinking."

"Do you really? How amazing."

"And it's perfectly revolting."

I glanced at the sky. "I'm sorry to hear it."

Her face grew flushed, her eyes sharpened; her voice started to tremble.

"You're just a ridiculous old maid. Perpetually snooping and prying. It's quite ludicrous, my pet. And excessively vulgar."

"I see. The shoe fits."

"You're being loathsome," said Stella.

"It's no business of mine, naturally."

"It certainly is not," said Stella fiercely. "Row me back to the shore, please. I see no point in continuing this discussion."

I rowed back. We walked down to the Plaza without a word. I paused for a moment by the gilded statue of General Sherman.

"Well, good-bye," I said softly.

She glanced at me frostily. "Good-bye."

And she vanished in the traffic at Fifth Avenue and Fifty-Ninth Street.

Ten days later I found a letter lying on my pink Navajo bedspread. I immediately recognized that languid, rotund hand, with the little balloons floating over the i's.

"Henry dear:
I've behaved like a pig. Forgive and forget me. I'm sailing on Thursday.
                                    S."

An icicle slid through my heart. I felt for a moment like suffocating. I stared at my elephants and my Gauguin, and out through the window at the welling twilight, and finally I dozed off over my thumb-worn Baudelaire.

8

The heat fell and the city took on an ominous stillness, as though struck by the plague. The streets were chasms in some harrowing landscape, like the pictures I had seen of the Cappadocian deserts. And late at night the towers rose threateningly, the very air seemed to churn and a fiery vapor covered the sky, like the glow from a volcano.

In the horror of late July the footsteps echoed in the empty side-streets and the sound of the traffic resembled the roar of a distant waterfall. And in the half-light of dawn it turned into a city of hallucinations, of heart-broken manias and murderous obsessions.

I began to hate the smells and the noises, the very pulse of the place. And yet, from that very bleakness, from that chaos and compulsion, a certain splendor did emerge, frail and illusory, like a rainbow. At dusk the tall buildings, suffused with an apricot brightness, seemed to blend with the air, to grow impalpable, like a *fata morgana*. The sky grew murky in the distance, as though a hurricane were brewing. The leaves in the park turned to a deep irascible mauve. There was a hidden suspense, a touch of fever in the air. Suddenly the lights were turned on and a thousand windows began to glow. The tension broke, the multitudinous struggle between darkness and light crumbled away, no wind stirred, the stars glowed and a huge serenity swept through the city.

I was lonely, of course. I kept brooding about Stella. I had a dream, as I'd had in Llewellyn, but very different in its flavor and plangency. I was wandering through some tropical city, hurrying this way and that. I turned a corner and caught sight of a silhouette in the distance. It was Stella: and suddenly I knew that I was desperately in love with her. She disappeared through a crumbling archway; I started to run down the street. Finally I saw her again, standing in the middle of a piazza. She had turned into a boy. Her hair was clipped; she was twirling a cane. And all of a sudden the air grew blurred, the minarets turned into palms and Stella herself turned into a panther who looked at me with smouldering eyes, as in a Douanier Rousseau, and then vanished among the grasses.

One evening I was sitting alone in Central Park, leafing aimlessly through *The Wings of the Dove*. A slender girl in ballet slippers came strolling down the path, glanced at me in a casual way and sat down on the bench beside me.

"Beautiful, isn't it?" she said, pointing to the skyline in the distance.

"Yes, it is."

"What are you reading?"

"Henry James."

"How frightfully clever of you."

"Are you English?" I said pleasantly.

"Heavens, no. I'm from Quebec."

"Do you dance?"

"Oh, a bit." She shrugged her shoulders. "It's hideously hot, isn't it?" She looked at the stars, which were beginning to twinkle. I was struck by the glow on her cheeks, the coppery lustre of her hair, and the snowy sheen of her catlike teeth.

She turned around with an indifferent air. "Would you like to come home with me?"

I caught my breath and looked at her warily. "Oh. Thanks. Yes. I would."

It was in the basement of an old, dusty house on Seventy-seventh Street. An African head hung on the wall and a wilted fern stood on the table. On the floor lay a copy of *Vogue,* an album of Mozart and an empty tea cup. We silently threw off our clothes and flung ourselves on the couch. The room was dark but a ray of light drifted in from the street-lamp. The passing shadows of the pedestrians kept floating across the curtains. She lay motionless, with closed eyes, her silky hair flooding the pillow, her lips parted, her flesh moist, the pulse of her heart throbbing unevenly. I caught the fragrance of her sweat, brisk and sour, like a quince. And as we lay there with our limbs interlaced, glued together, scarcely moving except for an occasional tremor or a wild, sudden kiss, her face gradually took on a beautiful, peaceful anonymity; as though drained of all tension, all thought, all emotion. We fell asleep. It was nearly midnight when we woke up again. The yellow rectangle of light still shone on the sleek Oubangui head. And a new excitement surged over us, we hurled ourselves on each other, we sweated and writhed, we groaned and wrestled, we grew grotesque, we grew macabre, until at last we fell back on the tangled sheets, limp and weary.

After a while I turned and looked at her. "What is your name?"

She glanced at a shadow on the curtain. "Why bother with names?"

I held a flame under her cigarette. "Do you do this often?"

"Oh, now and then. As the spirit moves me." There was silence for a while. She held her cigarette in the air and stared intensely at the glowing ash. Suddenly she said in a low, hoarse tone: "I'm sorry. I lied to you. This is the first time in my life that I've slept with a man. . . ."

9

On the following morning, under the spell of some half-blind compulsion, I walked down Fifth Avenue in the boiling sunlight. I walked block after block, glancing vacuously through the narrow shop windows, staring at shirts and cravats, at sapphire cufflinks and pigskin wallets. Finally I stepped through an open door into a room plastered with travel posters and booked a passage on the *Aquitania*, third class, for Le Havre.

VII

THERE WERE NIGHTS when I wandered back to my room
a little later than usual. When I paused on the Pont
Royal and breathed the cool, swampy air and watched
the early mist spreading like steam over the river. Here
and there a tiny barge squatted in the gloom like a hippo-
potamus. Sleeping beggars lay on the quay, covered with
old dirty newspapers. Once or twice I lay on the railing
and stared at the stars, waiting for their light to grow dim
and for the vegetable carts to come rattling. I watched the
illuminated clock on the Gare d'Orsay grow gradually
fainter and the clouds over the Louvre grow tinted with
gold. And suddenly the dome of the Grand Palais burst
into a fiery mosaic, the veil of fog slid from the dew-
varnished banks, the smell of coal-dust and coffee seeped
over the bridge and the insect-like noises of the awakening
city filled the air.

Finally I rose and walked back to my miserable room on
Rue du Bac.

The Hotel de L'Univers was a dilapidated old house with peeling walls, broken windows and lop-sided shutters. A little sign over the entrance said *"Tout comfort. Eau courante."* I entered a courtyard filled with mildewy baskets and broken flower-pots. I rang the bell. Five minutes later the wart-faced concierge opened the door and I entered a rambling hall which stank of dead rats and garlic.

I climbed the stairs, which shuddered and wheezed like an old slattern. A chamber-pot stood on the landing with a cockroach floating in the amber liquid. Finally I turned the key in the lock and entered my foul little room with its sagging bed, its frayed curtains, its rusty bidet, its leaking wash-basin.

Still, what I felt during those first few weeks was a continual golden joy. The very squalor seemed to glow with a Carolingian splendor. I saw a tortuous human mystery in the little alleys by Notre Dame. I sniffed at the crumbling old masonry and caught the musk of the Middle Ages. I peered through dark cellar windows and guessed at murderous intrigues. I browsed among the bookstalls on the quays; I explored the urinals like a roaming mongrel. And as I strolled through the Luxembourg gardens or along the Boulevard Malesherbes I saw the shades of Swann and Odette, of Oriane and Palamède.

I discarded my turtle-neck sweater and bought a cheap velvet jacket. My hair grew longer and I cultivated a silky brown mustache. I sat in the Café du Dôme and read the poems of Appollinaire. I visited the wine-shops near the Halles and the shady bars on Rue de Lappe.

I wondered occasionally about Stella. I mentioned her name once or twice. I checked periodically at the Embassy.

But no one had ever heard of her. It almost seemed that my new, libidinous passion for Paris had obliterated her from the world as well as from my heart. Uneasy memories still stirred in my mind, but little by little they grew dimmer. And after a while I stopped wondering; she became a dark, dwindling phantom.

2

One day I stood in the Louvre, looking at a painting by Le Nain, when I noticed a tall, brittle figure stroll past. I turned sharply and tapped him on the shoulder.

"I beg your pardon. Are you Latimer Peck?"

Latimer winced imperceptibly. "Sorry. I'm not aware that I have the pleasure of. . . ."

"It's me," I said. "Henry. Don't you remember me, Latimer?"

"Merciful Heaven," said Latimer in his high, throbbing voice.

"I've changed," I said, "I suppose."

"You most emphatically have, dear."

"Come," I said. "Let's go for a drink in the Place des Pyramides."

Latimer too, I thought, had changed. He was carrying a silk umbrella and wore a blue flannel suit with a rose in the buttonhole. His mouth had a pinched, parsimonious expression. He sipped at his Byrrh with a martyr-like air.

"Well," I said, "what are you up to nowadays, Latimer?"

"I teach Sophomore English in South Dakota," said Latimer.

"That must be amusing," I said.

"It is perfectly deadly," said Latimer. He gazed at me acidly. "And what about you, my dear Henry?"

"I'll be staying in Paris for a while."

"Writing poems, or something of the sort?"

"In a smallish kind of way."

"Well, you certainly look Parisian."

"I live on a shoestring," I admitted.

"Well," said Latimer, "I'm not surprised. You always had a bee in your bonnet. *La vie de Bohême* and all the rest of it."

"I'm afraid you're right," I said guiltily.

"Maybe Paris will do you good. Maybe you'll learn to appreciate people like Mallarmé, or Modigliani."

"You must feel a bit lonely in South Dakota," I hinted.

"Comme çi, comme ça," muttered Latimer dryly.

"You're still working on your novel?"

Latimer's features grew mellow. "I've revised it again," he said. "I've turned it into a series of antiphonal monologues."

"It sounds splendid," I said. "I hope you find a good publisher for it."

"It doesn't matter, really," said Latimer. "I didn't write it for the vulgar public. I wrote it as a kind of spiritual purge, a catharsis."

"Still," I said, "it would be a shame if nobody reads it, don't you think?"

"It is a matter of the most consummate indifference to me," said Latimer loftily.

We started walking down Rue de Rivoli, under those

gloomy arcades with their little windows full of cream-puffs and old Chinese ivories. Then we entered the Tuileries gardens and paused near the puppet show. The Devil was beating Punchinello over the head with a club while the children were clapping their hands with delight.

"Have you ever stopped to consider," said Latimer, "what you want out of life?"

"Yes," I said. "Rather gropingly."

"And what have you decided?"

"I'm not sure," I said cautiously. "I'd like to taste new experiences. To roam about. To explore. To be in love. To be happy."

"To be happy," said Latimer wearily. "Who in the world is ever happy? And to be in love. My dear Henry, I feel sorry for you. I really do."

He stood rigid and motionless under the twilit trees. His jutting teeth were glistening in a peculiar, broken smile.

We walked slowly toward the Orangerie. Neither of us spoke for several minutes. Finally we entered the Place de la Concorde and I said, "Good-bye, Latimer."

"Good-bye, Henry . . . I really wish . . . I just wish that . . . Well, never mind."

And he hurried off toward the dusky glow of the Rue Royale.

3

I made friends with Maggy and Boris. Maggy was a dancer and Boris was a sculptor. I met both of them one morning at the swimming pool in the Seine, where they were basking in diminutive *cache-sexes* and rubbing their bodies with cocoanut oil.

They took me back to their little studio behind the Quai Voltaire for a glass of wine. Boris showed me his sculptures, which were in the manner of Maillol, with a soupçon of Mestrovic and a fleeting suggestion of Thorvaldsen. There was one of Leda and the Swan and another of Niobe Weeping, and a rather imaginative version of Danaë and the Shower of Gold.

"Maggy posed for them," said Boris. "She has a magnificent pagan body."

"He is planning the Rape of Prosperine," said Maggy, with a wink.

"It will be my *chef d'oeuvre*," said Boris, gazing at the ceiling.

"Would you care," said Maggy, "to pose for it? You'd be Pluto and I'd be Prosperine."

"There wouldn't be much money in it, mind you," said Boris thoughtfully.

"A mushroom omelette, perhaps, with a glass of Beaujolais," said Maggy.

"Still," said Boris, "it will be my masterpiece. Please consider yourself flattered. Don't you wish that you'd been the model for the Discus Thrower, or the Dying Gaul?"

So I started on the following morning to pose for Boris' new allegory. It was strenuous work. I held Maggy precariously suspended from my shoulder, upside down, with her hair dangling loosely across my bare knee. In the heat of September we both dripped with sweat. When November arrived we both began to shiver. After an hour or so we wrapped ourselves in thick flannel bathrobes and

Maggy would light the stove to cook a bowl of spaghetti.

"The world," said Boris, raising his glass, "is staggering through the dark like a maniac."

"True," said Maggy. "The old landmarks, the old traditions have vanished."

"And the artist," said Boris in his thin sad voice, "has grown hysterical."

"Look at Picasso," said Maggy vigorously. "Look at Giacometti. Look at Ernst."

"What we need is the old barbaric zest," said Boris with a sigh. He was a small, owlish man with a red goatee and slavic cheekbones and a look of impenetrable innocence in his pale gray eyes.

"People's notions of beauty," said Maggy, stirring her coffee, "have been tarnished."

"They've become a fraud," said Boris. He shook his head. "They've become a parody."

"People are drifting away from their elemental instincts," said Maggy.

"People are turning into robots and charlatans," said Boris gloomily.

One day Maggy tuned to me briskly and said: "Henry. I have an idea."

I blew a smoke ring. "Oh. Do you?"

"Have you ever danced?"

"Now and then."

"Creative dancing, I mean, dear."

"Oh. Not much, I'm afraid."

"You could do it beautifully, I'm sure," said Maggy, "if you really put your mind to it. And you could slip a bit of cash into your pocket while you're at it."

Maggy was a gypsy-like woman with a long narrow nose,

kinky hair, encircled with ribbons, and intelligent, cynical eyes. Twice a week she danced in a night club called the Box of Sardines. The rest of the time she was available for private recitals in colorful numbers such as her "Brazilian Fire Dance," "Comanche Funeral Song," and "Prayer of the Congo." She called herself Mahala Swali and posed as half Ceylonese, half Inca.

"I've been toying with some new ideas," she said. "An Eskimo dance, for example. And maybe some things from Greek mythology, like the Rescue of Andromeda."

So I started rehearsing some dances with Maggy. By the end of the year we had built up a respectable repertory. I made my debut on New Year's Eve at a private party given by a Cuban millionaire in an elaborate apartment on the Avenue George Mandel. There were some flamenco singers first, followed by a pair of tumblers and a Polish magician. Finally Maggy and I stepped forth for our "Zulu Love Dance." We had both dyed our bodies a nutmeg brown from head to foot. On our faces we had painted elaborate golden patterns. We were naked except for infinitesimal raffia aprons. The musical accompaniment was an elderly Negro with a drum and a rattle.

The chandeliers were extinguished; an orange spotlight was turned on us.

"Ready, dear?" whispered Maggy. "Don't be shy now. Plenty of feeling. . . ."

The drumbeats grew louder, the rhythm grew more emphatic. We wriggled our arms, twitched our legs, shook our bellies and ground our hips. Finally we sank to the floor, still quivering and writhing. The drumbeats rose to a climax. We heaved and lay motionless. The lights went on and there was an enthusiastic ovation.

We gave similar recitals from time to time, each adjusted to the particular occasion. For the Theosophical Society's tea we gave "Apollo and Daphne" and "Manchurian Harvest Dance." For the Bachelor Dinner at the Travellers' Club we gave our "Etruscan Fertility Rite." Finally I appeared one snowy night at the Box of Sardines. We did "Europa and the Bull," followed by an "Abyssinian Spear Dance."

"Darling," said Maggy at the end of the evening, "you were really quite marvelous. They all agreed that they'd never seen a more ravishing bull." She winked playfully. "Don't tell Boris, but it wouldn't surprise me in the least if we get an offer from the Folies Bergère. . . ."

4

How can I tell of the excitement that ran through my blood? The fever of lust, the hunger of expectancy, the sheer delight of being alive? A veil had fallen abruptly from the visible world all around me, revealing creatures and objects with a strange wine-like brilliance. A loaf of bread, a raw carrot, two love-birds in a cage—everything shone with a startling, prismatic sort of vividness. My morning coffee tasted exquisitely pungent and earthy. The evening light on the Quai Voltaire was like a mystical illumination.

I explored the city with an adventurous, half erotic kind of zest; almost as though it were the body of some beautiful woman, no longer young but still desirable, no longer blooming but still fascinating and with the whiff of past amours still lingering about her.

I sat in my room after breakfast with my pen in my hand, waiting for the moment when a magical phrase might descend on me. I'd stare at the mattress on my bed, with its cotton stuffing beginning to leak; at the portable wooden bidet with its white enamel cover; at my Baudelaire, my Kafka, my *Crime and Punishment,* my *Golden Bough;* and finally at the ceiling which was sagging directly over my head, disfigured by yellowish veins which wriggled across the paint like streaks of lightning.

And then I looked out of my window at the dingy buildings across the street. There was a strange fascination in the half-seen movements behind a curtain, in a hand resting on a windowsill, in an empty glove beside a geranium pot. Powerful, enigmatic dramas seemed perpetually to transpire behind those dirty little courtyards on the Rue de l'Université. They took the place of the enchanted frogs and buried emperors of my childhood.

And then the people themselves. As I walked through the parks or peered through my window I developed a habit of watching, of appraising, of speculating. I noticed the way my Breton chambermaid rolled her haunches as she carried the linen. I kept wondering about the young Algerian who pushed his applecart along the quay. I invented love affairs for the pot-bellied news-vendor and the freckled girl in the pastry shop, for the limping lady with the parasol, for the elderly Syrian with the poodle.

And finally at dusk, after my daily orgy of imaginary eavesdropping, I wandered along the Seine toward the Box of Sardines.

5

One night in March, after an unusually wearing performance, Maggy and I stopped for a nightcap at a place
near the Rond Point called La Vie en Rose. It was
considerably more lavish than our little Box of Sardines,
where the walls were covered with humorous posters and
faded old photographs. Baroque mirrors hung on a background of thick crimson damask; a chubby young man
was playing softly on a grand piano.

Maggy and I chatted aimlessly over a glass of champagne. "We should seriously consider," she observed,
"touring the provinces next summer. I know of some
places where our 'Hottentot Rhythms' might do nicely."

"Do you really think that we ought to focus on that
particular kind of appeal?"

"Definitely not," said Maggy firmly. "But it might be a
springboard. I know of an actress who started her career
by posing for pornographic postcards."

"You don't say."

"It gave her a certain unshatterable dignity. She has
done beautifully ever since. She has a villa in Cannes and
a suite in the Crillon."

The lights grew softer at this point and a spotlight was
focused on the dance-floor. A curtain parted and a slender
girl in purple satin stood by the piano.

"She's rather pretty, don't you think?" said Maggy.

"A bit too thin," I began. I caught my breath. Was it
possible? I put down my glass and rubbed my eyes.

The girl sang in English. Her voice was low and caressing, with a strange little undertone of tropical plangency. She sang "Lady Be Good," and then "Someone to Watch over Me," and finally, as an encore, "Body and Soul."

After the first little shock I felt amused, then faintly embarrassed. Her voice had a mournful throb, but it wavered, it slid, it stumbled. She looked strangely pathetic, with her tight little dress and crystal earrings.

"She seems to fascinate you," said Maggy.

"She definitely does. She's my cousin."

"Oh, really?" said Maggy, somewhat sceptically. "I don't see the family resemblance, quite."

"Poor little Stella," I said pityingly. "I hope she'll be a success."

"She's not doing badly," said Maggy, glancing around astutely.

"Excuse me for a moment," I said, after the singer had slipped through the curtain. I found her in a dingy little dressing room, sipping absently at a lemonade.

"Heavens above," she cried. "Henry! I do keep meeting you in the weirdest places."

"Congratulations," I said solemnly. "You were absolutely stunning."

She shrugged her shoulders. "You're an angel. I was utterly hideous. And you know it."

"Miss Weinberger was perfectly right. Paris has given you poise."

"Oh, Henry, my dove, what a joy. You're like a breath of fresh air!" Her voice grew cajoling. "You look brutally healthy."

"I've been getting quite a lot of physical exercise lately."

She leaned closer suspiciously. "Bless my soul. You're wearing make-up."

I blushed. "It's just a bit left over from the performance, I imagine."

She smiled wickedly. "I can't believe it! It's too divine,
it really is."

She flung her arms around me joyfully and kissed me
vigorously on both cheeks.

6

I lunched with Stella the following noon in a little bistro
near the Madeleine. We started with artichokes, continued
with frogs' legs and ended up with a fine, ripe Camembert.

"We're being desperately French today, aren't we?" said
Stella.

"We certainly are. You especially. You've taken to
Paris like a duck to a duck-pond."

"It hasn't been easy, mind you, dear. There were all
sorts of problems. Still," said Stella, placing a Gauloise
in her holder, "it's been worth it. All in all."

Her little face, half veiled by a spiral of lilac smoke,
looked suddenly solemn. A shadow passed over her eyes;
just a flicker of panic. She drew her fingers along her
tapering throat and smiled vividly. "Do you think I've
changed?"

"You look older, a bit."

Her face grew mellow. "Anything else?"

"More mysterious. More sophisticated."

"Well," she said, lowering her lashes, "things are beginning to look up a trifle. René Bloy wants me for a film.
Set in Venice. In the middle of April."

"Splendid," I said.

"And Lecoq is interested. For something in Morocco. In July."

"Marvelous," I said.

"I could do with a bit of cash, to be quite frank with you," said Stella.

"Well," I sighed, "so could I. But one manages to survive in Paris, somehow."

"Yes," said Stella, with a far-off look. "One usually does. With a bit of luck."

I emptied my wine-glass and picked up the bill. "Where do you live, by the way?"

"With Alphonse, naturally," said Stella.

"Who in the world is Alphonse?"

"Oh," said Stella, "you haven't met him?"

"Not," I said, "as I recall."

"Alphonse is a dream," said Stella softly.

"Lord," I said. "Are you married?"

"Bless you, no," said Stella rapidly. She crushed her cigarette in the saucer. "I wouldn't dream of marrying Alphonse. Alphonse is a dear but incurably penniless. . . ."

I met Alphonse three days later at the Café Deux Magots. He wasn't quite what I had expected, somehow or other. He was a thickset man in his forties with shaggy hair, an undisciplined beard and lascivious eyes like a satyr's. He had thick, powerful hands with purple-edged nails and shiny mauve lips, like snails drenched in garlic sauce.

He shook my hand with an exuberant bone-cracking grip. "Sit down, Henry. I've been hearing about you. What will you drink? A glass of beer? Well, I'm glad to see that you're not like the rest of these Left Bank non-entities. You look wholesome and idealistic. You're a dancer, eh? I wouldn't have guessed it."

"Alphonse paints," put in Stella. "He's a bit of an iconoclast."

"Fiddlesticks, child," said Alphonse gustily. "I believe in the truth, that is all. Truth with the cobwebs cleaned away, with the barnacles scraped off, with the sediment drained out, with the moth-balls thrown into the garbage."

"Alphonse," said Stella affectionately, "is an experimentalist."

"Depending, of course," growled Alphonse, "on what you mean by experiments. I have no use for all these ridiculous little artists around here. All these semi-cubist and semi-surrealists, semi-Lesbians and semi-pederasts, semi-lunatics and semi-prostitutes. They're all dead, dead, dead! They're anti-life! They're anti-reality! They squirm in the scum of their own frustrations!"

"Alphonse thinks that they've fallen behind the times," ventured Stella.

"They're as dead as door-nails!" roared Alphonse. "What we need is a new approach. Something clean and relentless as a surgeon's scalpel!"

I was taken that same evening on a visit to Alphonse's rooms, which lay at the top of a dingy building in Rue Saint-Dominique. The general effect of his studio was very different from Boris'. There was nothing human, nothing domestic, nothing démodé about it. The paintings were geometrical patterns of puce, beige and fuchsia, dotted with strange little shapes that resembled spermatozoa.

"I try to go back," said Alphonse vibrantly, "to our

earliest tribal memories. Before the cave-man. Before the glaciers. Back to the fish and the tadpoles."

"It's most impressive," I said.

"It's colossal!" bellowed Alphonse. "I've gone back to fundamentals! To the grandeurs and miseries of the womb!"

7

After this I saw Stella and her lover with growing frequency. Sometimes for lunch in a neighboring bistro, sometimes for a drink in the studio, sometimes for coffee along the quay or a little nightcap near the Opéra after Stella was through at "La Vie en Rose."

With the warm April weather we used to drive out into the country in Alphonse's rattly little Peugeot. We'd buy a bottle of Burgundy and some thick country sausages and lie down under a tree in the Vallée de la Chevreuse. Or we stopped at one of the cheap little inns near Bougival and ate *truite au bleu* and wild strawberries on the banks of the river. We sipped lazily at our wine and watched the barges glide past and then sauntered along the tow-path, pausing to pick a jack-in-the-pulpit or waving merrily to the sweating oarsmen. Spring was filling the air with a kind of heady opalescence. Nothing mattered but the pure brainless joy of being alive, eating and drinking and laughing under the green-smelling arbors.

Sometimes Alphonse lay down in the grass with a napkin over his face while Stella and I wandered idly among the poplars.

We paused for a moment in the shade. She tossed a pebble into the water. She wore her hair hanging loose over her shoulders, like a school girl's, and her dress was a lemon-hued smock patterned with roses. Something stirred in my memory: the scent of cedars came back to me, of raw sunlit figs and of mulberries crushed on the asphalt.

"Tell me frankly," said Stella. "What do you think of Alphonse?"

"I find him thoroughly refreshing. Full of spice. Full of gusto."

"I used to think so too," said Stella. "But it's only a façade, I've discovered. He's exactly the opposite. He's weary and impotent and jaded."

"He's good company, at any rate, isn't he?"

"When he's drinking," said Stella. "There are times when he's sober, and then he's a stupefying bore."

"I'm sorry to hear it," I said. "I thought you were blissfully happy."

"I was," said Stella, "until recently. But something's gone wrong. I feel restless. I'm afraid that I need . . . well, something a wee bit different."

She glanced at me slyly. The April sunlight slid over her cheeks, delicately filtered by the network of young spring foliage. I noticed a subtle but unmistakable change in her face. That lean, sullen, greedy, flamingo-like look was gradually melting into something mellow, elusive, adroit. Was she merely shedding her adolescence? Or was the change more hidden, more intricate?

We passed a flowering apple tree and Stella reached toward the buzzing fragrance. She broke off a twig and held the blossoms under her nose. And quite abruptly, as though some frail interior mechanism had been released, I felt a familiar, tremulous warmth glide through me once again—a mingling of zest and vulnerability, of a lurking delight and an indefinable fear.

"Wouldn't it be marvelous," Stella was saying, "if we both were a wild success?"

"It certainly would," I said absently, fondling a branch of pussy-willow.

"And made masses and masses of money? And could do whatever we pleased? I'd buy a Hispano-Suiza and drive to Morocco."

"You'd be too busy, wouldn't you, really? With those movies in Venice, and all the rest of it?"

"I might sail to Tahiti, even," said Stella, tossing her head.

"But what about Bloy, and Lecoq, and your little job in 'La Vie en Rose'?"

She flung her arms joyfully, scattered a fistful of apple-blossoms, which danced through the sunlight and lit on the glossy water. "I wouldn't care! I'd ignore them! I'd be as free as a humming bird! I'd pick cocoanuts off the trees and sleep with all those gorgeous savages!" She glanced at me playfully. "What's wrong, Henry love?" She leaned over and kissed my cheek. "Do I shock you dreadfully? Do I really?"

8

The chestnut-trees in the Champs-Elysées bloomed with thousands of candelabras, which exuded a powerful phallic aroma. Stella and I met occasionally for a cup of tea at Ledoyen's. We'd sit under a striped umbrella and watch the children play on the lawn and the nursemaids stroll past with their little pink carriages.

"Guess what happened to me yesterday, Enrico." Stella was developing a habit of calling me by a variety of nick-names—*mon coucou, mon petit lapin,* and things like Bibi, Pouff-Pouff, Po-po, and Enrico.

"I can't imagine," I said. "Do tell me. What happened?"

"I was sitting in front of Weber's, innocently sipping my *café filtre,* when a tall, dusky gentleman sat down at the neighboring table."

"How intriguing. Could it be the one that Madame Slama told us about?"

"He wore diamond cuff-links," said Stella, "and a gardenia in his button-hole. He kept staring at me in the most lascivious manner."

"It sounds like Willoughby Pratt, almost. Except for the button-hole," I said.

"Don't be beastly, please Henry. He ordered a whisky and soda. Then he leafed through the London *Times.* Finally he introduced himself."

"Yes? Who was it?"

"Guess!" said Stella.

"I can't possibly."

"It was the Nizam of Hyderabad!"

"Amazing," I murmured.

"He started by talking about the weather. But he ended by making some rather indelicate proposals."

"Well, I hope you slapped his face."

"Please, my dear, don't be a lunatic. I am not a virgin and I certainly don't intend to become one."

"Are you going to see him again?"

"It all depends," said Stella cryptically.

"Well, it might," I said crudely, "help you on your way to Tahiti."

I could see, as the days grew warmer, that her character was changing. Her air of restless caprice was tinged with a speculative glow. Her voice grew softer and more inquiring; her glance grew probing and equivocal. There was no question about it. She was turning into a beauty.

Soon it was warm enough to go for an occasional dip at the Bains de Ligny. We lay sunbathing in an ocean of moist, peeling bodies, whose aroma was tinged with the odor of chlorine from the pool and a whiff of fried porkchops from the little terrace restaurant, where the oil-lacquered bathers played chess and drank wine. We listened to the jazz on the gramophone and nibbled at blood-red cherries and occasionally we chatted with some gilded Diana or bronzed Adonis. There was André, for example, a philosophy student at the Sorbonne, who lay by the edge of the pool with his paperbacked American novels—*La Route au Tabac* or *Lumière en Août,* and one day even *Les Raisins de la Colère.* He was a good-looking fellow with the body of a Discobulus and tiny blond curls like golden watch-springs all over his chest.

"What fascinates me about Americans," he said, "is the way they go to extremes."

"What do you mean?" said Stella, wide-eyed, rubbing her shoulders with nut-oil.

"In art, for instance. They carry a notion to its logical conclusion—which is usually absurdity. And in sex they seem to believe in a kind of mass-production—do they call them 'gang-bangs'? And in human relations they usually end by resorting to violence, from all I hear. They are the harbingers of a new, thrilling era of self-abandonment. . . ."

"He's a darling, isn't he?" said Stella as she watched him dive from the edge of the pool. "He has such an old-fashioned, romantic picture of Americans. Look at you, for example. There is nothing violent about you, is there, dear? Though I'll admit that you look much more masculine than you used to, with that clean-cut jaw and those big brown pectorals. I used to think in the old days that you had a bit of a pansy streak in you—those fancy poems you kept reading, those corduroy pants. I was wrong, of course, needless to say. You were just pretending. You were trying to be sophisticated."

One day, as she sucked at an orange, she suddenly announced: "I've brought you a present. Pierre Ducasse took it last night when I wasn't looking. It's rather chic, don't you think? I look positively French in it."

It was a snapshot of herself amid the damask draperies of "La Vie en Rose." Her face looked abnormally pale and strangely flat, almost Mongolian. Her eyes were dilated and her teeth were glistening, and her dress clung to her body like scales to a fish.

"Do you like it?"

"It's charming!"

Actually, I detested the picture. It wasn't Stella at all, it was some vulgar and vapid nonentity who must have slipped into her clothes and darted in front of the camera. But I kept it and tucked it into my copy of *The Shropshire Lad,* where I used to glance at it occasionally, whenever I grew weary of my obsession.

What a contrast with the dark little animal who was lying beside me! That exquisite body, with the sinuous hips and tight little buttocks of a cicisbeo, that marvelous skin, an incandescent sort of *café au lait,* made velvety by the peripheral haze of golden down that shone in the sun like the scales of a swallowtail.

9

It was in the middle of May one rainy night that we both met Paolo. We were relaxing at "La Vie en Rose" after Stella had finished "Stardust." He invited us to his table for a glass of champagne.

"Excuse me. May I introduce myself? I am Prince Galeassi. Call me Paolo, if you'd like. You sing like an angel, mademoiselle."

He was a frail little man with intense, nervous eyes, anxious lips, pleading hands, and a melodious, grieving voice. He wore a blue shantung suit and a white silk tie with an emerald pin. There was a curiously childlike, bereft expression in his face. On the table lay a cigarette case of greenish gold encrusted with rubies.

"You have a very magnetic flavor, mademoiselle," he said gravely. "You should go far. I am surprised that you aren't famous already."

"Alas," said Stella, batting her eyelashes. "It's a terrible struggle here in Paris."

Paolo glanced at me cautiously. "And this is your . . . brother?"

"No," said Stella, with a meaning look. "Just a far-off cousin. He dances."

"I see," said Paolo caressingly. He fixed his squirrel-like eyes on me. Then he purred: "He too has a future. I feel it in my bones."

Three days later Prince Galeassi drove us into the country in his Mercedes. His two poodles sat in the back: Aucassin and Nicolette. We stopped at a rustic little spot in the forest near Barbizon. Small white tables with checquered cloths stood on the edge of a stagnant pond. There was a ping-pong table on the lawn and a swing was dangling under a plane tree.

"Oh, what fun," cried Stella daintily. "It reminds me of my childhood. Come, Enrico. Give me a push." And she climbed into the swing.

"How delicious she looks," said Paolo as she soared through the foliage.

"Higher!" cried Stella. "Higher, darling!"

"Like a Fragonard," said Paolo thoughtfully.

Finally the artichokes were brought to the table. We sat down in the shade.

Paolo turned to Stella politely. "Where were you born, may I inquire?"

"In Boston," said Stella promptly.

"A very dignified city, I'm told."

"My mother was Spanish," said Stella solemnly. "She was the daughter of a marquis. A great beauty in her day. The toast of London and Paris."

"And your father?"

Stella sighed. "He was a magnificent horseman. And a champion polo player. But he came to a heart-breaking end."

"I am grieved to hear it," said Paolo tactfully.

"He squandered his fortune at Monte Carlo. One night, in the Casino gardens, he put a bullet through his brains."

"What a pity," said Paolo. "He doesn't sound like a typical Bostonian."

"Not in the least," said Stella brightly. "He was a kind of Don Juan. He didn't spend much of his time in Massachusetts, naturally."

"Half Bostonian and half Spanish," said Paolo. "How remarkable."

"I'm terribly pleased that you think so," said Stella, with a mousy expression.

"A definite oddity," said Paolo. "I have always been fascinated by oddities. I collect them, in fact. Papuan butterflies, Moldavian Easter eggs, Peruvian skulls, Aztec funeral masks, Etruscan dildoes and triangular postage stamps."

"How delicious," said Stella.

"You must come and look at them," said Paolo.

Stella rested her chin on her palms and watched a wasp on the edge of her wine-glass. Her eyes grew dreamy. She smiled. "I'd utterly adore to," she whispered.

10

A new life began for Stella. One bright morning in June she packed her bags and asked me to carry them down the stairs in Rue Saint-Dominique.

"It's better this way," she said, kissing Alphonse on the beard. "No tapering off. No squabbles. No recriminations. God bless you."

And she took a taxi to the Quai de Passy, on the opposite bank of the river.

Her new apartment was done in the modern style, lightly touched with exoticism. Paolo helped her to choose the furnishings—large, squat chairs covered in cowhide, Finnish chests carved with penguins, leather cushions from Fez and agate obelisks from Florence. At the end of the room a Lalique statue of a naked faun was set in front of a lacquer screen dappled with fish, crabs and lobsters. Her bed was covered with an enormous spread of chinchilla. On the wall hung a bowl of orchids by Odilon Redon.

And little by little her clothes, her manners, her habits of life altered likewise. Her French improved noticeably. She read Gide and Cocteau. Copies of *Minotaure* and *Verve* lay on the ebony coffee-table. She took an interest in the ballet. She spoke of Bakst and Stravinsky. She went to exhibitions of modern paintings on Rue du Faubourg Saint-Honoré.

She began to dress rather grandly—cocktail ensembles by Chanel, evening dresses by Lelong and trim little suits by Schiaparelli. She wore her hair in a great shiny coil on top of her head and on her wrist she wore bracelets from

Cartier's or Boucheron. The smell of fashionable perfumes lingered deftly about her. She dined regularly with Paolo at Maxim's or Lapérouse or in one of the outdoor restaurants in the Bois de Boulogne.

Her voice grew delicately melodious, tinged with subtle nuances. Her skin grew silken; her brows grew arched; her glance grew veiled and ambiguous. Her very body seemed to go through some curious metamorphosis. Her tense, nervous gestures grew indolent, feline.

She gradually developed a *salon*. Every Tuesday at five she served tea and champagne, with tiny cakes from Rebattet. Here I met forgotten actresses, Chilean painters and Balkan diplomats, and now and then a soprano from Copenhagen or a gigolo from Rome. We chatted with animation about the latest novel by Colette, the latest play by Giraudoux or the latest ballet by Massine.

There were days when I still saw Stella alone, however. Sometimes she phoned me at noon and asked me to take her to lunch.

"In one of those simple little places on the quay, don't you think? I'm so weary of all this nauseating *chi-chi*. . . ."

She left Paris in August: a fortnight in Biarritz, a fortnight in Beaulieu. Early in September she phoned me at the Hôtel de l'Univers.

"So you're back. Did you enjoy yourself?"

"Not frightfully, I must say. I loathe those stuffy, pretentious places. Take me to lunch, won't you, Po-po?"

We wandered idly along the quay and sat down under an awning.

"You look different," I said suddenly.

"Do I really?" said Stella.

It was true. She was sitting calmly in the green wicker

chair: or rather poised, like some tropical bird, in her azure-blue dress, knees crossed, eyes lowered, smiling faintly as she raised her glass. And quite abruptly it struck me that she was wildly, flamboyantly beautiful. Like a rose that has finally opened, revealing unimagined hues, disclosing unsuspected marvels of texture and fragrance.

"I used to think you were rather homely," I said. "Odd, isn't it?"

"I'm sure that I was," mumbled Stella. She didn't seem to be listening.

"I've noticed the people all staring at you. It can't be the clothes. Or the jewels."

"I couldn't conceivably care less," said Stella, rather sulkily.

"Tell me, Stella," I said. "What is your notion of perfect happiness?"

A momentary brightness passed over her face, followed by a small, lingering shadow.

"Happiness? Really, Enrico, what quaint, old-fashioned words you keep using."

"But it still exists, don't you think? Now and then? Here and there?"

"Well," said Stella, "I've always had a picture tucked in the back of my mind. A little cottage on the edge of a beach. Palms. Butterflies. Bees."

"Yes? What else?"

"I dive into the water. All naked. Alone in the wilderness."

"Yes? And then?"

"I grow restless. I start fidgeting and yearning."

"Yearning for what?"

"Oh, for a beautiful young Tarzan, shall we say?"

"And what's wrong with that, may I ask?"

"Everything, dear. The dream crumbles. And something rather horrid comes creeping into the picture."

"The serpent. I see."

"Oh, it's worse than a serpent, darling. It's a terrible shaggy ape who keeps staring through the leaves. . . ."

We ate our lunch. And quite casually, as she stirred her coffee, Stella murmured.

"I have something to tell you, Henry."

"Nothing tiresome, I hope?"

"I had an abortion. In Beaulieu."

"Oh. My poor little Stella."

"Poor nonsense. It was merely a bore."

"Was it Paolo's?"

"I'm afraid it wasn't."

"Alphonse's?"

"Certainly not."

I grew thoughtful. "And what about Paolo? Was he miserable about it?"

"I told Paolo that it was the lobster soufflé we had at the Beach Club."

"Well," I said, vaguely puzzled, "as long as it's over. That's the main thing."

"Oh, it's over," said Stella. "Once and for all. Don't you worry."

We sat silently for several minutes, puffing away at our cigarettes and watching some kittens play tag among the flower pots. And quite suddenly, as I sat there, fondling the bulge of my coffee cup, a violent pang shot through me like the shock from a naked wire. My mind became a vacuum. All I saw at that moment was the savage blaze of her Tahitian loveliness, which came spearing through the air with all the glitter of a meteor. Those long silky lashes and sensual, caressive lips: the curve of her flaw-less chin, the lilt of her swan-like neck: and above all that glorious, petal-smooth flesh, which shone with a filmy brightness, as though a flame were burning beneath it.

She reached casually toward the floor to stroke one of the kittens. It seized her hand and bit savagely with its needle-sharp teeth. She gave a small cry: a drop of blood clung to her wrist.

"We'll ask for some iodine," I said. "It might get in-fected, you know."

She sucked at the tiny wound and shrugged her shoul-ders impatiently.

I called briskly to the waiter and ordered a fresh pot of coffee.

Suddenly Stella said quietly: "You really despise me, don't you, Henry?"

I was startled. "Of course not."

"Well, I know what you're thinking." Her voice grew throaty and tremulous. "You think I'm a plain, common harlot."

"It really," I said, "hadn't occurred to me."

"Don't be sarcastic with me, please." She glared at me furiously. "I know what goes on in your sneaking, de-generate mind."

I toyed nervously with my spoon.

"You're every bit as bad as I am!" Her voice shook. "Or even worse! I know all about you! Don't think that I don't!"

"Really, my dear, I don't see what. . . ."

"Never mind. Don't bother to explain, please. I've

learned through bitter experience not to believe a word you tell me."

"Well, of course, if that's the way you. . . ."

"It's high time that somebody spoke to you. You pretend to be so wholesome. What a farce! You're nothing but a hypocrite! You and your poetry! Don't make me laugh, dear. You're nothing but a lazy, promiscuous tom-cat."

"You seem unusually excited about it all," I retorted.

She reached feverishly into her purse and tossed a banknote on the table. "Here," she said. "I don't want to feel that you're making sacrifices for me." She rose briskly and straightened her dress. "Good-bye. And happy hunting!"

And I watched her disappear among the shadows of the quay.

VIII

THE COLD WEATHER CAME. The brittle armor of purplish bronze that shielded the Luxembourg gardens gave way to a dull, misty gray. The cool sun of October faded from the banks of the Seine. The boughs drooped disconsolately, like an old lady's shawl. All the shutters were closed along the Avenue Gabriel and the walls sank into a pattern of tarnished grays and wrinkled purples. The whole city looked shadowy, haunted, impenetrable.

I didn't see Stella for almost a month, as it happened. I still posed for Boris whenever I felt like a good hot lunch and twice a week I danced with Maggy at our Little Box of Sardines. She had devised a whole series of beguiling new dances, including "Ganymede and the Eagle" and a "Dance of the Patagonian Moon-Goddess."

The rest of the time I indulged in my usual speculations. I'd sit by my window with a scrap of paper, scribbling away at little poems which I called "The Absinthe Drinkers" or "The Martyrs of Guernica." Or I sauntered down to the Dôme and sipped at my lukewarm coffee and wondered about the lives of those emaciated philosophers, with their Christ-like faces and long, dirty fingernails. I leaned over casually and caught fragments of their chatter. I followed their fleeting love affairs with a beady eye. I waited faithfully every evening for the familiar faces to appear—the dilapidated dandy with the monocle, the formidable old Lesbian with the ear-trumpet.

But all the while I was aware of some ill-defined absence: a tingling vacancy in my being that at times grew so acute that I felt a sickening stab, like a needle prodding at the pit of my belly. My mind recoiled from giving a name to this aching absence but my instinct knew perfectly well what it was. It conjured up certain smells—fresh nasturtiums, or warm sun-oil—and certain colors—black, azure—and even at times certain gestures—the poise of a long cigarette-holder or the tilt of a head on a swan-like neck.

Maybe I really fell in love when I first discovered her innocence. That is what one loves in people, ultimately: their deep, unshatterable innocence. With all her lies, her fads and her postures, her promiscuity, her insatiable greed, she somehow never quite lost that first childlike lustre. Maybe the greed and all the rest were actually facets of her innocence. In any case, whatever she did, I could never rid myself of the notion that she was deeply naive, profoundly pathetic, and unalterably pure.

I found it utterly impossible to tell her about my feelings, of course. I took it for granted that they would never be reciprocated. I knew that if I were to say to her one day, "I'm in love with you, Stella," she would merely laugh, or shrug her shoulders, or be slightly *gênée*. Her fate was to drift through the world from one Paolo to another: there would be a Pedro, and then a Pavel, and then an Anton, and then an Ahmed, until she had finally explored the full boundaries of her exile. And all I could ever be to her, in the course of this triumphal march, was a kind of tolerant playmate, a simpering little *confidant*.

Sometimes I awoke from a dream in the middle of the night. I gripped my pillow and writhed about in a spasm of yearning. Once or twice even the tears began to stream from my eyes. For I knew it was a yearning that, under it all, was wholly destructive: that would never be stilled, that could never be comforted.

2

Late one morning I found a message at the Hôtel de l'Univers.

Monsieur:
I saw your charming performance in the "Abyssinian Spear Dance" last night. I thought it vivid and sensitive. Would you have tea with me on Thursday?
                    Isabelle de la Harpe.
                    23 b Quai d'Orléans.

So I wandered across to the Ile Saint-Louis on the following Thursday. All of Paris was sparkling. The first snow had fallen. The sea-nymphs in the Tuileries were tufted with foam and Joan of Arc in the Place des Pyramides wore brilliant white epaulets.

Finally I arrived at the Quai d'Orléans. The place was dark, dank, cavernous. Mould clung to the marble; the walls were peppered with stains. The chandeliers hung suspended in the cavernous recesses like stalactites, and a watery echo swam about me as I climbed the great staircase.

An elderly butler with ochreous teeth and hennaed hair led me into the drawing room.

"Madame la Comtesse will be with you in a moment," he said, with a glint in his goatish eyes.

I looked around. There were little cabinets filled with Meissen and Sèvres. On the walls hung pastoral paintings by Boucher and Greuze. There was an Aubusson rug covered with bouquets of roses and a tulip-wood desk mounted in bronze doré. There were tables sprinkled with ivory snuff boxes, gilded coffee cups, and porcelain baskets. And the Louis Quinze chairs were tapestried with all sorts of monsters—basilisks, unicorns and griffons, surrounded by garlands of heliotropes. But the general effect was rather depressing. The cold winter sunlight which slid through the velours curtains lit on the cracks in the china, the chips in the acajou, the rips in the rug.

"Oh, you're here. How delightful!" said a velvety voice behind me. I turned: it was a small, delicate lady in lilac chiffon. Her face was taut and curiously pale, almost phantasmal, like fine old vellum. Strands of gray, like oxydized silver, shone softly on her temples. She looked like a distillation of the fragile and faded atmosphere that hovered about the nick-nacks and draperies.

But this spectral impression dissolved the moment she spoke.

"Sit down, my dear boy. Here on the canapé beside me.

You'll have some tea? It's an exquisite Darjeeling. Isn't Paris superb after a snowfall? Bitter and wicked and heart-broken: that's how it strikes me during the winter. These little plum-tarts are from Rumpelmayer's. They're not as good as they used to be. You dance divinely, I must say. I thought your Patagonian moon-thing deeply intui-tive. And your Narcissus revealed a delicious adolescent sensuality. I thought both of them entirely convincing. One lump or two? And a bit of lemon? I've never danced, I'm afraid. But I used to act way back in my teens. I played Célimène, I distinctly remember, in my school down in Pau. As well as Phèdre and Andromaque. And even Cleopatra in some silly old play. Do tell me about yourself, my dear. You have something unusual about you. Poetic and a bit *farouche*. Are you in love, by any chance?"

I stirred my tea. "Not exactly."

"Obviously not. Try to avoid it. It's a wearisome ex-perience. You might be rather a success in the ballet, it suddenly occurs to me. You have the right sort of body. Narrow hips, sculptured buttocks. And well-developed calves, of course. I started to sing when I gave up acting. That was back in my early twenties. I did songs by Fauré and Debussy and dear old Reynaldo Hahn, who was a friend of the family's. After that I did water-colors. Flow-ers, chiefly—roses and peonies. And an occasional nude, of course. That was my real Bohemian period. I knew Van Dongen and Berthe Morisot. I met Proust one day in the Bois. I was very inquisitive, to phrase it delicately. I slept with every man I could lay my hands on. I took cocaine. I even tried Lesbianism. All quite innocently, mind you. It's different nowadays, I can't help feeling. The zest, the freshness have gone. These new young people have no élan. They're depleted and infinitely weary. Another cup? Please call me Isabelle. And I'll call you Henry, if I may. . . ."

3

The second time that I called on Isabelle was on a foggy afternoon. The whole of the Ile Saint-Louis was shrouded in a blue pungent melancholy. I found her gracefully reclining on a Régence *chaise-longue*. On the tea-table beside her lay a copy of Montaigne. She was wearing an amethyst gown with a Nattier-blue sash.

"Forgive this informality, please. I feel rather attenuated. I like to keep the curtains closed and shut out the pedestrian world. Well, my pet, what have you been up to? Any amorous adventures?"

"None," I said, "in particular."

"Nonsense," she said, adjusting her robe. I could see the outline of her breasts gleaming faintly, like cockle-shells. An odor of lily-of-the-valley hung in the atmosphere. "You are heavily sexed, that's easy to see. Your bone-structure. Your wrists. Your thumbs especially. And your neck, of course. But at the same time you are a romantic. You take your emotions rather seriously, don't you, my friend?"

"What is a romantic, would you say, Mad. . . . I mean, Isabelle?"

She arched her brows. "A romantic, my duckling, is

someone who believes in the unpredictability of things."

"I'm not sure," I said cautiously, "that I believe in the unpredictability of things."

"Of course you do, dear. I can see it in your eyes. You write poems, I hear. Do you know any of them by heart?"

"I'm afraid that I don't, Isabelle."

"My English," she said, "is somewhat limited. But I've always adored"—her pronunciation was almost unrecognizable—"Ed-gahr Al-lain Poë." She leaned over and drew a volume from the lower shelf of the tea-table. "Here you are. I want you to read to me. A poem by Poë, if you don't mind."

I leafed dejectedly through the pages. Finally I cleared my throat and read:

> *"The skies they were ashen and sober;*
> *The leaves they were crispèd and sere,*
> *The leaves they were withering and sere;*
> *It was night in the lonesome October. . . ."*

I could feel her shimmering gray eyes watching me slyly as I read.

> *"Here once, through an alley Titanic*
> *Of cypress, I roamed with my Soul,*
> *Of cypress, with Psyche, my Soul.*
> *These were days when my heart was volcanic . . ."*

I could hear her sighing appreciatively as she ran her fingers along her collar-bone.

Finally she said: "Stunning, my boy. And very appropriate to the season. Do you like Debussy, by any chance?"

I nodded. "Yes. Rather."

"I shall sing you," she murmured, "a bit of Debussy."

She rose from the cushions, her gown trailing, and sat down gracefully at the Pleyel.

> *"Il pleure dans mon coeur*
> *Comme il pleut sur la ville.*
> *Quelle est cette langueur*
> *Qui penètre dans mon coeur?*

> *"O bruit doux de la pluie*
> *Par terre et sur les toits!*
> *Pour un coeur qui s' ennuie*
> *O le bruit de la pluie!"*

She turned her head and looked at me expressively. "What did you think of it, *mon petit Nijinsky?*"

"Very pretty," I said. "Full of sadness and subtlety."

Her eyes grew reflective. "Henry," she said, "would you do me a kindness? These beautiful songs positively cry for a dancing accompaniment. Go into the bedroom, my dear, and slip off those dreary clothes. The room is reasonably well heated. And we'll try some Terpsichorean interpretations."

"Well," I began, "I rather doubt whether. . . ."

"Nonsense, child," said the Countess. "One mustn't be shy when it comes to Art. The naive freshness is all-important." And she started to leaf through the slender album.

"But really, Isabelle, don't you think that. . . ."

"Not in the least. You don't need a costume. A scarf or a veil will do perfectly. You'll find plenty of them in my boudoir. I'll just run over the notes once or twice while you change."

So I ended by dancing to the strains of:

> *"C'est l'extase langoureuse,*
> *C'est la fatigue amoureuse,*
> *C'est tous les frissons des bois*
> *Parmi l'étreinte des brises,*
> *C'est vers les ramures grises,*
> *Le choeur des petites voix. . . ."*

Finally the Countess closed the album and gazed at me tenderly. "You have no idea, my dear Henry, how restful it is to find a man who responds to this frail, mercurial music. I can see that you harbor unsuspected depths in you. . . ."

After this I began to see my friend Isabelle quite regularly. Every Wednesday at tea-time we interpreted the songs of Debussy together. As time went on these little recitals grew more intimate, more experimental. And in spite of her sagging flesh I began to find a certain allure in Isabelle's body—there was something in her caresses which was mellow and reassuring. I even began to find an abstruse beauty in the lines of her throat and the creases of her breast, as one might admire the delicate nuances in fine old taffeta. Gradually I lost my timidity. I dropped my restraint. There were moments when even Isabelle was a little bit shocked.

One day in mid-February she said: "Would you do me a favor, dear?"

"With pleasure."

"I don't happen," she murmured, "to care for the cut of your clothes particularly."

"I'm sorry," I said, blushing.

"I have a suggestion. We'll call tomorrow on M. Laboulaye in the Rue Castiglione. I shall phone him in the morning. He did my husband's suits for him. And then we'll go to Duvivier's. You need a few good shirts, I suspect. And *en route* we'll stop at Charvet's in the Place Vendôme. . . ."

4

By the end of the following day's excursion I found myself equipped with three pairs of shoes, three shirts of muslin and three of silk, a fine umbrella, a splendid hat, socks, cravats, pyjamas from Sulka's and a faun-colored vest from Washington Tremlett, as well as a pair of moonstone cuff-links and a cigarette case from Van Cleef and Arpels; aside from the suits which Isabelle very tactfully helped me to choose—a dark blue flannel, an English plaid, a pin-striped worsted and an elegant dinner-jacket.

Ten days later, on the first of March, I finally appeared in my new splendor. I wore a carnation in my buttonhole as I strolled into the Ritz. I walked slowly down the corridor, pausing to look at the vitrines—the beautiful scarves, the expensive wrist-watches, the alligator leather, the perfume. I entered the bar at the back and ordered a glass of champagne. Then I opened my cigarette-case and drew out a Balkan Sobranje.

I heard a low, familiar voice: "Well, God help us. If it isn't Henry!"

I turned swiftly. I saw Paolo sitting at a table in the corner. Beside him sat a beautiful young blonde with a vivid sun-tan. For a moment I didn't recognize her. Then I walked over briskly.

"Why, it's Stella!"

"It is, I'm afraid."

"I wasn't sure. . . ."

"Nor was I!" She cast a shrewd, appraising glance at me. "Bless my soul. You've turned into a dandy!"

"You certainly have," said Paolo mournfully.

"It's rather a change," I said, "isn't it?"

"Not for the better, I'd say. You look like a gigolo," said Stella.

I blushed. "I'm terribly sorry. It's nothing to be ashamed of, really, is it?"

"Mercy, no. Not if you do it cleverly. Sit down, Henry. What will you have?"

"I'm expecting someone, I'm afraid."

"How delicious. Male or female?"

"A musical countess," I said nervously.

"I can't believe it," said Stella. Her eyes grew veiled and equivocal. "Well," she said in a low dry tone, "now that you've grown so *soigné*, why don't you have dinner with us tomorrow?"

At that moment my friend Isabelle appeared in the doorway. I excused myself hastily and led her to a banquette near the bar.

"Who," she said, narrowing her eyes, "is the exotic blonde, may I ask?"

"A cousin of mine," I said carefully.

"Cousin," said Isabelle. "How charming."

"She used to sing at 'La Vie en Rose.' Songs by Gershwin and so on."

"She has switched to a new profession, I gather," said Isabelle caustically.

"She's an odd sort of girl. Restless and moody. Unpredictable."

"Just as I thought," said Isabelle gently. "You are enthralled by the unpredictable. . . ."

We had dinner at the Crêmaillère. Portuguese oysters and poached turbot, followed by a *blanquette de veau* and a delicious *pêche Melba*.

Isabelle chatted vivaciously. Suddenly she turned to me and said:

"Would you enjoy a trip to Egypt?"

"I'd adore it," I said.

"Good. That's settled then," said Isabelle, "I'll make reservations for the fifth of March."

"Oh, but I can't just suddenly go and. . . ."

"Why not, my dear child?"

"There's the Box of Sardines, you know. And Boris is counting on me for Diana and Actaeon."

"Please my lamb, forget about Boris and those drab little sardines."

"And Maggy is planning a recital at some place in Neuilly."

"Forget about that silly Maggy. The Sphinx is more important than Maggy."

"I'm frightfully sorry," I said. "I wish that I could."

"You're being," said Isabelle, "unusually tiresome."

"Poor old Maggy is counting on me. I can't just suddenly go and desert her."

"How preposterous," said Isabelle. She sipped at her

brandy and sighed. "It seems so wasteful for you to consort with all that riff-raff. With your talents . . ."

A feeling of oppression crept over me. I felt dizzy, slightly feverish; as though I were hovering on the brink of some dangerous malady.

Finally we stepped into a taxi and drove back to the Quai d'Orléans.

"You're coming in?" said Isabelle casually.

"I don't think I'd better."

"Oh. Why not?"

"I feel queer."

Her lips tightened. "How so?"

"It might be the turbot," I said.

She regarded me coldly. "Well, tomorrow, then?"

"T-tomorrow?" I stammered. "I'm busy for dinner, unfortunately."

Her face grew taut, then drooped slightly. "With whom?"

"My cousin Stella."

"The exotic blonde?"

I nodded wistfully.

She gazed past me into the night. She looked rather frightening in the glow of the street-lamp; as though her face had collapsed into a phosphorescent tissue.

She smiled gently. "I see. Well, *au revoir,* my dear boy. . . ."

She closed the door softly. I strolled back over the bridge.

5

The following night after dinner we dropped in at the Petit Trou, just around the corner from the Café Flore, on Rue Bonaparte. It was Saturday night and very crowded. The usual clientèle was there—chubby Turks; willowy Oxonions; girls in slacks; boys with bracelets.

"Where," said Stella, "do you think we ought to go for the summer, Paolo darling?"

"I thought Deauville," said Paolo humbly. "Or Juan-les-Pins, if you'd rather."

"How about something more colorful? Like Iviza or Dubrovnik?"

"We might take a villa on Lake Como, if it appeals to you," said Paolo.

"It sounds rather stuffy and démodé, from what I hear."

"There's Brioni, of course," said Paolo. "And Rhodes. And Corfu."

"That's more like it," said Stella. "Or some idyllic little fishing village." She placed her arm on my shoulder tenderly. "Oh Henry, my pearl, how nice to see you again. You look so wide-eyed and American among these old-world depravities."

The door swung open and a puff of cold, sooty air shot past us. A young man in an Alpine costume strolled up to the bar. He wore gabardine ski-slacks and a crimson sweater patterned with reindeer. He had narrow green eyes and curly black hair, a cleft in his chin, long black lashes, a scar on his cheek, a deep suntan. I watched

him carefully for a minute or two. Then I walked up behind him.

"Tony," I whispered.

He spun around, with a look of alarm tinged with co-
quetry. Then his eyes gradually softened; his teeth glittered lazily.

"I can't believe it," he purred. "Dear old Henry. Well,
well."

"What a surprise," I said brightly. "I thought you'd be
in Samoa."

"I've been in Kitzebühel for a couple of weeks. Skiing
and bob-sledding, and so on."

"What about your painting?" I said.

"It's coming along," said Tony placidly. "I've hit on a
marvelous new manner. I'm almost ready for an exhibition."

"Come," I said, "and meet Stella. I used to tell you
about her, didn't I?"

Tony frowned. "Oh. That wild little cousin of yours in
Texas?"

Stella's eyes grew cool and alert when I introduced her
to Tony. Her glance ran over his body with a lightning
rapidity; and a velvety glow suffused her features, a kind
of honey-like lambency, as though she were gazing into a
bed of hot coals.

"Tony is an old friend of mine. He is doing a trip
around the world."

"How very nice," remarked Stella, touching her chin
with her forefinger.

"He plans to paint exotic people. He will paint the
Balinese," I said, "and maybe a few Fiji Islanders, or even
the headhunters of Sarawak."

"I could show him," said Stella, "some exotic types right here in Paris. Such as Paolo, for instance. Wouldn't you like to have your portrait done, Paolo?"

Paolo's rhesus-like gaze was fixed thoughtfully on Tony. He said softly: "May I ask who your favorite painters are, monsieur?"

Tony raised his brows languorously. "I rather enjoy Uccello. And Piero di Cosimo in his more whimsical moments. And I've always had an affection for dear old Bosch."

"You sound," said Stella suspiciously, "wildly sophisticated, I must say."

"Do you really think so?" said Tony. "I thought my taste was rather primitive."

"Would you like," said Paolo softly, "to drive to Fontainebleau with us tomorrow?"

"I'd love to," said Tony, lowering his eyelashes slightly.

"We'll have lunch at the Grand Véneur."

"An excellent spot," said Tony, nodding.

"And then we'll visit the château. We might have tea at the Aigle Noir. And we'll come back for a cozy supper at the Tour d'Argent," said Paolo eagerly.

"It sounds charming," said Tony.

"It really does, doesn't it?" said Stella.

"We might even," said Paolo excitedly, "stop at one of those antique shops in Barbizon. I happen to be looking for a Louis-Philippe mirror for my guest room. You must come," he said softly, still gazing intently at Tony, "and look at my apartment. I have a splendid collection of Papuan butterflies. . . ."

After Tony had left us Stella lowered her voice. "Well,

you certainly made an ass of yourself, didn't you, my dear?"

"What do you mean?" said Paolo innocently.

"You know exactly what I mean."

"I felt," said Paolo, "that I ought to be hospitable to an old friend of Henry's."

"I thought him hideously affected. And nauseatingly conceited."

"You are most unkind," murmured Paolo.

"Don't be an idiot," said Stella. "I know perfectly well why you liked him. I can read your mind like a book."

"Well," said Paolo with dejection, "we'll forget about tomorrow."

"It's too late," said Stella wearily. "We'll have to go through with it, I'm afraid."

6

April came once again. They were selling violets in front of the Crillon and a curious malaise was beginning to spread through my system. I'd sit at Weber's and stare at the thick black columns of the Madeleine and grow aware of an ugly odor, like rotting flesh. Or I'd climb the stairs in my hotel and see a greenish stain creep over the walls, as though some deadly acid were devouring the masonry.

I was still in love with the city; but it was a drugged, unhealthy love. There was something about the place which was both radiant and ominous—like a landscape trapped in the bilious brilliance before a hurricane. It was a city of contradictions. Of delight and desperation; of exhaustion and gusto; of the exquisite and the horrendous. There were moments, as I strolled along the quay in the light of dusk, when I felt a surge of happiness that bordered on ecstasy. And there were times, late at night near the Odéon for example, or walking home through the drizzly dullness of Rue de Lille, when all my hopes seemed to disintegrate among those rat-like façades and the whole bitter city seemed to be poised on the brink of suicide.

And a violent yearning took hold of me, so suddenly that it took my breath away; the sound of breakers, the smell of pinewoods, the taste of the sea and the heat of the sand: the glow of an endless blue sky on a long yellow beach: a sail tucked on the horizon, like a snow-white feather; and the cool glassy waves gliding across my tingling belly.

I decided to take a trip. To some island, if possible. To Corsica. Or Capri. Or maybe one of the Balearics.

7

But with the coming of May this feeling of *angst* disappeared again. The rains ended. The airs ripened. The season shed its caprice. The long boughs down in the Tuileries spread their leafy marquees and scalloped umbrellas burst into bloom along the boulevards.

Tony had joined our little circle. We were all the best of friends. We took excursions every week-end in Paolo's green Mercedes—to Chartres and Compiègne, to Sens and

Beauvais. Paolo always made a point of bringing along his Guide Michelin, and we lunched on *oeufs Bibesco, caneton en chemise* and *poires Hélène.* Paolo rather fancied himself as a connoisseur of wines: he always took care to pick the most stately and elegant vintages. We visited the cathedrals in the morning, admiring the sculptural details; and after lunch we usually explored some out-of-the-way little château, pausing to feed the fish in the fish-pond or tossing crumbs into the aviary.

We'd stop at sunset for a cocktail in some pleasant little square and then we'd have a light supper at a two-star inn along the way—a *mousse de saumon en gelée,* or a *poulet à la Vallée d'Auge,* with fresh raspberries or an apricot soufflé for dessert. Then we'd stroll through the woods by moonlight, our brains reeling with armagnac.

"Look," said Paolo, "at the stars. I've never seen them so brilliant."

"Millions and millions," said Stella. "It's rather terrifying, isn't it?"

"Just think, dear," said Paolo. "We're nothing but grains of dust in the universe."

"It makes life seem desperately short. And utterly pointless," said Stella.

"Come," said Paolo, somewhat nervously, "let's change the subject. Let's talk about Art."

"Tony's paintings," said Stella, "for instance. What are they like, dear? Terribly stark?"

Tony smiled. "Not in the least. Pierre Lejeune compared them to Magnasco. And Claude Lepic, who writes for *Figaro,* said they had a whiff of Salvator Rosa."

"How perfectly marvelous," said Stella.

"One needs luck," said Tony stoically. "Especially right

here in Paris. Just consider. There are thousands of painters in Montparnasse, not to mention Montmartre. One
out of ten has a shred of talent. One out of a hundred
makes money."

"It's a pity," said Paolo, "isn't it?"

"It's a tragedy," growled Tony.

He glanced at me with a little wink. I was never certain,
quite, about Tony. Passionately sincere at one moment,
and a moment later coyly ironic.

8

Tony and I took to wandering about in the sun-dappled
streets. We'd go and prowl through the medieval alleys on
the Ile de la Cité or pay a visit on the Post-Impressionists
in the Galeries Charpentier. Once in a while we went to
the baths in Rue de Penthièvre or Rue d'Odessa and I'd
sit in the calidarium, primly flexing my muscles, while
Tony strutted about like a seasoned roué. And once or
twice we were picked up by a married couple in the Bois
and driven back for an "intimate evening" in some miserable flat in Auteuil.

Now and again we dropped in at Hédiard's on the Place
de la Madeleine and fondled the bowls of goose-liver, or
the jars of honey from Hymettus. The only thing that
we ever bought was a bit of zwieback or a box of raisins.
One day I noticed Tony slipping a glass of caviar into his
pocket.

"Rather risky, don't you think?" I said, as we stepped
across the square.

"It wouldn't be fun," retorted Tony, "if there weren't a risk, my dear fellow."

Some days later he stole some chocolates at the Marquise de Sevigné's, and not long after a piece of jade at the Yokohama on Rue d'Alger. Finally one day he made off with a first edition of Rimbaud at one of the little bookshops on Boulevard Saint-Germain.

He slipped it merrily under my arm as we hurried down the street. Finally we reached the Café Flore and sat down for a cup of coffee.

"Really," I said, "I think you're going a bit too far with all this nonsense. Sooner or later they'll catch you. And what will you say?"

"Don't you worry," said Tony breezily. "I'll turn on the charm. I'll chuck them under the chin and say that I did it on a bet."

"Well, anyway," I said virtuously, "please don't expect me to cooperate."

"What ingratitude!" said Tony. "I stole it especially for you. And what do I get? Moral sermons. It's disillusioning, to put it mildly. . . ."

One evening we had cocktails in the Deux Magots, just the two of us.

"I'm leaving for Venice on Wednesday, I've just decided," said Tony.

"So suddenly? Why?"

"I'm sick of France. Of all the intrigue. Of all the dirt and decay. Of all the harlots and impostors." He leaned back in his chair and ran his fingers through his curls. "France is an over-ripe fruit. Someone will come along one of these days. Some wicked German. He'll shake the tree. And the fruit will fall. Mark my words."

"You're a pessimist," I said.

"Well, in any case I'm leaving. I'm sick of your friends, to be quite frank about it. I'm heading for Italy."

"Sick of my friends?"

"Take Stella, for instance. She's pretty. She's amusing. But she's dangerous."

I looked shocked. "Poor little Stella. She's impulsive, that's all."

Tony looked at me pityingly. "Poor little Henry. He's a fool, that's all."

He placed his glass on the marble table-top and glanced at the sky. A spider hung dangling from an overhanging bough. I watched the thread gradually lengthening until it almost touched the table. Finally it lit on Tony's hand. He looked startled. He smiled at me drowsily.

We sat silently for a while. Finally I said: "What will you do in Venice?"

"Paint," said Tony. "And keep painting. Till I'm blue in the face."

"Well, I wish you the best of luck."

"Thanks," said Tony. "I may need it." He looked at me slyly with those beautiful sea-green eyes where ice and fire, scorn and affection, lust and loathing seemed to mingle. "By the way. Could you lend me a hundred dollars, old boy?"

"That's rather a lot," I said dejectedly.

"I really need it," said Tony. "There's nobody else I can turn to. You're my only friend in the world."

"How about fifty?" I said guiltily.

"Make it sixty," said Tony. "After all, we live only once. What's ten dollars more or less?"

I drew out my wallet and signed my name to some

traveler's cheques. "Here you are. But be careful. Don't squander them, please!"

Tony rested his warm, powerful hand on top of mine. Then he rose. "Someday, Henry, you'll be proud that you knew me."

"And what about Stella and Paolo?"

"Well," said Tony, "what about them?"

"They'll miss you,'" I said, "I imagine."

"Tell them I've left for the Riviera."

"Very well," I said calmly. "Good-bye. And *bonne chance!*"

And he hurried across the street and disappeared in a pissoir.

IX

A SUDDEN HEAT fell on Paris. The leaves hung stiff in the Tuileries gardens. The noonday air shook like a jelly in the arid wastes of the Place Vendôme.

One sizzling morning Stella called me up out of the blue and said briskly:

"Are you up, *mon petit?* Have breakfast with me, won't you? I'll see you at Fouquet's in twenty minutes."

She looked drawn and rather pale as she strolled toward my table. She wore a dress of ivory muslin and a big white hat with a yellow rose.

She looked, I couldn't help noticing, unmistakably like a Parisian. The flavor of the city had finally penetrated her flesh. No one would have guessed, as she minced along the boulevard in delicate wayward steps, nonchalantly patting her belly, resting her fingers in mid-air, gazing dreamily at a passing gigolo, stifling a yawn, belching urbanely: no one would have guessed what she really was: a little ragamuffin from Texas.

"Forgive me, dear. I'm hideously late. I'm on the verge of collapse."

"It must be the heat."

"Not only the heat. There's something in Paris which utterly exhausts me."

She plucked fretfully at her croissant and dipped it in her coffee. Then she drew a Gauloise from the gold enameled case which Paolo had given her.

"Something is slipping through my fingers, slipping away, slipping away. . . ." She gazed at the clouds. "Tell me, sweet. Am I losing my looks?"

"Ridiculous," I said. "You're as pretty as ever."

Stella pouted. "Pretty. How boring."

"I meant beautiful. You're as beautiful as ever. Especially now that you're a brunette again."

She sighed wistfully. "Enrico, dove. You're my only friend in the world." She stole a glance at me slyly, then looked quickly away again. She stared desolately up the boulevard toward the Arc de Triomphe. "There's something wrong with all this. Desperately, sickeningly wrong."

"Wrong with what?"

"With the way we live. Don't you see, dear? It's all so meaningless. Months are passing and years are passing and we're withering away, like flowers in a desert."

"I hadn't thought of myself as a desert flower, exactly."

"Oh, don't be an ass, dear. You know what I mean."

"Maybe you ought to go back to 'La Vie en Rose.'"

She shrugged her shoulders. "Perhaps. But it's deeper than that, *mon chou*. Our life has grown terribly hollow and hot-housey."

"Maybe we ought to grow tulips. Or breed Irish wolfhounds."

"Don't be cheap, darling, please. It's not in the least a laughing matter. Sometimes I wake up in the night full of a mysterious kind of horror." She looked me suddenly in the eyes. Her voice sank to a whisper. "I feel my face turning into a mask. I feel my body turning to sawdust. I feel my heart floating away in the dark like a puff of smoke."

I said after a moment: "Have you quarreled with Paolo?"

"Oh, God, really, Henry. As if Paolo had anything to do with it. It's something bigger and much more frightening than poor little Paolo."

"It's something in the air," I said soothingly. "It's this worry about a war."

Stella stared through her cigarette smoke. "It might be a relief. Having a war."

I watched the traffic race by. There was a hint of something feverishly ephemeral in all that noisy, sparkling animation.

"Paolo has bought me a car, by the way," said Stella absently.

"Oh, really?"

"Nothing special. Just a small, cozy Lancia."

"How very nice."

"Listen, Henry. Would you like to take a trip with me?"

"Where, for example?"

"Wherever you think. Cannes, *peut-être*. Or Monte Carlo."

"Why not Holland?"

"I couldn't bear it. With all those windmills whirling around."

"Or Switzerland?"

"I'm not interested in clocks, my pet. Or in chocolates. Or peace."

"Very well. The Riviera, then."

"You're serious?"

"Of course I'm serious."

"When do we start?"

"Tomorrow morning?"

"Oh, Henry, dearest, you're perfectly marvelous." Her eyes sparkled suddenly. "I knew I could count on you. I'll tell Paolo to join us in a couple of weeks down in Nice." She crushed her cigarette, leaned over and kissed me on the cheek. "I'll have to dash, sweetie pie, and pick up some things *pour la plage.* I'll fetch you at ten o'clock sharp in Rue du Bac. . . ."

2

We didn't start until noon. It was a blue, leisurely day. A delicious lightness filled my heart as we drove through the Porte d'Italie and entered the enormous highway to the south. I had visions of tinkling waterfalls and Roman amphitheatres, of misty châteaux and pigeon-flecked gargoyles, of breeze-silvered poplars and even, who could tell, a casual caress in some ivied little inn.

We drove down through Fontainebleau, where we looked at the castle, and then southward through Sens, where we studied the cathedral, and spent the night in Avallon, where we dined on fried prawns and a *poularde flambée* with a delicious dry white wine.

Stella had grown remarkably lovely and cheerful overnight. Her eyes glowed with excitement as she flicked at the steering wheel. I felt a lurking expectancy, a kind of hovering delight, such as I felt on New Year's Eve when I waited for the bells to start ringing.

"Do you remember the little games we played in Texas, Enrico?"

I lowered my eyes discreetly. "I certainly do. Out in the canna bed."

"Blind Man's Buff. And Button, Button. And Hide-and-Go-Seek," murmured Stella.

"And other games too. Puppy Dog's Tails and Sugar Bowls."

Stella looked rather distant. "What odd little names. I don't recall them."

"And once we looked for some ghosts in a haunted house. Do you remember, dear?"

"Did we really?"

"And I gave you a funny little bracelet with forget-me-nots."

"You don't say."

"And I wanted to be your husband. But I wasn't rich enough. Remember?"

"Really? How quaint of you, dear. You were such a solemn little boy."

"It seems terribly long ago, doesn't it?"

"And terribly far away."

"And yet, somehow or other. . . ."

"Yes?"

"More real than Paris, in a kind of way."

"Not to me," said Stella crisply. "I can hardly remember San Pedro. It's like a horrible, hazy dream. I was wretched there. I really was."

"You were just an ugly duckling. Waiting to turn into a swan."

"America terrifies me, Henry. God knows why. It simply terrifies me."

She tipped her glass and watched the lights of the chandelier play in the wine. "I do hope that we won't meet any Americans on the Riviera."

"We probably will," I remarked.

"Well, not Tony, at any rate."

"There's not much danger," I said carelessly.

"Oh? Why not?" said Stella quickly.

"He's in Venice," I said.

Stella's face grew suddenly pale. "Venice? Really? But I thought you told me. . . ."

"I probably did. He changed his mind."

"But why didn't you tell me?"

"Does it matter?" I said.

"Not in the least," said Stella snappishly. "But I don't like people who lie to me."

Her joy, her playfulness had vanished. She looked cold, hard and alien.

3

We headed for Lyons the following morning. But some twenty miles from Avallon Stella turned to me casually and said: "Let's have a look at the map, dear, shall we?"

I passed it to her obediently. "Here we are. Down through Saulieu. And then straight along the Rhône. We'll spend the night in Avignon."

"It sounds dreary, somehow."

"We might try the Dordogne."

Stella's eyes were fixed on the map. "What about Dijon? And then Switzerland?"

"It's rather a detour," I said cautiously.

"I'd love seeing some mountains. Such a relief in this sticky, enervating heat."

"Well," I said. "we'll drive through Aix."

"Darling," said Stella, "let's forget the Riviera. I'm simply not in the mood for Monte Carlo."

"Very well," I said thinly.

"What about Zurich? And those marvelous Dolomites?"

"And then Venice, I presume?"

"Well, why not, after all? Venice has a lot more to offer than that dreary Cannes, when you stop to think of it."

"All those churches and palazzos."

"And those marvelous canals."

"And the Tiepolos, naturally."

"Not to mention the mosaics. . . ."

So we turned into a side-road and headed for the east. We cruised through the meadows of Burgundy, which lay sleek as Cockaigne. The pigs looked glossy and crisp, as though fresh from the spit. The fruits in the orchards looked ready to burst; pools of wine lay floating in the courtyards.

Marvelous clouds hung overhead, like great puffs of sea foam. We tossed our Baedeker aside; we forgot about culture. Instead of peering at old crypts and romanesque vestibules we strolled on grassy ramparts, we prowled through ancient cemeteries, we picked wild cyclamen in the woods and bought tartelettes still warm from the oven and so feathery light that they seemed to float through our fingers.

We stopped for lunch in Dijon. Everything reeked of obesity. A row of dusty jereboams stood on top of the sideboard and jugs of fresh butter were squatting on the tables. We finally ordered a *truite au bleu,* followed by a *bavarois aux fraises.* Then we finished our *filtre* and strolled back into the sunlight.

We passed through Dôle, turned southward, crossed the border near Pontarlier, passed by the lake of Neuchâtel and stopped in Bern for a cup of tea.

"We could spend the night here," I said. "It's rather cozy, don't you think?"

Stella gazed through the medieval arch at a gilded fountain in the square.

"We could, I guess," she said amiably. "It's rather early in the day, though. Switzerland is marvelous to look at but one doesn't feel much like lingering. . . ."

She was rapidly recovering her spirits. We reached Zurich at dusk and spent the night in a charming old inn beside the Limmat.

We dined on the edge of the lake and took a stroll through the park. We paused by the shore and looked at the swans paddling silently under the starlight. My feeling of elation, of quivering expectancy had withered away: and instead I felt a deepening, accelerating tension.

Stella sat on a stone and trailed her fingers in the smooth black water.

"Do you remember the day," I said, "that we rowed in Central Park?"

"Did we row in Central Park? I'd quite forgotten," said Stella.

"You trailed your fingers in the water. A butterfly lit on your neck. And we ended by having a rather nasty squabble, as I recall."

"I was a vicious little idiot, I'm afraid," said Stella.

"You kept talking about a man called Willoughby Pratt who was in love with you."

"Willoughby Pratt? Heavens, dear. There was no such person as Willoughby Pratt."

"You made him up?"

"Of course I did. I was a fiendish little liar."

"Oh. I see."

"I still am, dear. Don't ever believe a word I say."

We sat silently for a while. The neon-lights on the opposite shore darted about in the inky water like rainbow-colored eels.

The swans looked porcelain-white against the dead black water. Everything was still, hollow, hushed, as though the city were in the grip of the plague. I suddenly saw something sinister in all this precision. I longed for anarchy. I longed for dirt. I longed for the smell of humanity.

Stella whispered: "What do you think, dear? Should I marry poor Paolo?"

"Has he asked you?"

"Dozens of times. With tears in his eyes. It's quite pathetic."

"Do you think you'd be happy with Paolo?"

"I'd be bored to death with Paolo."

"Well, don't marry him, then."

"It isn't as simple as that, my pet."

"Why not?"

"Don't be obtuse, Henry. Something might happen one of these days."

"Such as what?"

"Something frightening."

I said blithely: "A war, for instance?"

"Nonsense, dear. There's nothing frightening about a silly old war."

"Well," I said, somewhat edgily, "maybe you're best off with Paolo. You'll have a roof over your head. And plenty of nick-nacks from Cartier's."

Stella sighed, closed her eyes and ran her palm over her brow. "Really, Henry, there are times when you sound like an absolute imbecile. Here you've known me since I was a baby. And rather intimately, if I may say so. And you haven't the foggiest idea what I'm really like, deep inside. . . ."

4

Everything glittered. The mountainous pastures shone with scallops of sunlight. The lakes gleamed in the distance like bowls filled with quicksilver. Even the cows grazing in the grass looked curiously bright, like painted Nymphenburg. Everything shone with the weird exactitude and immobility of a dream: the vacancy, the strange, intangible menace of a dream.

We crossed the frontier at Feldkirch and entered the mountains of the Tyrol. Everything changed as though by magic. The air grew mild and lilac-tinted, and all around

us we saw the drugged, ox-like gaze of the Austrian moun-
tain-dwellers. The clock-like precision melted into a casual, pastoral drowsiness. There were villages with shadowy
arcades where the paint had peeled from the walls. There
were inns whose façades were decorated with stags, grapes
and angels. There were wilted flowers in the rustic shrines
and chipped madonnas in the stucco niches. The air
was heavy with the aroma of gentians and evergreen.

We had goulash and white wine in a little tavern beside
a waterfall. Then we sat under an umbrella and looked
out over the valley. I felt a pang of delight when I caught
the old, familiar fragrance: fresh coffee and old masonry
and sweet, sun-baked horse-dung.

"What's wrong, dear?" said Stella.

"It's the mountain air, I guess."

"You look ready to cry."

"I just happened to think of something."

"Well," said Stella, "I know what it is. It's the blood
in your veins. I felt it one day when I walked through the
Kasbah in Algiers."

"How very interesting. I didn't know that you had Arab
blood in your veins."

"I do, *mon cher,* believe it or not. I used to think it was
Polynesian. But that day in Algiers it all came back to me
in a flash. My mother's family came from Seville and of
course that explains it. There's a tinge of Arab blood in
every family in Andalusia. . . ."

We sipped at our wine and looked down at the sunlit
waterfall. A rainbow hung poised over the pirouetting
foam. A flock of geese came waddling over the foot-bridge
and the little goose-girl dipped her toes in the torrent.

"That's why Tony wanted to go to Italy, I suppose,"

said Stella absently. "The Italian blood in his veins. It explains a lot about Tony."

"I'm sure that it does," I said quietly.

"That shifty streak in him, for example. You're never sure what he's up to. That's typically Italian, don't you think?"

I gazed sadly up at the Arlberg.

"Tony baffles me," said Stella. "He seems so cocksure and conceited. And yet, you know, I keep thinking. . . ."

"What?"

"That maybe he's frightened of life, like all the rest of us."

"Am I frightened, do you think?"

"Of course you are, darling. Look at your eyes. They're like a deer's. You're just a waif in the wilderness."

"I didn't know that you were capable of such insight," I murmured.

"You're pitifully naïve, my dear Henry. That's your trouble. You're only a baby."

5

We slept in Innsbruck that night and the following day we drove through the Dolomites. The fields and pastures vanished away and the air grew brittle, explosive. The giant cones pierced the sky like a landscape in hell: naked and phallic, obsessed, tinged with a fiery opalescence.

"Italy," said Stella. "I can smell it. I can feel it in the air."

"Yes. It smells like a suntanned peasant who's been treading on grapes."

"And look how beautiful they are. Especially the men. Have you noticed?"

"Their teeth are unusually white, I must say," I said sulkily.

"Not only their teeth, dear. Their eyes. And above all their bodies. They really look as though they were fabulous at love-making, don't they?"

We followed the foam of the Adige and picnicked in a meadow: sausages and cheese and black peasant bread and a bottle of cheap Chianti. We rode south from Bolzano toward the shimmering hills by Rovereto. We passed grim, derelict villages and spruce modern garrisons. And wherever we looked we saw those teasing brown eyes and felt that soft-fingered, pagan sensuality. The magic of the Italian peninsula, so corrupt yet so human: so beautifully poised; so smilingly cunning.

We rode through little piazzas where dusky beauties peeped through the shutters; past Renaissance churches where silvery saints shone in the candlelight; through streets where obscene drawings were scrawled on the plaster; past farms where the cows stood motionless in the crimson haze and ducks ruffled their feathers under the dusty plane-trees. And as we rode I felt enveloped in a haze of delight. Everything sang, everything sparkled, the world had never seemed so exquisite.

Finally, just before sunset, we entered the gates of Verona. We shared a hot tiny room: the only one left in the hotel. There was a dresser of varnished pine and two little beds with paisley coverlets. A narrow door led into the bathroom, which was painted a sickly rose.

"Is it wise, do you think?" I said.

"Don't be a prig, please," said Stella.

She opened her goatskin valise and tossed her bathrobe over the chair.

"Very well. Just as you say."

"I shan't try to seduce you, dear. I still think of you as a wistful, innocent brother."

"I see."

"And I'm sure you still think of me as a scrawny little sister, don't you, dear?"

"Naturally," I said.

"So it's silly to be stuffy about beds, really, isn't it?"

I nodded.

She smiled at me blandly. "It's rather a relief, you know, Henry, to be with a man who isn't perpetually trying to drag me to bed with him."

"It must be," I mumbled.

"Except Tony, of course," said Stella. She sat down on the edge of my bed and thoughtfully drew off one of her slippers. She ran her fingers through her hair and looked dreamily through the window, where a dragon-shaped cloud was floating across a copper crescent.

"What do you mean? About Tony?"

"Nothing especially," said Stella. "It's just that Tony seems to have no sexual interest in women."

"Well, I wonder," I said.

Stella glanced at me sharply. "What do you mean, dear? Precisely?"

"Only that Tony is rather flexible."

"Oh," said Stella. She kept peering at me from the corner of her eye. "He's been having an affair, has he?"

"I haven't the faintest idea."

"Maybe that's why he left for Italy."

"It's conceivable," I murmured.

Stella sighed, lowered her head and drew off her other slipper.

"I don't believe that Tony is capable of passion," she said drowsily.

"Quite possibly," I said.

"Or of deep, genuine love."

"What is love? Would you say?"

"Goodness, Enrico. What a question. Either you feel it or you don't."

"Have you ever been in love?"

"Certainly. Twice, dear. *Au moins.*"

I paused for a moment. "Anyone I know?"

"No. Unfortunately," said Stella.

"Not Alphonse?"

"Mercy, no."

"Not even Paolo?"

"Not for a moment."

"Well, it shows how terribly little I really know about you, doesn't it?"

"I suppose it does. You'd be hideously shocked, my puss, if I told you about those episodes." She glanced up at me coyly. "And what about you, dear? Have you ever been in love?"

"Twice," I said.

"Really? How fascinating. Anyone I know?" said Stella softly.

"Yes, unfortunately," I said. "You'd be hideously shocked if I told you."

Stella's eyes grew veiled and teasing. "Don't be an idiot,

mon enfant. You're just trying to sound mysterious. You've never been in love and you know it. . . ."

She stepped into the bathroom and turned on the water. Then she tiptoed back to the bedroom, slipped out of her clothes, turned her back for an instant, and flung her bathrobe around her.

"I won't be a moment," she said. "It's quarter past eight: time for dinner. I'll turn on your bath as soon as I'm through, shall I, dear?"

She skipped gayly into the bathroom, humming "Constantinople." She left the door open. I could see her reflection in the wavering mirror, pausing for a moment beside the basin, tossing her robe over the hook, stepping daintily into the water and vanishing nimbly into the tub. I could hear her splashing and singing; I could hear the lick of the lather; I could hear the gurgle and hiss as she finally drew out the plug.

She threw a towel around her waist and waltzed merrily back into the bedroom. She smiled at me brightly. "Hurry up, sweet," she said. A little lock of her wet hair clung to the back of her neck and a few shiny drops still hung from her honey-skinned breasts.

I sat motionless, dizzy, half-blind with desire.

"Come, darling. I need a drink. Don't keep dawdling," said Stella.

"Stella," I whispered. "Will you do me a favor?"

"Certainly," she sang, pointing her toe at me.

"Take off your towel and let me look at you."

"Goodness, darling. Of course, if you'd like." She dropped the towel on the floor and stood naked in front of me. She glanced at me slyly from the corner of her eye.

"Am I pretty?" she murmured.

My voice shook. "Yes. Glorious."

She placed her forefinger on her chin. "Thank you, dear. You're an utter angel. And now hurry. The bathtub's full. I'm dying for a nice, strong martini. . . ."

6

I hardly slept that whole night. I kept twisting in my bed, glancing again and again at the silhouette that lay on the bed beside me: motionless, supine, almost saintly: frighteningly serene, like a corpse.

The following morning, after we had visited the beautiful church of San Zeno and she lingered in the breakfast room to dash off a letter to Paolo, I leaned over her suitcase and prowled among her clothes—those crumpled pink underthings that had touched her intimate flesh. I fondled them lovingly and held them against the light, eager to detect some faint residue of the limbs they had enveloped. I pressed them to my face, striving to catch that fruit-like fragrance, half sweet and half acrid, like a ripe nectarine. I drew out one of her handkerchiefs, faintly tinged with a hint of lipstick and embroidered in the corner with a serpentine S, and quickly tucked it into one of the pleated pockets of my bag, where it lurked with *The Shropshire Lad,* with its sad, wilted dandelion.

7

We arrived in Venice at noon. We left the Lancia in the big garage and took a gondola to our little inn, which was called the Concordia.

Our memory of a place is a haunted thing. Haunted by the ghosts of our own experiences, which merge mysteriously with the ghosts of a myriad other experiences: so that the atmosphere of a locality becomes a miraculous distillation of all the passions and experiences that have been endured there over the centuries. At least, so it seems whenever I try to recapture them: the wolves that lurked in the Carinthian woods; the violent aridity of San Pedro; the sensuous loneliness of Prairie du Loup and the furtive hankerings of Cliffdale; the false bravado of Llewellyn; the feverish search of New York; and the adventurous, multitudinous cunning of Paris. They were all a bouquet, infinitely subtle and variegated, of my own dark emotions and the million emotions of a nameless past. I instinctively became a part of every place that I lived in. Like a chameleon I partook of its coloring—azure, gray, puce, pistachio. So that, however minutely I still remember each detail, the real truth lies in the unrememberable; the aroma; the mystery.

Was the feeling of passionate exultation that filled Venice that day only a result of the brilliant sunlight that fell on those façades? Or was it something in the heart of the city, the human accretion of centuries? Or was it something that I caught from Stella—some quivering breath of anticipation? Or was it only that I myself felt a strange, crazy happiness, all the sharper because it was tinged with frustration and foreboding?

As we rode along in our gondola the great palaces slid past. The piercing light seemed to reduce those stupendous old walls to a painted *coulisse,* a hovering illusion of rust and lavender. The clouds above looked solid as ice and the sky beyond impenetrable as turquoise. But the city itself looked as frail as a butterfly's wing, ready to wilt and disintegrate.

We left our bags at the Concordia, which was a small crowded hostelry with red damask on the walls, dusty chandeliers in the dining room, and a little glass fountain filled with goldfish in the lobby. Then we strolled down a dark, narrow alley toward the Piazza. We passed a fruit shop where the plums lay glittering in the sun like globes of glass, and then a glass shop where the grapes lay tucked on the shelves, like real fruit. Everything seemed to be reversed, like the lights and shadows on a film. The dark canals looked massive as marble; the mirrored walls looked sinuous and liquid. The light of the sun felt strangely cool and the dark arcades were hot and stifling. The willowy men minced like women and the haunchy women strode like men. The smell of the sea seeped out of the lavatories and the stench of excrement welled up from the sea.

We passed a baroque chapel and then walked under a cobwebbed archway. I caught my breath. The vast arena of the Piazza lay before us. After those dark, crowded corridors and spindly little bridges the effect was of infinite space, of blinding radiance, of feverish opulence. Tiny figures passed in the distance among those endless colonnades: they looked faceless, dehumanized, like the hooded dancers in a *bal masqué* or the small china dolls in some elaborate puppet-show. I stood spellbound for several minutes. Had I been here before? I had, surely: I was absolutely convinced of it. I felt like bursting into tears.

We threaded our way through the café tables and wandered out toward the Piazzetta. A hunchbacked woman was selling little porpoises of gold-peppered glass and some boys in striped jerseys were scattering seeds for the pigeons. An ice-cream vendor came rolling his bright nickel wagon. A blind little girl sold glacé walnuts pierced on a wire.

Stella said: "Well, it's just as I imagined it. Rather harrowing, in a way."

"Harrowing? Why?"

"It's so intense, dear. Everything seems so theatrical. People would drown themselves for a love-affair in Venice, don't you think?"

"I do indeed."

"I'd hate being trapped in a love-affair in Venice, I must say."

"You probably will," I said wryly.

"Don't be preposterous," said Stella. "I'm not in a mood for any nonsense. I'll be too busy looking at those marvelous Tiepolos."

We stood by the water and looked at the isle of San Giorgio in the distance.

"Speaking of paintings," said Stella. "Do you suppose that Tony has much talent?"

"I haven't seen any of his work," I said, "I'm afraid."

"I doubt whether he has. He might, of course. He's such an enigma."

We went sauntering past the aisle of green wicker tables. The little band was playing the Estudiantina Waltz by Waldteufel.

"Tell me, dearest," said Stella. "What was he like when you first knew him?"

"More or less what he's now. Rather adventurous. A shade unscrupulous."

"Disgustingly selfish, even then?"

"Tough and cocky. And selfish."

"Was he terribly good-looking?"

"I suppose he was. In his way."

"You had a crush on him, didn't you?"

"What on earth makes you think so?"

"I can sense it, somehow."

"What a lunatic notion."

"Don't deny it, please, dear. I can read you like a book. You always grow tense the moment I mention his name. . . ."

I said: "Look!"

"Yes? What?"

"Over there. In the second row."

Stella turned; she grew pale. "It's Tony," she muttered. "With a woman."

"He's as brown as a berry," I said.

"How utterly incredible," said Stella. "A small, blowzy Jewess. I wouldn't have thought it of Tony."

We strolled casually toward Tony's table. He smiled up at us brilliantly. "Well, well. What a surprise. This is Melanie," he said.

Melanie gazed at us gently through her long black lashes. She was a shy, sad-eyed creature, slim and alert, like an elf. She wore a smock patterned with butterflies and small scarlet sandals and on her arm an elaborate cobra-shaped bracelet. Tony was wearing a crimson shirt and canary-hued slacks. His skin was dark as a Hawaiian's and his hair was long and unruly; little curls, dark and wiry, clung to the nape of his neck. He melted harmoniously into the bright Venetian atmosphere.

And Stella too, as I turned and glanced at her, seemed suddenly to have changed. She looked, in this southern light, like a real Mediterranean: graceful and glossy and olive-skinned, with a whiff of grape-vines about her. Her breasts looked a little riper, her hips just a trifle heavier. Her whole body suggested sunlight, fruits, wine, copulation, laughter.

We sat down at the table and ordered a *granita di caffé*. "Well," I said, "what's been happening? Have you painted away busily?"

"God, I have," said Tony impetuously. "I've been painting like a fiend. I've developed a new approach. I've been studying Tintoretto."

"How exciting," said Stella.

"I've met a man who runs a gallery. Count Alberti," said Tony. "He's going to arrange an exhibition."

"How perfectly thrilling," said Stella.

"My paintings remind him of Guardi. He's quite enthusiastic. He thinks that I have a great career ahead of me."

"How absolutely splendid," said Stella. "You'll be staying here long?"

"For the rest of August," said Tony. "Then I'm off to Morocco."

"Oh. How marvelous," said Stella. "You'll be painting the Africans?"

"Yes," said Tony, with a glance at Melanie. "I'll be painting those beautiful Africans. . . ."

8

We all met on the following morning and sailed out to the Lido.

Stella was wearing one of her smart new dresses from Schiaparelli: a simple sheath of azure linen, with a gold-braided belt. Poor little Melanie, in her Austrian *dirndl*-dress, looked rather dowdy beside her. As for Tony, he was wearing a pair of black velvet trousers and a shirt of green shantung with large golden buttons. He was carrying a beach-bag of thick, studded cow-hide.

"God, Tony," I whispered. "How on earth did you pay for all this?"

"I was given a small advance on my exhibition, naturally," said Tony.

"You look unusually vivid. Almost like an Italian," I said.

"I like to look vivid. There's Italian blood in my veins!"

We took a little cabana in front of the Hôtel des Bains. It was a brisk, windy day. The aisle of striped awnings rippled festively in the breeze and a row of small sail-boats slid southward toward Chioggia. We bought a basket of grapes, spread our towels on the sand, rubbed our shoulders with unguents and lay down in the sun.

I glanced furtively at the others. Stella's suit was of

heliotrope and so small that it barely covered her breasts and her abdomen. She looked almost naked. But her limbs were so elegant and her skin so beautifully golden that the effect was quite natural. Poor little Melanie looked very white and very frail, almost haggard. Her body was that of an undernourished child. And as for Tony, I immediately recognized the supple lines of his body: the bulging chest with its tiny nipples, the silky curls under the navel.

"Come," he said. "Let's swim out to the raft, shall we, Henry?"

We crossed the sand and waded out into the windpocked Adriatic. When I turned and glanced back the beach looked eerily far away. The mosque-like dome of the Excelsior in the distance, the interminable row of cabanas, the fluttering marquees, the blue umbrellas, the gleaming sand, the glittering waves: once again I had the impression that I had seen it all before, in some earlier incarnation or maybe a vague, prophetic dream.

We climbed on the gently rocking raft and lay down in the sun.

I said softly: "Tell me, Tony, are you having an affair with Melanie?"

"Not especially," said Tony. "She paints. We met in Basel."

"What does she do? Oils? Temperas?"

"Pastels mostly. Nudes and so on."

"You've probably posed for her, haven't you?"

"Now and then. As a kind of favor."

"Have you slept with her?"

"Once."

"Is she in love with you?"

"Madly."

He said it in his cool, light-hearted way, as a simple statement of fact. I began to feel rather uneasy about poor little Melanie.

"Tell me, Tony," I said. "What do you feel about Stella?"

Tony glanced at me drowsily. "I've already told you. I despise her."

"Come, come," I said gently. "You're exaggerating a little, aren't you?"

"Not in the least. Stella's a bitch. Stella's a hysterical, vicious woman."

I turned over on my belly and stared out at the sea. A small steamer was heading eastward, toward the coast of Dalmatia. The sunlight had a tense, almost delirious sheen to it: everything looked unnaturally clear, like a landscape viewed through a stereopticon.

I glanced furtively at Tony. He was certainly superbly handsome, in a sexual, sardonic, Caravaggio sort of way: that little cleft in his faunlike chin, those eyes as green as a Triton's, those curls all stiffly coiled, like a Babylonian emperor's. Something of my old adoration swept over me for a moment. It was like a tang in the lazy air, a remembered whiff of dank water lilies.

"She's in love with you, I'm afraid."

"Don't be a fool," snorted Tony.

"She really is. I'm convinced of it."

"She's incapable of love. She's a whore."

When we stepped back on the beach again we saw a stranger in front of our cabana: a tall young man, intensely sun-tanned, with a typically Venetian face—soft gray eyes and a long sharp nose and a mop of wet, coppery hair.

"This is Massimo," said Stella.

We shook hands with young Massimo.

"Massimo has a glass-shop," said Melanie.

"Oh," said Tony. "How amusing."

"You're a marvelous painter, I hear," said Massimo.

"Well, I paint," muttered Tony.

"It would be a privilege," said Massimo courteously, "if you'd allow me to visit your studio. . . ."

9

Tony's studio was in a small, dingy house near the Merceria, just a three minute walk from the basilica of San Marco. We stopped beneath the bell-tower and then entered the thronging alley, passed a leather-shop and a lace-shop and entered a dark, tiny courtyard. We climbed a narrow stone stair-case, passed through an ill-smelling tunnel, crossed over a terrace draped with laundry and entered the glass-enclosed studio.

The light from the low-lying sun fell on a row of fresh oil paintings, one of them still on the easel, the rest placed casually along the wall—on the floor, on the dresser, on the washstand, on top of the book-case.

"Magnificent," said Massimo, after a moment.

"Utterly fascinating," said Stella.

They were imaginary landscapes filled with beasts, birds and castles. There was a hint of Claude Lorrain, a suggestion of Dossi, a tinge of Chirico. There was a half-ruined palace in the middle of a desert, with a torrent gushing through a window and an enormous snake coiled over the door. There was a harbor surrounded by obelisks, minarets and temples, with an ivory-white skeleton lying on a half-sunken barge. There was a garden with a tall ivied tower in the background: bats were flying out of the roof and lions were prowling among the bushes and under a pergola sat a naked young lady combing her hair.

Tony glared at me. "What do you think of them?"

"They're highly imaginative," I said.

"Yes? What else?"

"I'm not sure. I'd have to get used to them," I murmured.

"I can see you don't like them."

"I do like them. Enormously."

Tony brightened. "Really? You do?"

"Especially the one with the obelisks."

"Well," said Tony, "I'll make you a present of it."

"I'd be thrilled," I said anxiously.

"After the exhibition, that is."

"You're wonderfully generous, Tony."

He smiled at me gratefully. And for the first time since I'd known him I saw in his eyes something vulnerable, something childlike and pleading.

We said good-bye in front of Florian's. Stella and Massimo stopped for a drink; Melanie walked back to her rooms and I went sauntering toward the Rialto. The sun was setting and a cool, brackish breeze swept through the alleys. I caught the musk of each little shop: of sizzling olive oil and onions, of ripe peaches, of shell-fish, of soap, of Chianti. I parted the thick leather curtains and stepped into a small, musty chapel. The smell of incense and

tallow swept out of the coolness. The arrowing flames
played gently on the baroque candlesticks and the gilded
cherubs. Two old ladies in black were praying in front
of a crucifix.

I entered the Campo San Luca and sat down for a cup
of coffee. I felt strangely at peace. The whole world, the
whole universe, seemed gently and miraculously to fall into
place. Not, as in America, through the power of the
wilderness, nor, as in France, through the force of the
intellect, but quite calmly and inevitably through the
insistence of the flesh. The loaves of bread, the velvet
slippers, the scent of urinals, the smell to olive oil—
everything joined in a paean of praise of the physical
reality of man. Not man's hopes or man's fears, not man's
soul or desires, simply man's body with all its appetites, its
warm secretions, its childlike vanity. I watched a child rolling a hoop, three young sailors, an old beggar woman: and
after a while the anonymity of it all began to frighten
me. There was something strangely sad and rather primitive and even cruel in this casual surrender to animal
mortality.

10

I returned to the Concordia after an hour or thereabouts.
There was no sign of Stella. I sat down and wrote some
postcards—to Maggy and Boris, to my old Aunt Ursula.
Then I took a quick bath, dressed for dinner and returned
to the Piazza. I paused in front of a glittering shop win-

dow. A little box caught my eye: it was shaped like a sea-
shell, with flakes of gold in the fluted amethyst.

I strolled out toward the Campanile. Suddenly, with a
start, I saw Stella. She was standing in front of the basilica,
looking up at the four bronze horses.

I cried: "Stella!"

She swung around. "Well, my cuckoo. Where have you
been?"

The moment I looked into her eyes I grasped what had
happened. A wave of nausea welled up in me; my eyes
grew clouded; I started to tremble.

"It's time for dinner, nearly," I whispered.

"Don't be a glutton, please, darling. Come along and
have a peep at the Bridge of Sighs with me, won't you?"

We walked down past the Doge's Palace toward the
Hotel Danieli. Stella peered at me coyly. "Goodness, dear.
You're as red as a lobster."

"Too much sun, I presume."

"And you're dripping with sweat!"

I smiled thinly. "Oh, really?"

"You're in a huff. I can sense it."

"Not in the least," I said hoarsely.

"You certainly are. You're in a tantrum."

"Not a bit. I'm as calm as a cucumber."

Stella glanced at me sidelong. Her face hardened
abruptly. "I know perfectly well what you're thinking.
Yes. You're right. I slept with Massimo."

I closed my eyes for a tiny instant. A peculiar stillness
passed through me: the whistling steamer, the chattering
motorboats, the screaming vendors grew inaudible.

Finally I said: "I've bought you a present, by the way.

I hope you like it." I gave her the little box, which was wrapped in pink tissue paper.

"Oh. How sweet."

"Do you like it?"

"It's silly of you, dear. You can't afford it."

"It's not from Cartier's, unluckily."

"Don't be catty, please, Enrico."

I paused and stared at the filmy, grape-skinned lagoon. The tiny lights on the Lido were beginning to twinkle. Over the spire of San Giorgio a dark cloud hung suspended, like a purple balloon poised on the tip of a knife.

"Was it fun," I said, "with Massimo?"

"Perfectly charming," snapped Stella.

"I knew that Venice would agree with you."

"You were right. I utterly adore it."

The bell in the bell-tower rang eight o'clock. We returned to the Piazza. Tony and Melanie were waiting for us in front of Lavena's.

"You're beautifully punctual," said Tony.

"Thanks," I said. "We timed it perfectly."

"You looked flushed. Have you had a fight?"

"It's the sun. One has to get used to it."

We sat down and ordered our drinks. We both took *negrones*. The sky quickly darkened and the lights flashed on in the colonnades.

And for a moment, as I stared across at the Procuratoria Nuova, I was struck by that rich, almost nightmarish splendor. It wasn't merely the dusk that darkened that marvelous arena. It was history, it was mystery, it was infinity, it was love. The glow from the flood-light fell on the walls of the Campanile, which soared skyward, roseate in its lonely erectitude, while the endless ripple of arches all around it pulsated with a cavernous, seething femininity.

"Well," said Tony, turning to Stella, "you've been sightseeing busily?"

"*Mais naturellement,*" said Stella. "The mosaics. And those heavenly Tiepolos."

Tony gazed at her cunningly. "How is Paolo, incidentally?"

"Doing nicely. Staying with a friend up in Deauville for the weekend."

"He'll be coming to Venice?"

"It's unlikely," said Stella.

"Don't you miss him?" said Tony.

Stella glared. "Why should I miss him?"

Tony grinned and winked at Melanie. "Paolo's a dear. He really is. I'm devoted to little Paolo. Paolo has a beautiful, subtle mind."

"There's no need for being sarcastic, my dear boy," said Stella softly.

She bit crisply at an almond and stared fixedly across the Piazza. A sudden breeze swept in from the sea. There was a mumur of far-off thunder.

"Our life without Paolo would be just a little drearier," said Tony, "wouldn't it?"

"Would it really? I hadn't realized that you were so infatuated with Paolo."

"I find him spiritually irresistible. And physically devastating," said Tony.

"Come," purred Stella. "What would your dear friend Count Alberti say if he heard you?"

Tony's eyes grew suddenly sharp. "What do you know about Alberti?"

"Nothing at all, my little pet. But I can imagine him quite vividly. Tall. Lean. Aristocratic. Beautifully dressed. Terribly sensitive. Prefers Debussy to Beethoven. And 'Mon Rêve' to 'Moustache'. . . ."

There was a small, pungent silence. Tony's face had grown pale. He looked stonily at Stella. "What do you mean, may I inquire?"

"Nothing unusual," said Stella melodiously. "We all know that you're a bit of a gigolo."

Tony drew a deep breath. "Oh, I see," he said silkily. "That's rather a compliment, I take it. Coming from an old *cocotte* like you."

Stella's eyes were quite expressionless. She gazed placidly at Tony. Then she reached over the table and slapped him viciously on the cheek.

"Come," she said. "Let's go, Henry." She took her bag and rose languidly. "It's rather stifling here in the Piazza. Pay the bill, won't you, sweet?"

11

We left Venice the following morning and followed the road toward Vicenza. The first gold of autumn shone in the fields beyond Mestre.

"What a relief," declared Stella. "It's an evil, degenerate city."

"You didn't see it quite at its best, I'm afraid," I said bleakly.

"I shall never speak to that swine again," she announced, "as long as I live."

"An excellent idea," I said softly. "He's a cold-blooded rascal."

The road twisted through Padua and entered a smooth rolling country, aromatic with vineyards and studded with iron-dark cypresses. Here and there rose a weather-streaked Palladian villa, with a headless Bacchus or a crumbling Pomona lurking among the bushes. The sheen of an oncoming storm still hung in the air. A greenish light played over the orchards, the stables, the pastures.

"Well, at least you saw the mosaics."

"And those ravishing Tiepolos."

"And you rode in a gondola."

"Yes," said Stella. "I rode in a gondola."

A gust of wind blew over the fields. Stella's hair danced like a pennant. I felt a strand of it whipping against my cheek, soft as thistledown.

I glanced at her wind-burned face in the mirror: her lips moved uneasily and a shiny tear rolled down her chin.

X

WE DROVE WESTWARD through the dead, dusty towns of the Veneto, with their seedy old palaces and fly-ridden streets; with their wine-shops and taverns tucked in the gloom like snails in a shell; and with their column-lined piazzas where old hags crouched in the shade, haggling behind pyramids of onions and *zucchini*. Here and there a dandified lieutenant or a spruce young black-shirt strutted by: and the townsmen sat at their tables with glazed, vacant eyes. The surface of things was touched with a feverish air of vitality. Bells rang: horns blew: voices screamed: dishes clattered. But beneath all this clamor lurked a deep inner stillness, not so much of decay as of a stale, ugly boredom.

We followed the shores of Lake Garda out to the Sirmione peninsula. A sultry heat hung over the water, which lay sleek and unruffled. Some tawny boys were splashing about in the slime-stippled shallows and further out, in a pea-green boat, two old graybeards were fishing for trout.

We stopped at the Hotel Catullo, left our bags with the *portiere* and strolled into the vine-covered pergola for lunch.

"Catullus. Was he an emperor?"

"No, a poet, I think, dear."

"How perfectly charming," said Stella.

"He was in love with a girl named Lesbia."

"Really?" said Stella, raising her brows. "Poor Catullus. I feel sorry for him."

"She must have been rather fascinating, judging from the poems," I said.

"It must be shattering for a poet to be in love with a Lesbian."

"I'm not sure," I said mildly, "that this particular Lesbia was a Lesbian."

"Don't be prudish, please, dear. That's what made her so fascinating. Poor Catullus was never sure of her. She baffled him. She eluded him."

They brought us some melons with slices of prosciutto, and after this came a rosy-flaked trout from the lake. We had a bottle of *soave* and plucked at the marvelous little grapes, whose frail, dusky skin was dappled with tiny beads of sweat.

We felt lazy and mellow. Stella puffed at her cigarette.

"It's such a change, isn't it dear? After that decadence in Venice?"

I nodded sedately. "Yes. You're right. It certainly is."

"We shouldn't have gone there in the first place. But I knew you were dying to see it."

I drained my little wine-glass. "Yes. Quite. It was very thoughtful of you."

She peered at me through her lashes: that sapphire-blue

gaze, with its sly, secret innocence and its delicate, solemn
mockery. It was those eyes, those incredible eyes, which
were the core of her power. They transformed her from
an affected and petulant trollope into a wayward, touching, enigmatical sprite. Everything she said grew ambiguous, everything she did grew suggestive under the
spell of those luminous, tantalizing jewels.

We stepped out on the terrace. Two young oarsmen
started to wave at us.

"Go for a boat-ride, signora? Over to Garda? Or
Dezenzano?"

They sat on the edge of the pier with their naked feet
dangling in the water. One was dark and the other blond:
powerfully built, like young blacksmiths, with their dark,
hairy flesh showing through their wet clinging jerseys. The
dark one had his arm cast over the blond one's shoulder.
They grinned wickedly at Stella. "How about it, signora?"

"Come," said Stella. "Just for an hour, shall we, dear?
I'd adore it."

We stepped down into the boat and the blond young
oarsman jumped after us. A swampy smell oozed up from
the water. *"Ciao,* Tullio!" shouted our oarsman. *"Ciao,*
Mario!" shouted his friend. We moved out and skirted
the shadowy point of the promontory and then headed for
the rose-tinted shore by Dezenzano.

A dusky veil hung over the northern stretch of the lake
and a curious light filtered through it, like the light under
water. Nothing stirred. We went gliding over a sheet of
green satin. I could see the fish stirring idly when I leaned
over the gunwale. Here and there a small minnow sprang
out after a gnat.

The young oarsman sat facing us. A yellow lock hung

over his forehead. I caught the musk of his bull-like torso as he tugged at the oars. His leathery feet were heavily calloused, like an animal's. Stella's gaze rested casually on his thick, bulging thighs.

A sudden breeze shot out of the east; the water grew ruffled. Three blackbirds flew past, calling down at us ominously.

The air cooled abruptly. I caught the smell of acacia. Then the light dimmed uncannily. It turned to a sharp, acrid brown. We could see the storm moving swiftly across the water from San Vigilio. A streak of lightning cracked the horizon and a moment later came the thunder—so low, so stupendous that it seemed scarcely audible: it was more like some vast and annihilating silence.

We could see the rain galloping toward us in a great milky curtain. Then it struck. Everything vanished. We saw nothing but water. Our faces and bodies were streaked with cascades. Even the lightning and thunder were dimmed by the downpour. Mario tugged at the oars and we headed back for Sirmione, digging miserably through the ponderous zinc-smelling torrent.

A pool of dirty water started to lap at our ankles. Little by little the squat, decrepit boat was filling up. The fuller it grew the more dangerously it swayed: tongues of water swept over the seat. Mario spat, cursed, panted. We were lost in the flood. He kept rowing but the boat zigzagged aimlessly in the storm. It sank deeper and deeper. Suddenly I felt it lean sideways. I clutched desperately at Stella and a moment later it slid from under us.

At that moment the rain let up. I could see the shore creep out of the mist. Mario was floundering close behind us, shouting pitifully *"Aiuto!"*

"Don't be an ass, dear," gasped Stella. She struggled away from my grip. "I'll head for the shore. Try to rescue that drowning idiot."

Mario was gulping and screaming. I grasped his chin under the crook of my elbow and laboriously dug my way toward the Hotel Catullo, which suddenly loomed through the drizzle only a stone's throw away. Three minutes later I dragged him out on the slimy green pier, where young Tullio stood flinging his arms toward the heavens.

2

"Well," said Stella when we entered our room, "you were an absolute hero!" She smiled gayly and pressed a quick clammy kiss on my cheek.

Little pools were beginning to gather on the floor around our feet. Stella ripped off her dress, then her shoes and her underwear. She ran naked into the bathroom and turned on the water.

"Hurry up, sweet. Don't stand there. Take off those horrible things."

I tossed my clothes into a corner and followed her sheepishly into the bathroom.

She was leaning over the sink, wringing her tangled black hair. I stood motionless for a moment: I stared at her long golden legs, at her lean, childlike buttocks and her dangling little breasts. Her face was hidden under a cataract of hair.

She turned briskly and glanced at the tub. "Heavens,

Henry! It's running over." She reached down and turned the spiggot. Then she glanced at me quaintly.

For a moment we stood there, face to face, totally naked. Suddenly Stella started to laugh. "Darling! Really! I'd never thought it of you!"

I blushed, reached for a towel and flung it around my waist.

"Bless you, dear, it's nothing to be ashamed of," said Stella maternally.

"You seem to find it very amusing," I muttered, "at any rate."

"Well, you know, it just occurred to me. I've never seen you in the nude."

"Apparently not," I said grimly. I glared angrily at the wash-basin.

"Darling," she said, "don't be *gauche*. I don't mind in the least, really. And do take off that ridiculous towel. We're not children, after all."

She looked beautifully relaxed, one hand resting on her hip and the other poised thoughtfully on the nape of her neck. My jaw shook; my eyes watered. She smiled at me slyly. I dropped my towel on the tiles and folded her gently in my arms.

3

I could hear the rain pattering on the roof, crisp and sharp, like castanets. Now and again a flash of lightning shot through the pale moiré curtains, scattering a sulphurous web of brightness over the sheets and turning Stella's flesh to a cold, rippled mercury.

"Darling," she whispered, "I didn't dream. . . ."

I kissed her on the forehead. "Yes? What?"

She sighed drowsily. "That you were so virile."

"Was I virile?"

"Shockingly, dear."

"Well," I said, "it's easy to be virile with someone so dazzling."

She smiled wistfully. "I wish I were, dear. But I'm not. I know I'm not." She gazed thoughtfully at the ceiling, where a brass candelabra hung suspended from a garland of plaster roses. "Oh, I'm pretty enough, I suppose. Prettier than most. I can't complain. But I've always had a dream. To be the loveliest thing in the world. To be absolutely devastating. To sweep princes out of their thrones."

"You do. Nearly."

"But not quite. That's the point. Just not quite. You know, Henry, I used to think I was hideously ugly. That day I called on Aunt Ursula, for instance. I burst into tears after I left. I felt so utterly dreary. It took me years to get over it."

"Well, as long as you're over it."

"But something else is beginning to haunt me."

"Yes? What?"

"Growing old. Growing dreary and droopy. Watching the creases come to my neck. Watching the bloom go from my skin. It's much easier for men, you know. It doesn't matter if they lose their looks so long as they're potent and, well, amusing."

"I wonder," I said.

"But it's different with women. Life is a tragedy for a beautiful woman. She blossoms for a year, or two, or three. And then she waits for the terrible moment. . . ."

"What moment?"

"That's the tragedy of it. It isn't merely a moment. It's a desperate succession of hideous little moments. She sits in front of her mirror day after day and watches it happen. The lustre fading. The freshness withering. The gloss and the glitter wilting away. And nothing coming to take its place. No peace. No wisdom. Nothing at all. To be finally undesired, dear: that's the last, unbearable horror."

The rain finally stopped. A few last drops still trickled melodiously. A ray of sunlight shot through the curtains and lit on Stella's abdomen, where it shone like a quivering golden girdle.

I leaned over and pressed my face between her cool little breasts. I could feel the throbbing of her heart—strangely abrupt and irregular, as though it might suddenly come to a halt. She ran her hands over my head: gently, soothingly, impersonally. And I felt at that moment that she wasn't Stella at all; that she was someone I'd never known, some exquisite stranger; and at the same time, paradoxically, someone I'd known through all eternity, some inherited image that I had slept with as long as I could remember.

I raised my head and looked down at her. The ray of sunlight had shifted. It lay cast over her thighs like a thin, fiery arrow. Her pubic hair shone like a tuft of incandescent wires. I leaned down and kissed that magical, tender little furrow, which had haunted my mind ever since that moment in San Pedro, that dark, dusty moment when I first saw her nakedness. I placed my hands under her knees and lifted them slowly. I opened her body like a fan. She closed her eyes and smiled lazily.

Ever so gently, imperceptibly almost, I finally entered her. It was like gliding after a storm into a smooth, sunlit harbor. It was like entering an oasis after the sickening glare of the desert. It was like diving from a rock into the cool, crystal sea. I slid deeper and deeper, savoring the poignance of relief. I moved hither and thither, probing new, hidden crannies. And gradually, with all the zest of a violinist with his Stradivarius, gathering an unsuspected sweetness as he moves his bow across the strings, I headed for the climax: I gripped at her shoulders: and I buried my face in the pit of her neck.

4

There are three kinds of happiness. There is the exultation of the strong young animal: the raw delight of the tingling flesh; the sting of the wind and the sea and the sun: the taste of grapes crushed on the palate or the smell of woods on an autumn morning. There is the happiness of relief: the peace that comes after suffering, the serenity after chaos, the reassurance of twilight. And there is the happiness of revelation: the thrill of wonder and insight in the presence of human achievement or natural splendor.

I felt all three of them that night as I walked on the rain-soaked shore, watching the moon creeping out from the mottled clouds over Garda. And this triple happiness —this fleshly elation, this deep relief, this moral harmony —was additionally sharpened by my awareness of its random, ephemeral quality. I knew it could never last. I knew it was only an accident. I knew that the moment it ceased it would be like some horrible amputation.

"Look at the moon!" said Stella, pointing. "I'd love to live there for a while. In those marvelous silver pools and cool, glassy catacombs. . . ."

A pearly mist rose over the lake. The shores of Garda disappeared. It was like standing on some desolate little isle in the Hebrides. Nothing stirred. Suddenly a fish jumped out of the water. I could see its body for just an instant, arched like a crescent, scaled with platinum.

5

We drove through Brescia and Milan and spent the night in Turin. We crossed the Alps the following morning. Suddenly we were back in the fields of France.

The change in the atmosphere was subtle but uncannily sharp and pervasive. No more slogans on the walls; no more emblems or uniforms. No more piazzas, no more fountains, no more arias or gesticulations. We were back in the shires of lucidity and reason. Even the plough-boys had a dry, caustic look on their faces.

We lunched on a chicken and sauterne under the pines on the edge of a cliff. Far below us a torrent coiled through the rocks like an adder.

"You look sad, dear."

"Do I really?"

"Are you sad?"

"I'm ridiculously happy."

"I just wonder. A penny for your thoughts!"

"I was thinking about Venice."

"Oh, really? What in Venice?"

"Those lovely murals in the Rezzonico."

"You weren't in the least."

"Maybe I wasn't."

"You were thinking about me, weren't you? Trying to figure me out. Trying to probe into my soul. Trying to pin me down, like a butterfly."

"Was I really? Maybe I was."

"But you'll never succeed."

"Maybe not."

"And I'll tell you why, *mon petit bébé*. You live in a world of your own, like a bird on top of a tree."

"You really think so?"

"I know so. You stare at life from a distance. You never get entangled. You're never caught in the hurly-burly."

We watched an ox-cart rumbling past, loaded with freshly cut logs. I caught the sweet juicy smell of the raw mountain timber. On top of the pine-logs sat a girl in a gentian-blue dress. She smiled at us shyly and tossed us a strawberry.

"Tell me, Henry," said Stella softly. "Have you ever slept with a man?"

I was startled, a bit. "Do you mean. . . ."

"Don't be an ass, dear. You know what I mean."

"Yes. Twice. Three times, maybe."

"I thought so. Was it amusing?"

"Not amusing exactly."

"Did you enjoy it, I mean?"

"Not conspicuously, as I recall."

"Well, then why did you do it?"

"*Faute de mieux,* I suppose."

"Don't be absurd. There's always a girl."

"I was frightened of girls."

"You've certainly changed, haven't you, my pigeon?"

"Not much. I'm still afraid of you."

"Oh, Henry, for God's sake, come off it." She peered scornfully through her long black lashes. "Afraid of me. Do you think I'll bite you?"

"Well, not bite me, precisely."

"You're frightened of life, that's your trouble. You're afraid of getting involved. You recoil from relationships."

I sighed. "I wish I did."

"Oh?" said Stella inquisitively. "Don't tell me you've slept with that faded old countess?"

"Of course I have."

"And that dreary Maggy?"

"Naturally," I said.

"And Boris, I suppose?"

"Well, why not?"

"Bless you, dear. At least you're frank about it. It's rather refreshing, for a change."

She threw a crust over the edge of the cliff: a tiny bird shot down from a bough, caught it deftly in mid-air, then swung back into the foliage.

Stella stared at me accusingly. "You have no morals, I'm beginning to realize. I used to think you were an idealist. But you're a lecherous, ruthless cynic." Her pupils narrowed; her lips trembled. Her voice grew ominously gentle: "You thought you'd fooled me, didn't you, dear? Well, thank God, I know better. You play your quaint little role of being an absent-minded poet. But under it all you're just a scheming, degenerate scoundrel."

I watched the smoke from my cigarette spiraling up through the shrubbery. "Yes," I said. "I'm a scoundrel. You're right. You're perfectly right."

6

We reached Cannes after sunset. Dusk was filtering through the avenues, spreading the smell of acacia and fresh, steaming asphalt.

We found Paolo in the bar of the Carlton. He was heavily sun-tanned and unusually cheerful. He was wearing a dark blue blazer with the Trinity College insignia. A magnum of Veuve Clicquot stood on the table beside him.

He kissed Stella on both cheeks. "You look dazzling, my dove. What will you have? Let's be lavish. Champagne and caviar? I have marvelous news for you."

"Yes?" said Stella, with an arrowing look.

"I've been left some money by my Uncle Pino. Rather a lot, in point of fact. He owned some mines in Venezuela."

"Oh," said Stella. "How perfectly heavenly."

"And I've bought a villa in Saint-Etienne. You'll like it, I think. A lovely pool and a beautiful tennis-court. Two cooks, five gardeners and thirteen maids."

"Darling, you're mad," said Stella thinly.

"Not in the least." He smiled triumphantly. "And I bought a Rolls yesterday morning. I'll be looking at some yachts later in the week."

"Paolo, my pet, you're insane."

"Look," said Paolo. "See what I've brought you." He reached into his pocket and drew out a box. He flipped it open: a magnificent bracelet, studded with diamonds as large as hazelnuts.

"Angel," cried Stella. "It's perfectly criminal of you."

"It's only a bagatelle," purred Paolo. "I can buy you a hundred more with those beautiful mines of my Uncle Pino's."

A bowl of caviar was brought to the table. Stella was blushing with delight. But as I watched her I saw a curious malaise creep over her face. The champagne glass shook in her hand. Her eyes grew bright with a hint of panic.

"Shall we go?" said Paolo presently. "I'm dying to show you our new château."

Stella glanced at me furtively. "Yes. Let's look at the new château."

We crossed the terrace and stepped into the canary-hued Rolls. Dusk was seeping like wood-smoke over the crowded Croisette. A few last bathers were gathering their towels on the pock-marked beach and orange lights were beginning to twinkle from the row of cafés. Down by the Casino the palms were aglow; music swam through the gilded lattices. The crowd was drifting along the esplanade like a horde of somnambulists.

"Wouldn't it be tiresome," said Stella, "if there were a war all of a sudden?"

"There won't be a war," said Paolo placidly. "It's all just hysterical chatter."

"Still," said Stella, "what if there were?"

"We'll sail to Tahiti," said Paolo.

We followed the coast by La Napoule along the road to Saint-Raphael. The air was sweet with midsummer. There was a smell of oleander, which mixed with the tang from the sea and the indefinable fragrance of holiday—the stench of petrol and tar, the odor of beach-fires and sun-oil. Night fell. The sound of dance-music hung over the seaside—cheap little radios down on the beach, cheap little gramophones in the bistros.

The road entered a pine wood soon after Théoule. All was dark and secluded. We could hear the sea playing in the inlets. We slowed down and entered an enormous castiron gate. On a white marble slab were chiseled the words: "Villa Flora."

7

It was an old decaying palace, rather in the style of Sans Souci, with gesturing statues and rusty fountains and symmetrical alleys of shrubbery. Overlooking the sea was a peach-colored gazebo, all entwined with wistaria and bougainvillea. A whiff of camphor still lingered in the dusty salons, which were filled with Empire consoles and Louis Quinze mirrors.

The day after we arrived, which was the eleventh of August, a battalion of workmen appeared: painters, plumbers, upholsterers. An ornithologist arrived from Nice with some tropical birds for the aviary. In less than ten days the whole place was transmogrified. The yellowing tubs in the bathrooms gave way to black marble pools, with dolphin-shaped spiggots and cupid-shaped lamps.

Thick Savonnerie rugs were laid over the bare *terrazza* floors. Great leather divans replaced the needlepoint bergères and the Fragonard prints gave way to Braques and Bérards.

"I can't help wondering," said Stella thoughtfully. "Is it really worth it all, dear?"

"Of course, my love," said Paolo amiably. "It's so much roomier than the Quai d'Orsay. We'll stay on till mid-October. Then we'll head for the Balearics. . . ."

For three weeks we lived in a state of almost lunatic largesse. We drove to Cagnes-sur-Mer and ate langouste with truffles. We played baccarat in Cannes and chemin-de-fer in Monte Carlo. We dined with princes on their yachts and maharajahs in their villas. Parcels arrived every day from Chanel and Cartier and cases of rare, costly vintages were installed in the cellars. Paolo developed a sudden interest in unusual first editions: he bought a magnificent set of Proust and a charmingly inscribed *Alice in Wonderland*. And for Stella he bought a spectacular set of Fabergé Easter eggs—of carnelian and lapis lazuli, dappled with emeralds and rubies.

Within three or four days he had surrounded himself with a kind of court—a bevy of waifs who lolled by the pool and devoured his *pâté de foie gras*. There was Cynthia, the English surrealist, and there was Geza, the Hungarian dancer. There was Trygve, the Norwegian baritone and there was Tita, the Portuguese poetess. Paolo had gathered them up from the *louche* little bars on the Rue d'Antibes; and he watched with joy and animation as Geza danced on the grassy lawn or Cynthia worked on a new *collage* of tattered burlap and orange peel.

He bought us all a set of rather lurid holiday costumes.

We went strutting about the beach in shorts of fish-net
or leopard-skin. Stella wore slacks of Burmese silk and
shirts of indigo from Hyderabad, and I wore sandals of
tooled morocco and a little vest of dyed chamois. Cynthia
appeared in a pair of sailor pants and Trygve in an
African burnous. Geza sprinkled his hair with gold-leaf
and draped a sari around his waist, while Tita dressed
herself like a nun, with a bird-of-paradise on top of her
head. People laid down their forks when we waltzed
into a restaurant in Juan-les-Pins, with our rainbow-colored absurdities and Paolo's new pair of Afghans, whom
he called Petrouchka and Scheherazade, and who wore
collars studded with amethysts.

I said to Stella on the beach one day: "Well, your
dreams have come true. A wealthy prince. Pearls and diamonds. A sumptuous villa on the Riviera."

"Oh, it's just a mirage. It will crumble to bits," she
said.

"There's no reason why it should."

"Yes, there is," said Stella, pouting.

"He's in love with you," I said. "You hold him in the
palm of your hand."

"I suppose I do. But it's all so silly. So meaningless. So
boring. . . ."

Now and again, at odd moments, I felt a flicker of sudden hope. Stella would smile at me slyly, or press my
hand under the table. But after our arrival in the Villa
Flora she took pains not to be alone with me. I felt sick
with desire as I watched her lying beside the pool, spreading oil on her thighs or feeding bon-bons to Petrouchka.
Gradually the episode in Garda grew painfully unreal,

like a trick of fantasy, and I sank into a torpor of sullen frustration.

Oh, those indolent, golden days! Even the sea basked in its languor, spreading its shiny blue arms under the late August sun. Those dazzling mornings out on the boat, watching the sails on the horizon, listening to Geza's mandolin, singing songs, sipping Cassis; those afternoons on the shore, watching the bathers among the pines, sinking my teeth into a peach and feeling the drops on my darkening skin; and those evenings up in the mountains, watching the farm-lights twinkling in the distance, smelling the wine and the garlic and listening to the hoof-beats on the road!

It all seems infinitely long ago. It is all a part of a vanished world. It is touched with the peacock brilliance, the ache and the emptiness of a chimera.

8

We used to sit and play games over our demi-tasses in the sunlight. We played Fruits, Flowers, Beasts, Historical Figures and Famous Paintings.

"What is Paolo, do you think?"

"A squirrel!"

"And Geza?"

"A flamingo, naturally."

"And Cynthia?"

"A bull, perhaps?"

"And what about Henry?"

"Oh. A chameleon."

Tita was a vibrant little woman with deep liquid eyes whose whites were tinged with blue and whose lids were sprinkled with silver. She walked about in the garden with an angular, Gothic air, plucking the petals from the Gloires de Dijon and turning the pages of her T.S. Eliot. Cynthia was large and heavily loined, with violent, rapacious eyes; she spoke in powerful ringing tones and wore her hair slicked back like a bathing-cap. Trygve was pink, shy and pudgy, with a cold Viking gaze, which looked rather incongruous in that baby-like face. And as for Geza, there was something tropical about his shape and demeanor: the red bandana wound tightly around his squirming buttocks like a snake-skin, the honeyed ringlets, the tinkling earrings, the painted toe-nails and the rich mascara, which gave him the air of some warrior from Dahomey, or maybe a bridesmaid from the hills of Bechuanaland.

In that Mediterranean light everything shone with a topaz brilliance. The water was so clear that when Stella dropped her comb from the raft one morning, it lay shining far below, as clearly as under a microscope, and we laughed with delight when Geza dove and fished it out again.

A bowl of figs, a frond of seaweed, the glitter of a rock washed by the sea—it was light, nothing but light that was the essence of things. Not texture, not solidity, not even the pulse of life itself. The world looked frail and inflammable under this cataract of light. It was exhilarating but numbing; it was like a bath of champagne.

And so, for a week or maybe a fortnight, it was all very pleasant. The monotonous chatter of the parakeets, the scent of lavender in the bedrooms, the mistral rattling

the plum-blue shutters, the shade of myrtles and tamarisks, the air drugged with brightness, the drowsiness, the
sensuality: it was all, for a little while, wonderfully sooth-
ing and luxurious.

But something, of course, was wrong. The air grew
tedious, oppressive. Even the house seemed to smoulder
under the falsification it had suffered. The stink of glue
clung to the library. The toilets refused to flush. There
were strange noises in the plaster beams and bulbous
cracks appeared in the ceiling.

And Stella, too, was growing restless. Her mouth had a
sullen twist to it and the light in her eyes was sharp and
tense, like a caged cheetah's.

9

And then it happened, at last. Cynthia strode into my
room one morning and announced in her low harsh
voice: "They've marched into Poland, the lousy bastards!"

"Good God. Have they really?"

"You know what it means, duckie, don't you?"

"I can't believe it."

"It's true."

"What will we do?"

"Does it matter?"

The rest of the morning was spent in panic. I sat glued
to the radio, listening to the latest reports from London
and Paris. Stella retired to her room with Petrouchka and
Scheherazade. She had lapsed into a strange, sloe-eyed
silence the past few days. Cynthia and Tita sat in the

gazebo, getting drunk on gin fizzes. Geza crouched by the phone, chatting hysterically with his friends in Cannes, and Trygve sat at the piano, singing arias by Puccini. Only Paolo displayed any semblance of lucidity. He sat poring over the map and then briskly announced:

"Well, I've made up my mind. We're heading for Spain tomorrow morning."

"Mercy," said Geza. "They've just finished a nasty war down there, haven't they?"

"Quite," said Paolo. "They'll be careful not to get involved in a new one."

We had lunch beside the pool. A table was set under the pergola, loaded with caviar, smoked salmon, cold lobster and chilled peaches.

"How delightful," said Tita. "Clean, cold and astringent."

"It's only a snack," said Paolo apologetically. "We'll have to be Spartans from now on."

As we sat by the pool the light seemed uncannily brilliant. Love had sharpened my sense of smell, my feeling of color, my taste, my hearing. The lobster was strangely delicious, the bougainvillea burned like a torch, and the sound of the waves was like a delicate march by Couperin. I still can see it all with the ominous exactitude of a prophecy—the blue tiles of the pool fluttering like wings under the rippled water; Tita with her harlequin sunglasses, looking rather like an insect; Cynthia mixing a cocktail, hair dripping untidily; Trygve pink as a newborn baby, Geza gleaming with almond oil, Paolo kneeling by the edge of the pool with a champagne glass in his hand, and my beautiful Stella casting her glitter over the scene, transforming it into a mythological allegory. Sometimes she looked like a butterfly, with her arms spread akimbo and the great red towel cast over her shoulders; or maybe a water-moccasin, as she slid through the water with diamonds of light dancing over her skin; or even a tigress, lying motionless under the bamboo pergola, with broad stripes of gold floating across her limber body.

After lunch Paolo and I drove to Cannes to arrange the visas. The roads were seething with traffic. The Great Holiday was disintegrating. The Brazilian playboys, the Austrian prostitutes, the Belgian merchants, the Siamese princes, all were racing along the highways to Grasse and Marseilles. Groups of gossiping, wide-eyed villagers stood clustered under the plane-trees. Men were smearing dark paint over the street-lamps and window-panes. Queues were gathering in front of the grocer's, the confectioner's, the butcher-shops. And when we finally arrived in Cannes a column of sad-eyed Moroccans, drab and dusty and sweating, came shuffling past the Casino.

"Well," said Tita that night at dinner, "the Moment of Truth has arrived."

"I don't believe it," said Geza. "It will all be over in a month."

"You'll see," said Tita sepulchrally. "It's the End of an Era, my pet. The Angel of Death is on the wing. The Powers of Darkness are descending!"

"And none too soon," said Cynthia, belching. "It will put a stop to all this frou-frou. All this decadent *blanc-mange*. It will bring us back to fundamentals."

"It's like the Fall of Rome," said Trygve, glaring fiercely at Petrouchka. "The Huns and Vandals are on their way. The West is crumbling like a rotten pineapple."

"Still," said Paolo, somewhat wistfully, glancing at his new pistachio draperies: "it's rather a pity, don't you think? We've all been happy, in our little way. . . ."

10

We rose at dawn the following morning, Paolo and Stella and I. We said good-bye to the drowsy servants and the two silky Afghans, loaded the Rolls with hampers of cheese, fruit, coffee and chocolate, and set off through the morning mist on the road to Fréjus. We raced through the pink, gleaming villages that lay basking beyond Hyères—Sanary-sur-Mer and Bandol, La Ciotat and Cassis. We had lunch in Marseilles on a vast steaming *bouillabaisse* and then headed for the wild, windy swamps of the Camargue. We passed Miramas and Arles, Montpellier and Béziers. We bribed the attendant with a five-pound note for a tankful of petrol in Narbonne. We followed the rock-littered coast through La Nouvelle and Leucate; the scenery began to shimmer with a tense, arid beauty. The light lay poised on the lime-trees and biscuit-hued beaches with a kind of desolate transparency, as though aware of the impending darkness. The blue of the sea, marbled with white, looked alien and dangerous. And the far-off hills, the gathering ranges of the dusk-fingered Pyrenees, looked terribly empty and old. The sheen of death hung about them.

XI

Barcelona was a vast and nightmarish city: a dirty and desecrated, scrounging metropolis. Even the buildings were touched with a rat-like grimace. Even the trees had a spiderish look about them.

It was nearly midnight when we arrived. We found some rooms just off the Rambla in a dingy little inn called the Catalonia Palace. We walked for a while along the streets, looking for a clean cheerful restaurant. Finally we found one in a cellar, not lavish but amiable, with white-stuccoed walls and Arabian carpets.

We had some dry Amontillado and ordered a big *paella*. They brought us a plateful of shrimps: fleshy, odorous little creatures.

"Well," said Paolo, "it's rather a relief to get away from it all."

Stella stared at him icily. "Away from what, darling?"

"From the Riviera," said Paolo. "With all that luxury and chi-chi."

"Luxury! Chi-chi! Don't be grotesque, dear. You're the one that kept looking for them."

"What do you mean?" said Paolo, wide-eyed.

"That horrible Cynthia with her crazy paintings! That pretentious Tita! That pudgy Trygve! That ridiculous Geza with his swishy dances!"

"They were rather sweet, I thought," said Paolo.

"They were sickening," said Stella.

The *paella* was brought to the table with a bottle of white wine from Malaga. We sat silently for a while, listening to a boy with a guitar. I saw that Stella's hands were trembling as she raised the glass to her lips. Her eyes were unusually bright; she was drinking more than usual.

She turned brusquely to Paolo. "Well, I've finally decided what's wrong with you."

"Yes? What?"

"You're a dilettante. Just a pampered little dilettante."

"Do you really think so?" said Paolo, rather woebegone. "Perhaps I am."

"You skate around on the edge of life! You never get below the surface! You dabble about with your Malayan butterflies and your Portuguese Lesbians! Just a collector, that's all you are! With art, with people, even with love! You think that money can buy everything! Well, you're wrong, my pet! You're wrong!" Her face looked haggard all of a sudden. The veins were throbbing in her temples. "Good God," she cried, "I keep looking for people and all I find are simpering parodies! I keep looking for genuine love! All I find is a box from Cartier's! What's wrong with the world? What's wrong with us all?"

Paolo's face grew wrinkled with worry. He stared

mournfully at Stella. "Hush, my pet," he said softly. "You're tired, that's all. The war and everything. . . ."

"War!" said Stella with a feverish air. "Don't make me laugh! What we need is a real catastrophe! Something to sweep away the sham and the lies and corruption! That's all it is! Just a substitute! We're not alive, that's the trouble! We go through our meaningless little gestures, we gossip and drink and lie in the sun, and when it's over we go to bed and we're another day closer to death! It's frightening! It's utterly horrifying! I'd rather live in the wilds of Borneo!"

"Well," said Paolo, with a mousy look, "I'll go to Cook's first thing in the morning. Maybe there's a boat leaving for Borneo. One of those new Italian liners. . . ."

2

The following morning Paolo rushed into my room in his mauve pyjamas, flourishing a slip of blue paper with a wild, blurred expression.

"Look," he gasped. "Look, Henry!"

I glanced at the note:

"Dearest P:
Forgive me, darling. I can't bear it any longer. Try to forget me. Life is short.
Love and kisses.
Your S."

"Odd," I said, "Where do you think. . . ."

"I phoned the concierge," said Paolo miserably. "She

left at four o'clock in the morning and took a cab to the station."

"Poor Stella," I muttered.

"She was out of her mind," said Paolo brokenly.

"She was drunk, just a bit, I fear."

"She was desperate, the little creature!"

We dressed quickly and drove to the station. There had been two trains earlier in the morning: one for Cadiz at half past six and one for Bilbao at seven-twenty. We checked assiduously with all the porters. Finally we found one who said, with a leer:

"Yes, señor. There was a young lady with a white leather bag. An American, I think. Very elegant. Very sun-tanned. She left for Seville."

3

We decided to follow the coast. We took the road through Tarragona and then south through the interminable orange groves by Nules and Sagunto. The land looked empty and lacerated. No smiles, no music, no young men. Only the old grief-stricken women and the scrawny young girls. And, of course, the hawk-nosed guards with their three-cornered hats and their air of suspicious, impenetrable hauteur. There were shattered churches and ruined nunneries on the way to Vendrell. The road lay ripped by Tortosa and the bridges were torn across the Ebro.

It was almost three when we reached Valencia. We had a quick, greasy lunch. Then we asked about the routes. It was shorter inland through Albacete. But the road, they argued, was in ruins; it was dangerous to start before morning. So we headed south for Alicante and the barren mountains of Murcia. The sun was setting when we turned from the highway on the rock-strewn road to Orihuela.

A hard, thorny land. The barren light fled toward the west, leaving behind the gesturing shadows of broken walls and twisted olive-trees. A few scrawny goats were standing motionless along the roadside, peering up at us with their cynical sea-green eyes. The towns grew more desolate as we entered the hills. Alcantarilla, Librilla, Totana, Lorca: grim, foul-smelling hamlets that crouched in the dusk like a pack of wolves, with a naked lamp dangling in the middle of a parched little plaza and no sound except the hoarse, hysterical clanging of the church-bells.

"Tell me the truth, please, Henry," said Paolo out of the stillness.

"What about?"

"About Stella."

"What do you mean, about Stella?"

"I mean . . . well, I mean . . . Do you think that she really loves me?"

I said carefully: "I wish I knew."

"Just a little? At least?"

"I'm quite sure that she's fond of you."

After a while Paolo whispered: "Tell me. Does she sleep with other men?"

"I have no idea. None whatever."

"Have you slept with her, Henry?"

"Certainly not," I said firmly.

"Do you think that Tony has slept with her?"

"No," I said, after an ugly moment. "I don't think so. I really don't."

The smell of dew-sweetened olive groves drifted in through the window, mingling with the scent of cigarette smoke and rich, dyed pig-skin. The probing aura of the headlights fell on the fields of twisted shrubbery, transforming them into a frozen, winter-white landscape. Once we passed an old man riding along on a donkey, and a little later the swollen cadaver of a goat, and once a flock of moths came dancing across the road: they shone like a flurry of little snowflakes.

Paolo's eyes pierced the darkness of the Sierra de las Estancias.

"She's strange, you know, Henry. She's utterly unpredictable. God knows I've done everything I could to make her happy. I gave her diamonds and pearls. I gave her a Lancia. I gave her an Ingres. I gave her all she could possibly want. And she runs off to Seville."

"She's a little bit mad," I said, rather gloomily.

"Yes," said Paolo, shaking his head. "You must be right. She's a wee bit mad."

We passed a town which loomed in the night like an enormous blue beehive. It was nothing but a network of caves in the mountainside. We saw women squat by the flames, stirring black steaming cauldrons, and half-naked boys dancing desolately among the boulders. Velez Rubio this was. It was nearly ten. We were growing hungry. But there was something about the place which was faintly alarming and we crossed the Sangomera and drove on toward Granada.

The road was deserted. Not a sign of life anywhere. We followed the banks of the torrent, which boiled like lava in the glow of the headlamps. On our right rose the great arid cliffs of the Sierra de Maria. The road curved and dipped; there was a tug at the steering wheel. The car stumbled awkwardly and came to a shuddering halt.

Paolo sighed and stared into the night.

"Flat tire," he said softly.

We stepped out into the gloom, which grew rich and enveloping. The great precipice reared, casting its black spicy breath on us. I pulled the jack out of the tool-case and we crouched by the gleam of the flash-light. Paolo drew off the hub-cap and I tugged at the bolts. Finally the lacerated tire came reeling across the gravel.

At that moment a low, furry voice said: "Señor!"

I dropped the wrench and turned sharply. At first I saw no one. Then, lithe and symmetrical, like three fish in a pool, three dark bodies materialized in the star-littered stillness. They stood on the edge of the road, perfectly casual and serene. Their faces shone like ice in the glow from the headlamps. I smiled thinly and rose.

"Trouble," I said, pointing to the tire.

One of the three nodded blankly. The other two stood expressionless.

I pointed west with an offhand air. "Beza," I grunted imbecilically.

The second of the three bared his teeth in a fetid little smile.

I glanced meaningly at Paolo. "What do you think?" I said softly.

"Bandits. Naturally," said Paolo, with a wistful expression.

I reached into my coat and drew out a package of cigarettes and passed them politely to the three dark strangers. They helped themselves rather languidly. I lit them one by one. Then I lit one for Paolo and finally a fifth one for myself. There we stood, in the pit of the black Murcian wilderness, quietly puffing at our gold-tipped Abdullahs.

No one spoke. No one moved. Finally the cigarettes were finished. One of the men pulled out a pistol and motioned quietly to the others, who stepped up to the car, swung open the door, pulled out the bags, opened them neatly, and with a delicately fastidious air drew out our *crêpe de Chine* pyjamas, our eau-de-Cologne, our Cantonese sport shirts and our Milanese bedroom slippers. Then they opened Paolo's jewel case, with its diamond cuff-links and emerald shirt-studs. They slipped the contents into their pockets with cool gracious gestures. There was also a wad of bank-notes tucked in one of the folds. These they scrutinized carefully and slid under their belts. Finally they strode up to Paolo and held out their hands. Paolo fumbled among his pockets and took out his wallet. The young bandits fondled it gently with their black, calloused fingers. They opened it thoughtfully, peered calmly at the documents, and handed it back with a baronial flourish.

Then they bowed with a kind of quaint oriental ceremoniousness, wished us a soft *"Buenas noches"* and strolled off into the night.

"Well," said Paolo, "they were really quite charming, when you stop to think of it."

"They certainly were," I agreed. "How much money did they take?"

"Nothing to fret about," said Paolo. "Two or three thousand pounds."

I nodded wryly. "It could have been worse."

"Oh, infinitely worse," murmured Paolo.

4

We reached Granada at midnight and spent the night in the Washington Irving, in a vast, echoing suite covered with bright heraldic tiles. We headed for Seville the following morning, racing through the glare of Andalusia— the glittering gullies by Loja, the snow-white walls of Antequera, the blinding sands of La Roda and the dusty orchards of El Arahal.

The air was abnormally clear, not a cloud was in the sky. The earth was all puckered like the skin of an old peasant woman. Shaggy donkeys came clattering down the steep mountain paths, dragging carts filled with bundles of spiky gray brushwood. Near La Roda a country funeral came winding down the road: even the mourners looked like corpses, with their dusty lips and hollow eyes.

I grew more and more nervous. As I stared at that desolate landscape each detail took on a cryptic, vaguely minatory significance. The shadows under the olive trees looked like bottomless crevices, and the windows in a farmhouse were as black as a gaping coffin.

I did finally begin to see, in those dingy white walls strung like vertebrae under the olive-strewn hills or gaping like the teeth of a monster under the blaze of the sky—yes, I finally detected a certain tragic intensity: the tinge of death under the bravado, the blood in the brilliance, the dread in the song. And I felt, by a kind of contagion, this sense of latent fatality gradually seeping into my own temper, my own moods, even my relationships.

My feeling toward Paolo grew sullen and cynical; my longing for Stella grew morbid, hallucinatory.

As we finally approached Seville my suspense grew almost feverish. I saw a silhouette in the distance on top of a hill—was it Stella? A woman in black stepped out of a church: could it possibly be Stella? A large Daimler raced past with a dark young man sitting in the back, and for a crazy little moment I thought it was Stella. My wild and beautiful Stella, who was no longer a single being but had spread her dark essence until she was a part of every landscape, a street in every city, a window in every house.

We reached Seville at half-past two and drove to the Andalucia Palace.

"Precisely, sir," said the young receptionist, a blue-eyed Austrian in a threadbare morning coat. "There was a charming American lady. She left in the bus right after breakfast. For Algeciras, if I'm not mistaken. And on to Africa, presumably."

"Ah. Thank you," said Paolo in a thin, reedy tone.

"You're quite welcome, I assure you," said the blue-eyed receptionist.

It was dusk when we finally stepped on the ferry to Tangier. "Rather a pity," said Paolo mournfully, gazing eastward toward Gibraltar. "Three little days for all of Spain. It isn't enough, is it, really?"

"Well, not quite, I'm afraid. We missed the bullfights. And the Goyas."

"Still," he said, "it's been most edifying. We've seen life in the raw."

"Quite," I said. "I'll never forget it. That sombre elegance. Those impeccable manners."

Gradually the walls of Tarifa sank back in the twilight.

The rocks of Malabata rose from the eddies like a fist. And out of the south rose the smell of another continent—faintly rancid, acidulous, like the smell of a toad.

5

Stillness and darkness: that was the feeling I first had of Africa. There was plenty of noise—horns blowing, carts rattling, radios blaring—but it all seemed to well out of a bottomless pool of silence. There was plenty of light—fluorescent lamps all over the city—but the effect was that of a firefly in a great black desert.

Up in the *grand socco* there was the rustle of haggling voices and of naked feet padding softly across the square. There was the smell of dyed leather—that ubiquitous stench of Moroccan thoroughfares—and the musk of warm bodies, and the stink of fresh excrement. And under it all hung some sweet indefinable perfume—hashish, I suspected, or opium. Later I learned what it really was.

We walked on through a labyrinth of dimly illuminated alleys. Finally we reached the *petit socco*. I heard the twang of a zither.

"There they are," I said softly.

Paolo halted and caught his breath.

They were sitting around a green café table, just the three of them. A turbaned waiter was leaning over, pouring brandy into their glasses. A yellowish glow seeped through the blinds and striped their bodies with light. Their faces were in shadow. They were chatting away casually.

I walked quietly up to them. "Well, you look rather cozy."

"Lord, it's Henry!" cried Stella. "How perfectly thrilling! When did you get here?"

"An hour ago," I said coldly. "On the seven o'clock ferry."

"How utterly divine. Sit down, sweet, and have a drink with us, won't you?"

"I have a friend along, as it happens," I said in measured tones.

"Poor little Paolo, I presume."

"Yes. Exactly. Poor little Paolo."

"Tell him to join us," said Stella merrily. "I've been horribly rude to dear old Paolo."

"He'll be delighted with the invitation, I'm sure," I said cuttingly.

Tony smiled at me slyly as he held out his hands. "Just like old times," he purred. "I can hardly believe it."

There was something a bit unpleasant, I thought, about his manner. His thick, coiling hair was even longer than usual. The little curls on his chest peered through a silk turquoise shirt. He looked flashily handsome; hyacinthine, corrupt.

As for sad, elf-like Melanie, she looked strangely cadaverous. Her eyes glittered tensely; her cheeks were sallow and sunken. Little wisps of damp hair clung to her high, brooding forehead. She smiled at me mournfully and lowered her eyes.

Paolo stepped through the crowd and approached the table at that moment.

"Paolo darling!" cried Stella. "*Quelle joie! Quelle surprise!* I never dreamed you'd pop up in Tangier!"

Paolo's worn, gentle face melted into a smile of relief. "Nor did I. It's rather cozy, isn't it? Shall we have some champagne?"

6

A harrowing heat fell on the city. Not a cloud. Not a breeze. The leaden sea lay squirming below us, sleek as molasses. The blazing slopes of the Kasbah reared stiffly in the distance, etched with caves and smouldering faintly, like a sleeping volcano.

Flies swarmed through the alleys in a buzzing blue torrent. Yellowish cats and hairless dogs lay panting in the shade, black with fleas. The smell of sweat seeped through everything—the sheets, the towels, even the soap. It came welling out of the kitchens. I could taste it in the coffee.

We all stayed at the El Minza for three blistering days. On the morning of the fourth Paolo announced that he'd rented a villa and that same afternoon we moved in right after lunch. It was a rambling white-washed house on the southern outskirts of the town, shadowed by eucalyptus trees and overlooking the Atlantic. The rooms were small, dark and cool, with vaulted ceilings and cushioned windowsills. The scent of lime-trees filled the courtyard. It was called the Villa Zuleika.

A week passed innocently enough. We sat in the garden in the mornings: Paolo with his Maugham, Tony with his temperas, Stella with *Vogue*, and I with *The Idiot*. Melanie stayed in her room. She was reading Saint-Simon. We gathered for lunch on the terrace, gazing at the sail-

boats in the distance and eating a spicy *kous-kous* prepared by Iqbal, the Algerian cook. After lunch we fell
asleep. At four we played bridge. At six we turned on the
radio and embarked on our cocktails. At eight we had dinner and after dinner we sat on the terrace and stared over
the war-haunted, moon-crested sea.

Paolo was suffering, it seemed, from some nervous af-
fliction. His jaw twitched spasmodically. He was developing a stammer. And poor Melanie was turning into a regular little skeleton. She kept gazing at Tony with those
houri-like eyes, encircled with mauve, drenched in centuries of lamentation. Love, passion, desire—or whatever
the proper word for it might be—was gradually destroying
her physical health, just as it was gnawing at Paolo's
nerves, just as it was sapping my own character, and hacking away at Stella's loveliness.

One morning I was sitting in the garden, having breakfast with Paolo.

"Tell me, Henry," he said pleadingly. "Why did she
c-come to T-Tangier?"

"God knows. Curiosity, maybe. Africa always intrigued
her."

"Did she know that T-Tony was here?"

"I doubt it," I said. "They had a nasty little quarrel
back in Venice, I seem to remember."

Not a cloud in the sky. Not a ripple among the leaves.
The broken flagstones were sheathed with moss and
trimmed with marsh marigolds, and the weather-streaked
walls were overgrown with seedy clematis.

Through the iron-grilled gate I could see a flood of
white arum lilies and beyond loomed the rich, black shade
of the cedars. A scarab beetle was crawling along the edge

of the pool, which was half full of dirty, leaf-littered rain water.

"Maybe I've been a bit of a t-tyrant toward Stella," said Paolo humbly.

"I hadn't noticed it," I said, pouring the cream into my coffee.

"Maybe I bore her," said Paolo sadly. "I'm not an Apollo, unfortunately."

"I really wouldn't give it a second thought, my dear Paolo."

At that moment the door swung open and our butler Mohammed stepped out on the terrace. He was carrying two handbags, a yellow raincoat and a picnic basket. He was followed by Melanie, dressed in a faun-colored suit and a little green turban on top of her head.

She seemed on the verge of collapse. Her whole body was shaking violently. Her eyes were a burning red and her lips were curiously twisted.

"Paolo, forgive me. It's terribly rude of me, I'm afraid," she said brokenly. "I've suddenly been called back to Basel. It's a terrible pity, really, isn't it? The *Giuseppe Verdi* is sailing for Genoa at noon, as luck would have it . . ."

7

The days floated by with a kind of limpid unreality. The African light seemed to freeze each passing moment like a fly in amber. Nothing cohered; nothing signified. The past and the future seemed to evaporate. And even the war, like distant thunder, gradually sank into an aimless rumble.

After Melanie's departure a listless stillness fell on the house. No more arguments about Berg or Bartok, no more chatter about Klee or Kandinsky, no more squabbles about Mussolini, no more references to Proust. Even Paolo's new parrot, who used to chatter the whole day long, lowered his head, blinked his eyes, and refused to utter a word. Only at six o'clock in the evening, when Paolo turned on the radio, did the flurry of distant conflict briefly impinge on our lethargy.

Sometimes Tony and I climbed down the thorny path and swam from the rocks. Toward sunset, when the heat had drifted out over the sea, a peculiar brightness hung on the smooth crimson flanks of Cape Spartel. Every line was accentuated, every tint was intensified, and the boats of the Arab fishermen were engulfed in a giant flame.

I glanced at Tony as he lay beside me. The salty drops had dried on his skin, leaving tiny white rings, like infinitesimal coral islands.

"How long do you think you'll stay here?"

"As long as I can," he said lazily.

"Do you really think it's worth your while?"

"Oh, I see. You'd like me to leave?"

"It's none of my business, I'll admit."

"Are you brooding about Melanie?"

"Not only Melanie," I murmured.

He peered at me lazily with his sea-green eyes. "I can't help what happened to Melanie. And I can't help what's happening to Stella, or Paolo, or even you. Call me a rascal if you want. I can't help it. I'm an artist. I'm heading for something bigger and much more important than the rest of you. I'm going to paint things that will make the whole world take notice. Things that will make even Picasso look like a dull, dribbling amateur . . ."

I left Tony down by the water and climbed up the path. Stella was sitting under a palm tree, quietly sipping a gin-and-tonic and leafing through a copy of Rimbaud that I had given her.

"Where is Tony?"

"Down on the rocks. Taking a sun-bath," I said.

"Oh. That beautiful brown body. He's revoltingly vain, don't you think?"

"Yes. He is. I'm afraid."

"A narcissus. Madly in love with himself." She puffed nervously at her cigarette. "I can understand that poor Melanie. Wilting away in front of our eyes. Turning into a hysterical old woman."

"Stella," I said. "Are you happy?"

"Oh, really. What a question."

"You seemed happy in Garda."

"Maybe I was. For a day or two."

"Are you happy in Tangier?"

"No, I'm not. To be perfectly honest."

"Come. Let's take a trip. Just the two of us."

"Goodness. Where?"

"Down to Fez."

"Yes? And Paolo?"

"Just tell Paolo that you need a change for a couple of days."

Stella looked at me quaintly. A quizzical smile shone in her eyes. Then she sighed and gazed absently over the gold-dusted sea.

"You're incurable, *mon ange*. You'll never learn about

people. Hasn't it occurred to you, dear, that I just can't bear to be happy?"

She turned her head slowly: and I saw a new light in her eyes, a spangled, exultant mercury cast over a blue and bottomless cunning.

Love! What more can one say about it? How can one define it? How can one measure it? Pang and delight: fear and triumph: rage and tenderness: darkness and light. A glittering climax, an interminable limbo. A labyrinth. A Gobi. A Sargasso Sea.

Oh my Stella, my beautiful Stella, my moth, my nightmare, my tiger-lily! What was it you really wanted? What was the secret of your terror? I never understood you and that is the truth of it. I caught a glimpse of the darkness occasionally, I could detect a mood or a motive: but the chasm underneath was too deep for me to penetrate.

She walked casually into the house. I sat quietly for several minutes, watching her half-smoked cigarette smouldering in the black china ash-tray. Finally I picked up my towel and stepped out into the garden. I paused for a moment by the gate, then strolled back toward the portico.

The sun had just set. A rosy haze hung over the shrubbery. The heady spice of the autumn vines sifted down through the lattices. And then the light suddenly died and dusk came shuttling over the sea: it covered the gulf like a vast umbrella.

I heard a voice through a bedroom window, furtive and intimate. I walked stealthily closer and peeped through the shutters. Tony was standing beside the dresser, dark, naked, erect. One hand was poised on his hip, the other was pressed against his thigh. He turned slowly toward the bed with a kind of voluptuous, mocking arrogance. He paused for a moment by the mirror; slipped on the contraceptive; and then leaned over the bed and drew Stella gently toward him.

8

The crises of our lives lie dark and blurred in the sea of memory, like sea-beasts afloat in a shadowy underworld; while certain small, random incidents lie gleaming like corals, brilliant, precise, bathed in a significance not quite their own.

Those autumn days in the Villa Zuleika are strangely hard to recapture. They have the pungency of sulphur, alien and dangerous, a bit satanic. I kept struggling against my old, ridiculous passion for Stella. My mind kept dwelling on the humiliation, the folly, the waste, and even the peril. But that brief twilit glimpse of her golden body in Tony's arms, far from sharpening my disillusionment, only intensified my hunger. I was fascinated by a mysterious hidden force which I couldn't fathom, by some powerful but elusive memory, like a shadow cast on a screen.

Sometimes I woke up in the night, vaguely aware of a lurking presence, some bestial imminence in the room, as though an ape were crouching in the shadows. A film of moonlight slid through the blinds, dropping its pattern on the tiles, and a shaggy black head seemed to rear over the bamboo night-table. I reached for the bed-lamp and turned on the switch: and a hard, glaring vacancy flooded the room.

One night I sat by the radio somewhat later than usual. Paolo and Stella had gone to bed; Tony had gone for his nightly prowl. A brittle voice with an Oxford accent was discussing the Maginot Line. I finally fell asleep in my chair.

A sudden cry woke me up. It came from the end of the terrace. Low, hacking, staccato, like the bark of a spaniel. I got up and stepped cautiously into the hall. There was a sound like the claws of a beast scratching the tiles. A strange torpor, a peculiar reluctance took hold of me. But then I suddenly knew what had happened. I stepped out into the darkness. The smell of lime-trees filled the air. All was still, but in the filigreed light that fell through the railing I saw two silhouettes leaning over a third. I stepped closer. No one stirred. Stella and Tony knelt motionless. Stella had a half-open robe flung over her shoulders and Tony wore nothing but a pair of green slippers. Paolo was lying on his back on the dew-varnished tiles. His eyes were still open. He was wearing his mauve pyjamas. A trickle of blood slid from the corner of his mouth.

9

The plea was self-defense. The trial lasted for seven hours. The Arab servants were blandly accommodating and the local authorities were appropriately cynical. When it was over we stepped on a bus and drove south toward Rabat. We spent the night in Casablanca. The following noon we were in Marrakech.

I am near the end of my story. I have often thought

about these violent days. I have tried to penetrate that hideous tangle toward some clear, central meaning. The pattern is there, the evidence is there. The symbols, the passions are there. But when I reach for the hidden core I am swept into a bottomless whirlpool.

What went wrong? I can only guess. We lived in a world of illusions. We kept listening to the sweet, deadly song of the sirens. We dreamed of luxury and glory, of dark châteaux, of golden promontories. And then, in the fever of our dream, in the very rapture of our search, we ruined the actual delight that lay in the palm of our hands. Like Odysseus, we kept roaming across the rose-tinted seas, looking for a new mysterious city, a new thrill, a new love affair. Like Odysseus, we were morbidly curious; we were wily and full of lust.

As for Stella and Tony, I kept watching and waiting. They were twins, of course, in a way. Decadent barbarians; *manqué* artists; beautiful and twisted adolescents. But in their very identity there was a fatal antagonism. Some new crisis was approaching. Which of the two would be the victor? The leaves were falling, the nights were deepening. I waited. I was mesmerized.

10

We took a cottage out in the palm-woods, not far from the Mamounia. It was small and rather dowdy compared to the Villa Zuleika. Tony and I were almost penniless but Stella had her magnificent jewels. She had sold a necklace in Casablanca for four thousand dollars.

For a fortnight all was calm. It was the middle of November. The days were glittering and crisp, the nights were cool and aromatic. Far in the south, beyond the palms, shone the peaks of the Atlas. To the east lay the plains that rolled gently to Mogador.

Tony was working on some landscapes, vaguely in the style of Delacroix. Stella had finished *The Waves* and was reading *Eyeless in Gaza*. I was working on a play in the manner of Pirandello and a sequence of sonnets in the vein of Stefan George. We strolled at dusk through the *soukh* and stopped for cocktails in the bar of the Mamounia. All was curiously peaceful. The real war hadn't started yet.

One thing I'll never forget. In the dust near the bazaar sat a row of blind beggars, each in a tattered old burnous. I gave a coin one day to the first one, a boy in his teens. He fondled it gently and then dutifully passed it to the next, who likewise stroked and caressed it attentively. In this manner it reached the last of the line, a scar-faced old ruffian. He glanced vaguely in our direction, tugged thoughtfully at his beard, and dropped it into his bowl with a toothless little smile.

Stella watched them with a look of wide-eyed fascination. Then she opened her bag and groped thoughtfully among the contents. Finally she drew out the little glass box I had bought in Venice. She gave it to the boy, who fingered it lovingly and raised it to his nostrils, as though it were some precious liqueur. So it passed down the line. Each of the beggars took the box, opened it carefully, smelled it inquisitively, and ran his fingers across the lid. Finally it reached the old battle-scarred patriarch at the end. He too stroked it daintily and sniffed at it slyly.

Then he bowed and smiled graciously and kissed the little box, rather in the fashion of an old aristocrat kissing a margravine's hand. Then he passed it down the line again till it reached the young boy, who pressed it to his cheek and gravely returned it to Stella.

The stars were unusually brilliant that night. We walked out through the palm grove to the Chichaoua gate.

"Isn't it odd?" said Stella quietly. "All those billions of blazing stars? So beautiful, so pure, so peaceful and gentle! And here we are on this little earth, squabbling and fretting and copulating! And staring up at the Milky Way! And waiting desperately for the day we die!"

11

Under the calm, sunny surface I knew we were heading for trouble. Tony was drinking uncontrollably and prowling in the streets night after night. Stella had grown intensely thin. She too drank alarmingly. She wore her hair clipped like a street-urchin's. Her marvelous beauty was disintegrating.

One day I said to her gently: "You're beginning to look like a boy."

"I always wanted to be a boy, don't you remember? In San Pedro?"

"Well, you're reasonably successful as a woman, don't you think?"

"Oh. I see." Her face froze. "I'm a whore. Is that what you mean?"

"Not in the least," I said softly. "You're mysterious and feminine."

"Don't bother to explain, please, my lamb. I know perfectly well what you think of me. You despise me. You pity me. You're even a little bit afraid of me. Listen, Henry. It's time someone spoke to you frankly. You and your drab, silly poetry. You and your ridiculous arty snobbery. You're worse than Tony. At least Tony has a dark, evil drive in him. But you sit in your ivory tower with your vague, airy words and what does it all boil down to? Nothing, my pet! Absolutely nothing!"

I looked rather woebegone and reached for a cigarette. "You have a point, I suppose. I ought to go and hunt lions."

"Don't be vapid, please, dear. I'm not asking you to be another Hemingway. All I ask is that you finally grow up. Have real thoughts. Feel real feelings. Stick out your neck. Show your claws. And become a real person."

"A real person?"

"Precisely. You're just a reflection, that's all. With me you're giddy and playful. With Tony you're naughty and reckless. In Italy you laughed and sang. In France you were sly and cerebral. Sometimes I wonder whether you really have any character at all. You just change color like one of those weird little lizards . . ."

That night was the first time she brought someone home with her. She left the house soon after dinner to have a drink at the Mamounia. I decided to stay in my room and finish *Dead Souls*. Two hours passed. Then a third. Finally I turned out my light. Our servant Ahmed was fast asleep. Tony was out on one of his escapades.

All was dark except for the bronze-hooded lamp in the loggia.

I heard the click of the garden gate and casually glanced through my window. Two figures were silently crossing the loggia. One was Stella. The other was a huge, black-skinned soldier in uniform—one of those broad-cheeked Sudanese that strutted about in the *soukh*.

My throat tightened queerly. I felt a rush of nausea. The waves of night rippled the curtains like the tongues of a flood. My whole body had burst into a violent sweat. Malaria, possibly? And then I knew what it was. Only a devouring fit of loneliness. The loneliness of the African midnight; of terror and jealousy.

Once or twice I heard the soft, cautious padding of naked feet. After an hour or thereabouts a noiseless shadow passed my window. He vanished quickly among the palms. Finally, toward dawn, I fell asleep.

12

Winter came. The winds from the Atlas cleared the air in the plains. The sunlight at noon grew as sharp as a scalpel. It seemed to peel away layer upon layer from the earth, exposing the brittle nerves, the throbbing arteries, the gleaming ribs. Under this fierce metallic light the most insignificant of things—a dead leaf, a green grasshopper— took on an oracular intensity.

And the city itself took on a patriarchal splendor, with its pock-marked skin, its sun-scorched furrows, its root-like odor, its relentless stare. Sometimes I went for a stroll in the big bazaar with Tony. He kept glancing at the Arabs with a kind of fascinated awe. He appeared to have lost all self-control; he was deep in the grip of a monomania. We'd wander from stall to stall in that lattice-spun haze and look at the chiseled knives, the leather *pouffs* and brass candlesticks, or maybe a cake of soap or a bottle of shaving lotion. He used to purchase quite regularly; I sometimes wondered where the money came from. But he wasn't interested in what he bought—only in that bottomless obsession which was eating away at his nerves like a parasite. His face had grown haggard and tense, ascetic; his eyes were ruthless and ravenous, like an egret's.

I still felt a pang of nostalgic tenderness occasionally, when a glint of the old, sly zest took hold of him for a moment or when his eyes grew suffused with a look of melancholy search. But it was a tenderness which had finally lost all trace of hero-worship and instead took on a tincture of alarm and compassion. He had given up painting except for an occasional nude of some little Arab whom he'd paid a few francs to come back to the house with him. Most of the day he spent sunbathing in the little walled garden, wearing a paisley bandana and a gold-embroidered skull-cap. His body was still muscular, lean and tight around the waist, with a wing-shaped embroidery of curls on his chest, like an Assyrian emperor's. But his face was prematurely lined, his lips were sagging, his voice was listless.

And I too was deteriorating. I was losing my gusto. I grew infected with the Moroccan lassitude, the anonymity, the insects. I lolled about under an umbrella, scribbling away perfunctorily. I gave up Dostoevsky and started to read Simenon. I still stared at Stella with a microscopic intensity—her petaled toenails, her tiny earlobes, the down on her arms, the poise of her fingers—but the sting of desire had grown stale with frustration. I had given up hope. I was ready to leave.

One night after dinner I sat chatting with Stella. It was warmer than usual. One of those rich, restless nights when the breeze seemed to be coming all the way from Nigeria, carrying the odor of sesame, snakes and incantations.

"I'm rather worried about our poor little Tony," she said. "He goes tom-catting about the *soukh,* picking up all sorts of riff-raff, and why something dreadful hasn't happened to him I can't imagine. Only yesterday a lift-boy from the Mamounia came to the door. He wanted a hundred francs. He was rather horrid about it. He said he'd go to the authorities if I didn't pay him immediately."

"Rather a bore, isn't it?" I said.

"And there's something else," said Stella.

"Yes? What?"

"Don't mention it to anyone, please, but do you remember the diamond bracelet that Paolo gave me in Cannes?"

"I certainly do."

"Well, it's gone."

"Good God. Call the police."

"I wouldn't dream of it, dear. I know exactly who took it."

After a moment I said: "Why stay on here, Stella?"

"What do you suggest?"

"Almost anything. Why not go to America?"

"I refuse to go to America."

"Why?"

"You know perfectly well." She looked at me darkly

and drew her fingers around the rim of the glass. "I'm an outcast. I was always an outcast. I was a rebel from the day I was born. Don't you remember San Pedro? What a viper I was? It was the same in Amarillo, and New Canaan, and even New York. I felt stigmatized, scorned. I wanted desperately to make up for it. I wanted power and fame, I wanted adoration and luxury! I wanted women to gasp with envy when I stepped into a restaurant. I wanted men to bristle with lust when I passed them on the street. I wanted duchesses to invite me to dinner and dukes to invite me to bed. I wanted to be cruel and exquisite and utterly ravishing."

"And now?"

"Well, I'm over it, thank God. And besides, what does it matter? The whole world is going to pieces, so what does it matter?"

The ice had melted in my glass. A moth was pirouetting around the lamp-shade and on the ceiling, directly over us, sat a small salamander.

"I suppose you hate me, don't you, Henry?" said Stella all of a sudden.

I looked at her sadly. "Perhaps. Just a bit."

"After all that I did to Melanie. And Paolo. And you." She raised her glass and held it tremulously under the peach-colored light. "I destroyed poor little Melanie. Deliberately and consciously. And I killed poor old Paolo. Through sheer bitter boredom."

"And me?"

"I'll probably end by killing you too, if you don't watch out. I bring misery. Nothing but misery. I'm a bitch. I'm a lunatic."

She suddenly looked quite old: her marvelous eyes

filmed with weariness, her neck lined, her beautiful skin dark and leathery, like an Indian squaw's. But as I watched her in the stillness, waiting for something to happen—who knows what?—she closed her eyes and seemed to fall asleep for a moment. And her features grew soft again, her flesh began to glow, and she turned into a kind of imperturbable deity—some sullen and satiated Aztec moon-goddess.

The moth rattled feebly against the wall of the lampshade. Then it dropped on the table and lay motionless on its back. At that moment the door swung open and a gust of air shot through the room. There was a short, eerie silence: and then the sound of someone falling.

We ran out into the loggia. There lay Tony, beside the entrance. The bronze-hooded lamp shone down on his face. He twisted his lips in a sickening grin and muttered hoarsely: "Oh, God in Heaven."

A black object, rather like an ice-pick, clung to his throat. Suddenly the blood began spilling. He twitched and lay still.

Stella flung herself on the floor, beating her breast and sobbing wildly. "Oh, darling! My darling! You've left me! You've left me!"

I ran in and snatched at the telephone and rang for the doctor. He arrived ten minutes later. It was much too late, of course.

13

The following morning I found a note under my bedroom door.

Dearest H:
Forgive me, sweet. I can't bear to stay on here.
No one knows where I'm going, so don't try to find out.
Love,
S.

And that was the last that I saw of Stella. Three days later I left for Lisbon. I spent six months in Sintra and early in March I sailed for America.

XII

I T WAS SIX YEARS LATER—that abysmal winter after the armistice. I still remember the train from Cherbourg grinding through the meadows of Normandy; the big white horses in front of the stables, breathing mist into the air; the leafless orchards and frozen ponds, the desolate ice-lacquered villages, and the shattered cathedrals etched in the sky like great talons.

Paris itself was stiff with the cold; the coldest winter in thirty years. Here and there on the walls I could detect little bullet holes, like pock-marks in some vast and abandoned torso. There were nests of grimy snow tucked in the shadows of the Tuileries but in the streets there was only ice: the Pont Royal was sheathed in ice, the stalls on the Quai Voltaire wore a cameo of ice.

People sat in their threadbare overcoats in cheerless cafés. Steam rose from their tea-cups and dissolved in the chilly gloom. Everything had turned to a dirty blue, the color of a bruise: the ice-flecked Seine, the naked trees, the slimy quays, the soot-streaked statues. The whole city radiated emptiness, not only a monetary and gastric emptiness but an absence of movement, of thought and desire, like an old *poule de luxe* who has finally given up love.

2

I thought that the Hotel de l'Univers would be a trifle too gloomy, so I stayed in the Regina in the Place des Pyramides. I spent the day after my arrival in a series of nostalgic pilgrimages: the Galerie l'Apollon in the Louvre, Hédiard's in the Place de la Madeleine, the Café Flore, the bar of the Ritz, the Turkish Baths in the Rue d'Odessa. But nothing was quite the same. There was an atmosphere of phantoms. I had dinner in a little bistro which I used to go to with Stella, and after dinner I went around to the Box of Sardines. But the door was boarded shut; there was soot on the windowpanes. So I strolled across the Road Point and down the street to La Vie en Rose. It had changed its name to the Mogador but everything else was still the same—the red brocade, the painted blackamoors, the Venetian glass chandelier. Even the tubby young man at the grand piano was still the same, and he played the same songs: "The Man I Love," "Body and Soul." It was thoroughly depressing. I drank my Drambuie and left.

The following morning I paid a visit to Boris' studio.

"Ah, monsieur," cried the concierge, a hysterical female with a hare-lip, "you're just the same, I swear you are! A little thinner of course. And you've got a scar on your forehead. The war, I suppose? Well, it could have been worse. You're looking for Monsieur Semenoff? Goodness me. How times have changed. He left at the beginning of the Occupation. For Costa Rica, if I'm not mistaken . . ."

So I got into a taxi and drove to the Rue Saint-Dominique. I thought it might be amusing to have lunch with Alphonse.

But the concierge, a cadaverous creature with a beak like a toucan's, bleakly declared: "Sorry, monsieur. He's taken a house in Provence. Somewhere near Arles, I understand. I'll give you the address if you want it . . ."

I thought for a moment of driving over to the Ile Saint-Louis. But my last encounter with poor Isabelle had been rather delicate. So I decided to spend the afternoon among the paintings in the Luxembourg and then had dinner at the Zanzibar in the Rue du Dragon.

It was infinitely sad, that little dinner at the Zanzibar. The filet mignon was the size of a chestnut. There were grayish wafers instead of bread. The *café filtre* was sour with chicory. There was only the Burgundy. I drank a whole bottle of it.

3

Then I strolled down the boulevard to the good old Deux Magots.

Here at least there had been no change. Or very little, at any rate. The waiters were a bit more harrowed-looking. And the coffee of course was hideous. But the red banquettes were the same as always, with their moth-eaten plush, and the clientèle was the same—the haggard misanthropes, the owl-eyed noctambules.

I felt a hand on my shoulder and glanced up uneasily.

"Well, well! If it isn't Henry!"

I blinked my eyes. Suddenly I remembered. It was the young philosophy student whom we used to see at the baths in the Seine, with the Discus-Thrower's body and the mania for Hemingway and Steinbeck.

He had aged rather strikingly. There were streaks of gray on his temples. His good-looking face had grown pointed and waspish. He was wearing a dark blue shirt and a corduroy jacket.

I shook his hand. "What a surprise! Have a drink, will you, André?"

He sat down on the seat beside me. "And what are you doing here in Paris?"

"Oh, little tidbits for some magazines. Nothing especially romantic."

"You've given up poetry?"

"Yes. I've given up poetry."

He seemed rather preoccupied, wrinkling his brow now and again and puckering his lips as he fondled his brandy glass. He cleared his throat, flicked his cigarette ash, and cast a sharp glance at me.

"It's a different place, isn't it, Henry?"

"Paris, you mean?"

"The whole world. You've changed and I've changed, but the world has changed even more. You used to look wistful and expectant. Now you look stoical and weatherbeaten. I don't blame you. You were . . . well, you were a bit infatuated in the old days, weren't you?"

I shrugged my shoulders and looked at the ceiling.

André smiled, somewhat wryly. "Well, you know, it's a funny thing. America always used to fascinate me. It still does, for all that. But in a different sort of way. I used to have theories about America. But I've given up theories. America's a mystery. It's an enigma. It keeps sprouting like a jungle. It shifts like the sea. And at the same time there's something lonely and horizonless about it, like a desert."

"Have you ever been in America?"

"No, I haven't," said André.

"Well, then . . ."

"Never mind. I know all about it," said André whimsically. He was silent for a minute or two, then he looked into my eyes and said gently:

"It was sad about Stella, wasn't it?"

"Stella?" It was like a jab in the ribs.

He scowled. "She never wrote you?"

"The last I heard of her was in 1940."

"Where was she then?"

"In Marrakech."

He nodded. "I see." He leaned back and ran his hand very slowly across his face. He gazed thoughtfully across the room at the two squatting mandarins whose black silhouettes dominated the room.

"Have you ever heard of Tamanrasset?"

"Mm. I don't believe I have."

"Well," said André, "I was stationed there during the last three years of the war. It's in the depth of the Sahara. Twelve hundred miles from Algiers. A desolate little town set among the cliffs of the Hoggar, which jut into the sky like the mountains of the moon. Try to visualize the place. Little hovels of reddish mud against a background of gutted sea-blue volcanoes. Beautiful in a way, beyond a doubt. You've never seen such sunsets. I used to sit with a glass of wine, listening to a record I had. The same old record, day after day. A Bach *Toccata* I think it was. Toward the end it was nothing but a dull, eerie scratch. And over the hills the colors shifted from a pinkish gold to a vicious purple. The Tuareg used to stroll with their camels past the barracks. They always wore white turbans and voluminous veils of faded indigo, and behind the veils were those soulful eyes with painted eyelids and eyelashes. Not once in three years did I see a Targui's whole face: only those harem-like eyes and maybe a hint of a nose.

"Tamanrasset hasn't changed in a thousand years, I imagine. The caravans come wandering along barely marked trails that lead from the swamps of Nigeria up to the Atlas and from the Sudan all the way to Fezzan. The distances are overwhelming. The lava mountains are utterly barren. The summers are flaming hot and the winters are icy cold. There was a handful of French officials, three or four doctors and a couple of teachers, as well as a few dozen Arabs, Mozabite merchants from Ghardaia. And of course there were the soldiers, a sprinkling of dapper young officers and a bevy of Nigerians, Sudanese, Senegambians. Lice and cockroaches all over the place. The stink of camel dung everywhere. And all day long, like a kind of madness, the monotonous tinkling of the caravan bells.

"A day or two after I arrived I was told about an American girl who lived in a cottage just behind the barracks. They all called her Coco. They never knew her real name. A trifle mad. Sick, of course. Drink, sedatives, cocaine. She needed a new man every day—sometimes three or four or five of them. She did it for nothing, naturally. Sometimes she even paid for it. She had her favorites—great stallions from the wastes of Mauretania. Occasionally she would dress in the evening, wearing a Schiaparelli gown and those wonderful emerald bracelets and ear-rings. She made friends with some of the officers who used to drop in after dinner and chat over a glass of lukewarm wine.

"Poor little Coco! I wouldn't have recognized her if she hadn't stopped me in the street one day, right in front of the mosque. She cried, 'André! My darling!' and kissed me on both cheeks. Twice a week after that I used to go for a drink in her cottage. She loved to talk about Paris— the lunches at Bougival, the dinners at Armenonville, the horse-racing at Longchamps and all the rest of it. I asked her how she happened to get to Tamanrasset, but she shrugged her shoulders and changed the subject. Believe it or not, she had a copy of Rimbaud in her bedroom. I wonder what they made of it, those mustachioed young officers. A Tamanrasset harlot reading *Le Bâteau Ivre!*

"Well, one day our poor little Coco just lay down and died. I'd seen it coming for weeks. She was looking like a corpse. I'll never forget those last few days—the hair all shaved from her head and that pitiful, worn-out face, all shriveled like a mummy's. Only the eyes were still the same—those marvelous eyes, do you remember? The day before she died she gave me her copy of Rimbaud. 'It isn't much,' she said when she gave it to me—'just a memory of old times.' And she smiled with that feverish, crazy little smile of hers. . . ."

4

I walked down the Boulevard Saint-Germain toward the Rue du Bac: past dreary little bistros and rusty pissoirs. In the dimly illuminated shop windows I discerned mysterious objects—dusty bottles and scalloped sea-shells, artificial legs, baroque candlesticks.

The Seine was as black as ink. I stood for a while on the Pont Royal, thinking back to the days when I first arrived in Paris. Slowly the moon rose up over the Ile de la Cité. I was shivering with cold. I felt violently alone. And yet, somehow or other, in spite of the terror, in spite of the loneliness, a strange sort of harmony hung over the city.

I walked slowly toward the Rue de Rivoli. The ice squeaked under my footsteps and the trees on the quay were all shining like crystal.